DEATH RIDING IN

"How fast is Vic Delay?" Cotton asked.

"Fast, accurate, deadly."

"You ever seen him?"

"Once," Shaye said, "years ago, in Abilene." He handed the telegram back to Cotton. "Jeb Collier is on his way here with Vic Delay and six other men. Can you get any more deputies?

"Not with any experience."

"When this is all over," Shaye said, "you might consider getting the town council to let you bring in some experienced men—especially if your bank carries as much money as you say."

"Well, if I come out of this alive, I'll take it up with the council," Riley Cotton said.

"You'll come out of it alive, Riley," Shaye said. "We all will."

"How can you be so sure?"

Shaye shrugged and said, "Thinking about the alternative doesn't appeal to me."

Books by Robert J. Randisi

The Sons of Daniel Shaye

PEARL RIVER JUNCTION
VENGEANCE CREEK
LEAVING EPITAPH

THE SONS OF DANIEL SHAYE

PEARL RIVER JUNCTION

ROBERT J. RANDISI

HarperTorch
An Imprint of HarperCollins*Publishers*

This is a work of fiction. Names, characters, places, and incidents are products of the author's imagination or are used fictitiously and are not to be construed as real. Any resemblance to actual events, locales, organizations, or persons, living or dead, is entirely coincidental.

HARPERTORCH
An Imprint of HarperCollins*Publishers*
10 East 53rd Street
New York, New York 10022-5299

ISBN-13: 978-0-06-058364-4
ISBN-10: 0-06-058364-9

First HarperTorch paperback printing: April 2006

Printed in the United States of America

Visit HarperTorch on the World Wide Web at www.harpercollins.com

10 9 8 7 6 5 4 3 2 1

PEARL RIVER JUNCTION

"Rider comin'."

Thomas Shaye looked up at the sound of younger brother James's voice. Both young men were bare-chested and sweaty, as they were working in the mid-day Wyoming heat, sinking fence posts. Two gun belts hung from the most recently erected post and Thomas walked over to be near his as the rider drew closer.

"Can you see who it is?" he asked James.

"No, but I know it ain't Pa."

Dan Shaye had ridden into town to purchase more supplies for the work that needed to be done around their ranch, which they had only recently purchased. And he'd taken the buckboard, so there'd be no reason for him to be riding toward them at this time of the day. It'd be several more hours before their father returned from the town of Winchester.

"James."

James turned in time to see Thomas toss him his gun belt. He caught it at the last moment, but instead of strapping it on he simply slung it over one shoulder.

Thomas started to strap his onto his hips, but then stopped when he recognized the rider.

"Ain't that Rafe Coleman?"

"I think you're right."

Instead of strapping the gun on, Thomas simply folded the gun belt and held it in his left hand. There seemed less of a chance of needing it now that they'd identified the rider, but it would still be easy for him to draw it if the need arose.

"Afternoon, Rafe," Thomas said as the rider reached them.

Rafe Coleman was about Thomas's age, mid-twenties, and ran errands around Winchester. The man reined in his horse, but remained mounted.

"You know my brother James?"

"Yessir," Rafe said. "Howdy."

James nodded.

"What brings you out here, Rafe?"

"Got a letter for your pa."

"Pa's in town," James said.

"Truly?" Rafe asked, frowning. "Geez, I guess I coulda saved myself a ride out here, huh?"

"You didn't see him there?" Thomas asked.

"No, sir," Rafe said. He removed his hat and wiped his brow on his sleeve. "If'n I had I wouldn'ta rode out here."

"Guess not," James said.

"Sure woulda saved me some time, though," Rafe complained. "Damn." With that he turned his horse and rode on.

Thomas regarded the small envelope for a moment. The handwriting was small and cramped, somehow feminine. The return address said Pearl River Junction, Texas, but there was no name. Thomas knew that Pearl River Junction was a town not far from Epitaph, where their mother had been killed while their pa, Dan

Shaye, had been the law. He'd deputized his three sons and they'd tracked down the killers. They also lost their brother Matthew, killed by the same man.

Thomas shoved the letter into his shirt pocket, removed his gun belt, and hung it back on the post.

"Well, what is it?" James asked.

"Like Rafe said, just a letter for Pa."

"From who?"

"Don't say."

"Ain't you gonna read it?"

"It's for Pa."

"So?"

"I ain't openin' Pa's mail, James," Thomas said. "Now come on, let's get these posts in. We're both gonna catch hell if we don't finish today."

"What's the good of fencin' in land when we got no livestock?" James groused.

"The livestock will come later," Thomas said. "You know Pa's got plans."

"We ain't farmers, Thomas."

"No, we're ranchers."

"We ain't ranchers neither," James said, "We're lawmen."

"We were lawmen," Thomas said. "That's in the past."

"Thomas," James said, grabbing his brother's arms, "just 'cause Pa don't want to be a lawman anymore don't mean we can't."

"James—"

"No, listen," James said. "We could find a town that would hire us: you as sheriff and me as a deputy."

"First of all, you don't get hired as sheriff, you get elected."

"Marshal, then."

"And second, we ain't got the experience—or the years."

"You're old enough to be a marshal," James said. "I can be your deputy."

"James—"

"Why do we have to quit just because Pa wants to?"

"We don't," Thomas said. "We can go our separate ways and do what we want. Pa said so."

"Then let's do it."

"Separate ways, James," Thomas said. "If you want to go and be somebody's deputy, go ahead."

"And what are you gonna do?"

"Stay right here."

"For how long?"

"Until I decide what I want to do with my life," Thomas said, "or, little brother, at least until these fence posts are put it. Now can we get this done?"

In the town of Winchester Dan Shaye was waiting in the general store for his order to be filled. While he waited he went over to look at the new shirts. When he'd gotten dressed that morning, he'd realized that his shirt had no holes on the left side, where he used to pin his badge. There was a time, years ago, when his wife Mary had been doing the laundry and had pointed out how all his shirts had these pin holes in them.

"Why don't you just slide the pin through the same hole every time you put on your badge?" she'd demanded.

"Why don't you make every apple pie you make taste the same?" he'd countered.

"My pies do taste the same, Daniel Shaye," she'd

responded. "They're delicious every time. You say so yourself."

She'd defeated him with words as she usually did. He touched the new shirts, felt the smoothness of the cotton. He didn't really need any new shirts, but most of the ones he had at home still had the pin holes in them from his badge. If he was going to leave the law behind forever, maybe he should get rid of those shirts and buy some of these new ones.

"Wanna add some shirts to your order, Mr. Shaye?" the clerk asked from behind him.

Shaye stared at the new shirts for a few moments more, then removed his hand and turned to face the man.

"No," he said, "I don't think so. I guess I can still get some wear out of the shirts I've got."

2

When Shaye pulled the buckboard to a halt in front of the house, both Thomas and James came out to help unload.

"You boys finish those fence posts?" he asked, dropping down from the seat.

"Yeah, Pa," Thomas said. "They're all in."

"Good," Shaye said, "then we can start stringin' this wire tomorrow morning."

First they took in the items that belonged in the house, then Shaye told James to take the buckboard with the wire to the barn and take care of the team.

"While I'm doin' that, Pa," James said, "Thomas can show you your letter."

As James drove the team away, Shaye looked at his oldest son and asked, "What letter?"

"Rafe brought this out for you today," Thomas said, producing the letter from his pocket and handing it to his father.

Shaye read the front and said, "Pearl River Junction."

"We know anybody from there, Pa?"

Shaye thought a moment, then shrugged and said, "Not that I can think of."

Thomas waited a few moments, then asked, "Are you gonna open it?"

"Is there a pot of coffee on the stove?"

"Yes, sir."

"Well, let's get some and then I'll open it."

They both went inside and Thomas poured out two cups of coffee while Shaye sat down at the kitchen table and opened the envelope. Thomas sat across from him and set a cup in front of his father.

"Thanks," Shaye said. He took a sip before unfolding the letter to read it. It had been folded so many times to fit into the envelope that it took a second or two to open it. Thomas waited patiently while his father read. They'd bought this run-down ranch almost a year ago, and in all that time they'd never received a telegram or a letter. Thomas knew that some of his mother's family were still out there, but there wasn't any way they'd have known where to find them.

He watched his father's face and saw the change in it as he read the words on the page.

"What is it, Pa?"

Shaye lowered the letter and looked at his son.

"Do you know a girl named Belinda Davis?"

"Belinda..." Thomas repeated. "No, I don't think so. Is that who the letter is from?"

"Yes."

"Who is she?"

"I don't know," Shaye said.

"How did she find us?"

"The letter went to Vengeance Creek first," Shaye said. "Then it got forwarded here."

"How'd they know to do that?"

"Once we settled here, I sent word to Vengeance Creek that we were here," Shaye said.

"Why?"

"Just in case."

"Just in case...what?"

"I thought..." He paused and tried again. "Well, in case any of your mother's people wanted to find us."

"But why would—"

"It doesn't matter now," Shaye said, cutting Thomas off. He looked at the letter again, then lowered it as James entered.

"James," Shaye asked, "did you ever know a girl named Belinda Davis?"

"Belinda?" he said. "Sure."

"You did?" Thomas asked.

"Come on, Thomas," James said, "she was that gal in Epitaph that Matthew was sweet on. Pretty little black-haired thing?"

"Matthew was sweet on her?" Shaye asked.

"Yeah, Pa," James said, "Why?"

"That's who the letter is from," Thomas said.

"What does she want, Pa?"

"Well," Shaye said, "She says she's not doing too good and wants our help."

"How?" Thomas asked. "Does she want money?"

"Just says she wants help."

"So why would she ask you?" Thomas asked.

"Well," Shaye said, looking at both his sons, "apparently she thinks that I should take some interest in my grandson."

3

"Grandson?" Thomas asked, aghast.

"Your nephew."

"Nephew?" James asked, gaping.

Shaye nodded and said, "Little Matt."

"Pa," Thomas said, "what are you talkin' about?"

"This girl," Shaye said, "claims that she had Matthew's baby."

Thomas and James were both stunned. Then Thomas asked, "But...when?"

"She says the boy is two years old."

They had left Epitaph for good about two years ago. The girl could have gotten pregnant before they left, but...

"But Pa...Matthew?" Thomas asked. "I don't think Matthew was ever with a girl."

"James?" Pa asked.

James blushed and said, "Pa, I don't know. He never told me anything about bein' with a girl, but..."

"But he did know a girl by this name?'

"Well, yeah...I knew her too, sort of, but...I never thought he...he did anything with her."

"Why didn't I know her?" Thomas asked. "Why didn't I know he was sweet on a girl?"

"No offense, big brother, but Matthew tended to talk to me a little more than he did to you."

Thomas didn't argue. More than once he'd lamented the fact that he had not spent more time with Matthew while he was alive.

"James, what kind of girl was she?"

"I don't know... a nice girl, I guess..."

"A nice girl who got pregnant?"

"I told you, Pa," James said. "I didn't know her that well."

"The question is," Thomas said, "how well did Matthew know her?"

"Well," Shaye said, refolding the letter, "I guess we're not going to get the answer to that question here."

"You gonna write to her?" James asked.

"This letter was sent three months ago," Shaye said. "There's no telling if she's even still in Pearl River Junction."

"So are we going to go there?" Thomas asked.

"We're going to have to send some telegrams first," Shaye said. "Check the situation out. At least find out if she's still there."

"And then what?" James asked.

"She can't be tellin' the truth, Pa," Thomas said. "Not about Matthew."

"We'll have to see, Thomas," Shaye said. "If this girl's boy in Matthew's son, we're going to have to help her."

"And if it's not?"

"We'll see," Shaye said. He stood up. "I'm going to make supper tonight. I want you boys to go to the barn and take that wire off the buckboard and store it in a corner."

"Off the buckboard?" Thomas asked. "I thought we were gonna start stringin' it tomorrow."

"Tomorrow we're going to town to send those telegrams."

"We can start on the wire while you do that, Pa," James said.

"No," Shaye said. "I don't want to start on the wire if we're going to end up leaving town. Let's find out what we're doing first."

"But Pa—" James started, only to be cut off by Thomas.

"Okay, Pa," he said, standing up, "you're the boss. Come on, James."

James opened his mouth to say something, but Thomas grabbed him by the shoulder and pulled him toward the door.

"I should have supper ready by the time you're through," Shaye said.

"Fine," Thomas said and yanked James out the door with him.

"What're you doin'?" James asked as Thomas released his hold on him.

"You're the one who doesn't want to be a rancher," Thomas said. "We could be headin' for Pearl River Junction in a couple of days instead of stringin' wire."

"But I thought you wanted to get started—"

"I don't want to do this back-breakin' work any more than you do, James," Thomas said.

"But...but you act like you do."

"That's for Pa's sake."

"So you wanna go back to bein' a lawman?"

"I want to get back on the trail and see what happens," Thomas said. "Once Pa gets back on a horse and away from here, maybe he'll have a change of heart."

"And wanna wear a badge again?" As they headed

for the barn, James trotted to keep up with Thomas, whose legs were longer.

"A badge...maybe he'll just want to start man hunting again."

"You mean...like bounty huntin'?"

"Why not?"

"I don't know if I wanna be a bounty man, Thomas."

"James," Thomas said as they reached the barn and stopped in front of the buckboard filled with barbed wire, "anythin's better than this."

In the house Shaye threw together a quick meal, frying up some salted meat and opening some cans he'd bought that day. None of the Shayes were good cooks. Since Mary's death, meals had become totally different to them, just something to soothe the rumblings in their bellies.

Shaye prepared the meal by rote, his mind elsewhere. If there was a grandson out there—Matthew's blood, his own blood—it was their duty to make sure the boy was raised right. If it turned out not to be Matthew's son, then the girl needed to stop saying it was.

Shaye wasn't sure which way his hopes were leaning.

Thomas didn't like the town of Winchester.

The first time the Shayes rode into town, a year or so ago, he didn't like the way it felt. The people eyed them in a funny way, a way he knew his father could not miss, and yet Dan Shaye insisted that this was where they were going to settle. Not in town, but on a small ranch just outside of town that he knew was for sale cheap.

Every time Thomas rode into Winchester, he had the same feeling—and this was no exception. Maybe this girl's baby wasn't Matthew's son at all, but maybe the little tyke was going to pry them away from Winchester, Wyoming, once and for all.

The three of them reined in their horses in front of the telegraph office and dismounted.

"Go over to the café and get a table, boys," Shaye said. "I'll join you for breakfast after I've sent my telegrams."

Eating at the café—at any café—was a treat for Thomas and James and they were looking forward to it today. Eating away from home was the only time they really looked forward to a meal as something other than a necessity.

As they were shown to a table, Thomas felt the eyes of the other early diners on them.

"I don't know what they're so all-fired curious about all the time," James said.

"You feel it too?"

"Every time we come into town."

"I felt it the first time we rode in, but I didn't wanna upset Pa," Thomas said. "He seemed so set on settling here."

James took his hat off and set it underneath his chair, then ran his hand through his hair.

"I reckon we got to talk more, brother," he said. "I didn't know you felt the same way I do."

"You're right, little brother," Thomas said. "We do have to talk more—to each other and probably to Pa too."

"God," James said, "we've spent the better part of a year here, not really knowin' what each other was thinkin'? That's sad. Thomas, I woulda told anybody that we was a close family."

"Reckon we ain't as close as we thought we were at all."

James was going to say something else, but the waiter came over and asked what they wanted. Thomas ordered three steak and egg breakfasts and a pot of coffee.

"He acts like we ain't never even been in here before," James complained, "and I know he's waited on us more'n once."

"James, this letter is our chance to get out of this town," Thomas said. "All three of us."

"Yeah, but...do you really think this gal's baby could be Matthew's?"

"No, I don't," Thomas said, "but I think Pa is gonna

be the one to decide that. And I guess this is gonna depend on how bad he wants to be a grandpa."

Dan Shaye sent a couple of telegrams to the town of Epitaph, Texas: one to the man who had replaced him as sheriff when he and the boys left and one to the mayor, Charles Garnett. One or both of them would be able to check with the authorities in Pearl River Junction to find out if a gal named Belinda Davis was still living there.

He told the clerk he'd be at the café across the street when a reply came in and then left to join his boys for breakfast. Crossing the street, he found himself thinking about Mary and how she'd longed for a grandchild. She'd always wondered which of her sons would marry first and make her a grandmother.

"Thomas," she would say, "because he's the oldest and the most charming."

Then, on another day, she'd say, "Probably James. He's the most sensitive and romantic."

But Shaye could not ever remember her guessing that it would be Matthew. His middle son was neither charming, nor was he romantic. Matthew, to the day he died, was childlike himself and never gave any indication that he'd change. The probability that he'd sired a child seemed small, and yet Shaye felt compelled to check it out for himself. If there was another Shaye out there... after all, they'd lost two in two years, hadn't they?

By the time Dan Shaye reached the table in the café, there were three steak and eggs plates on the table.

"Good," he said, seating himself, "you went ahead and ordered." He poured himself a cup of coffee and drank half of it down.

"You get the telegrams sent?' Thomas asked around a mouthful of steak and eggs.

"Yep," Shaye said, "I sent two to Epitaph. Either the sheriff or the mayor should be able to help us find out if this Belinda is still in Pearl River Junction."

"And if she is?" James asked. "Then we'll go there?"

"We'll outfit and leave tomorrow morning," Shaye said. He stopped with a forkful of food halfway to his mouth and looked at his two sons. "That is, unless you boys would rather not go?"

"No, no, Pa," Thomas said. "We wanna go."

"Yeah," James said. "We definitely wanna go."

Shaye put the food in his mouth and chewed thoughtfully.

"You boys have no desire to be ranchers, I know," Shaye said, "but that other life...the law...it's cost us too much."

"We know, Pa," Thomas said. "We know."

"I've always said you could make your own decisions," Shaye went on. "You don't have to stay on this ranch with me."

"We know that, Pa," James said. "We've stayed because we want to."

"And we'll go with you to Pearl River Junction for the same reason," Thomas added.

"Well," Shaye said, pouring more coffee, "whether we do that or not remains to be seen. Maybe we'll know by the time we finish breakfast."

There didn't seem much else to discuss, so the three men dug in and enjoyed their breakfasts, ignoring the fact that they were still the center of attention in the room.

5

Sheriff Adam Kennedy looked up as the door to his office opened and his deputy, Lyle Canton, entered. The look on Canton's unlined young face gave his news away.

"Where are they?"

"How did you know?" Canton asked.

"I can tell by looking at you when any of the Shayes are in town. Who is it this time? Or is it more than one?"

"All three."

"All three?"

Canton nodded with great satisfaction.

"What should we do?" the deputy asked.

"It's been what...a year since they settled here? And nothing's gone wrong, has it? No bodies, not even any shots."

"Yeah, but the mayor—"

"The mayor is an old woman."

"Sheriff—"

"Come on, Lyle," Kennedy said. "He's been mayor a year longer than I've been sheriff—and I've been sheriff for twelve years. After all that time I can say what I like."

"Yeah, but he's worried," Canton said. "They've got a reputation for—"

"I know what the Shayes have a reputation for, Lyle," Kennedy said. "Just relax. I'll have a look."

"I can go over to the café," Canton said. "I saw them goin' in there. First the two sons, then the father."

"Like I said, Lyle," Kennedy said, "relax. You stay here." The sheriff stood up, hitched up his gun belt, and put his hat on. "I'll be back in a little while."

"Sheriff—"

"Just watch the office, Lyle," Kennedy said. "I'll be back."

The sheriff left the unhappy deputy sitting behind the desk and walked toward the café. He remembered the day the Shayes rode into town. He recognized Dan Shaye from one dealing they'd had when both men wore badges. Shaye had tracked a man this far and together they'd arrested him. Since then Kennedy had heard about all Dan Shaye and his sons had been through, about the men they'd killed. Their presence in town made Mayor Ben Carter very nervous, and then when Shaye announced their intention to buy the old Tarver place, Carter went from nervous to scared.

"They're gonna bring trouble, Adam," the mayor said.

"That remains to be seen, Ben," Kennedy had replied. "Why don't we just wait and see what happens?"

What happened was that, for the most part, they remained on their ranch, came to town for supplies and—occasionally—for a meal, and the trouble Ben Carter had been afraid of never materialized. At least, not yet. Still, that didn't stop Adam Kennedy from talking with any of the Shayes who came into town. Yesterday he'd spoken briefly to Dan. Today, all three of them were in town. Maybe something was finally brewing.

When Kennedy entered the café, his appearance drew the eyes of the other diners to him and away from Dan Shaye and his boys. The lawman wondered how the Shayes could even stand coming to town at all. Not only did they have to deal with his presence every time, but with the stares from the rest of the townsfolk, who—like the mayor—were waiting for lead to fly.

"Sheriff," Dan Shaye said, "I've been expecting you. Have some coffee with us."

Kennedy pulled out the fourth chair at the table and sat down. He accepted the cup of coffee Thomas Shaye handed him.

"Two days in a row," Kennedy said to Shaye. "That's kind of unusual."

"I guess everyone else must feel the same way," Shaye said.

"Why don't they just all come over and join us?" James said. "It's like they're sitting with us anyway."

Kennedy and Shaye exchanged a glance. They were roughly the same age and they both understood the way the people of Winchester felt. Shaye had dealt with it himself as a lawman. Whenever somebody with a reputation came to town, trouble usually followed. However, Shaye was beginning to wonder how long he and the boys had to be part of this community before the stares and the fear went away.

"Anything in particular bring you back?" Kennedy asked.

"Telegrams," Shaye said. "I had to send a couple. We're waiting for the replies now."

"Waitin' for good news or bad news?"

"Depends on how you look at it," Shaye said. "We

get the right reply for you and the townspeople and we'll be leaving tomorrow."

"Leaving?" Kennedy asked. "For good?"

"I don't know," Shaye said. "Probably not, but for a while. Long enough to give you all a breather."

Kennedy put his coffee cup down.

"I know it's been going on a long time, Dan," he said, then looked at the boys as well. "I kinda thought it would wear off by now."

"So did I," James said.

"I didn't," Thomas said.

They all looked at him.

"This town hasn't felt right from the beginning, Pa," Thomas said. "I didn't want to say anything, but—"

"You should have said something, Thomas," his father said, "right from the start. What about you, James?"

"I...agree with Thomas, Pa...b-but I don't feel as strongly as he does about it."

"This is a good town," Kennedy told them. "You may not believe that now, but it is. We've just never had anyone like...well, like you living here before."

Shaye looked at his boys and then at the lawman. Finally, he looked around, saw that although the number of diners had thinned out, they were still the center of attention.

Maybe he should have noticed this from the beginning as well.

Shaye had seen the old Tarver place the first time he'd come to Winchester, tracking Dolph Jordan. Sheriff Kennedy had helped him take Jordan in, but before heading back to Texas with his prisoner, Shaye had seen the run-down ranch and thought it was the kind of place he could take Mary and the boys to. Later, once he'd returned to Epitaph, he'd forgotten about the place—until last year. Once he decided that he and the boys should stop carrying stars, he remembered the vacant Tarver ranch outside of Winchester, Wyoming. When he brought the boys here, he became so enamored with the idea of fixing up the old ranch that he hadn't seen or felt what they did when they first rode into town.

Now, sitting in the café with the boys and the sheriff, waiting for the answers to his telegrams, he realized what a mistake he'd made. But maybe it was too late, because if it turned out that Belinda Davis's baby was Matthew's, they were going to have to have someplace to bring her and the baby, a home for the child to grow up in, someplace that was not so close to the painful memories of Epitaph.

So much depended on what happened with Belinda Davis—and on whether or not it turned out he was a grandfather.

6

"I'm tired of waitin'," James said.

Sheriff Kennedy had left them and they had ordered another pot of coffee. They were almost to the bottom of that pot and Shaye was talking about ordering still another.

"I can't drink any more coffee, Pa," Thomas said.

"Ah...neither can I," Shaye admitted. "Okay, let's pay the check and get out of here."

Thomas and James stopped on the boardwalk outside the café to wait for their father. While they were waiting, they both saw the clerk from the telegraph office crossing the street toward them.

"Hey," Thomas said as the man started to go by them, "is that the reply for Dan Shaye?"

"Yes, sir," the man said, "he wanted me to bring it right over to him."

"That's okay," Thomas said, "we'll take it."

"But he said—"

"It's okay," James said. "We're his sons."

"Oh...o-okay." The clerk handed the telegram to Thomas, turned, and went back across the street.

"You boys ready?" Shaye said, coming out behind them.

Thomas turned to Shaye, holding the telegram.

"You got an answer, Pa."

Shaye took the yellow piece of paper from his son and unfolded it.

"What's it say?" James asked.

"Just an answer from Mayor Garnett," Shaye said. "He says he'll check on the girl and get back to me later today."

"Damn," James said. "So what do we do now?"

"We stay in town and wait."

"We're gonna make people nervous, Pa," Thomas said.

"That's too bad," Shaye said, refolding the telegram and putting it in his shirt pocket. "Boys, I'm sorry I've been so blind about this town."

"That's okay, Pa," Thomas said. "We know how you feel about the ranch, about wearin' a badge again."

"I tell you what we're going to do," Shaye said. "Let's get outfitted to hit the trail."

"We going to Pearl River Junction?"

"I figure we're going to have to go, one way or another," Shaye said. "If she's not still there, it's the last place we know she was. Maybe somebody there will be able to tell us where she went. We'll know better when we hear from Garnett again. Meanwhile, let's go over to the general store and get some supplies."

They stepped down from the boardwalk together into the street and started across.

From the window of the sheriff's office, Deputy Canton watched as the Shayes left the café and crossed the street.

"Looks like they got an answer," he said over his shoulder to Sheriff Kennedy.

"Lyle, get away from the window."

Canton turned and looked at the sheriff.

"Don't you think I should follow them, see where they're goin'?" he asked. "What they're gonna do?"

"I think you should leave them alone," Kennedy said. "I think we should all just leave them alone. They haven't done a thing wrong since they got here."

Canton gave Kennedy a funny look.

"Look, Lyle," the sheriff said, sitting back in his chair, "you want to follow them? Be my guest."

"Really?"

"Don't talk to them unless they talk to you," Kennedy instructed. "Do you understand?"

"Yes, sir."

"And try not to be obvious, Lyle," Kennedy said.

"I won't be," Canton said, "I promise."

The eager young deputy was out the door before Kennedy could ask him if he knew what the word "obvious" meant.

“What are you lookin’ at?” James asked Thomas.

They were in the general store and Thomas was standing at the front window, looking out.

“The deputy,” Thomas said. “He followed us here. He’s across the street.”

They both turned and looked at their father, who was standing at the counter.

“Think Pa saw him?” James asked.

“If I saw him, Pa saw him,” Thomas said. “Doesn’t matter, I guess. He’s not gonna do anythin’.”

“Think the sheriff sent him?”

“No,” Thomas said. “I think Pa and the sheriff have an understandin’. The deputy’s on his own.”

“You boys lookin’ at the deputy?” Shaye asked, coming over to join them.

“Yeah, Pa,” James said. “You want me to go talk to him?”

“No,” Shaye said, “let him be.”

“Are we finished here, Pa?” Thomas asked.

“They’re holding our order for us,” Shaye said. “Let’s go back to the telegraph office and see if anything else has come in.”

The three of them walked down the street to the office with the deputy behind them.

Mayor Ben Carter opened the door to the sheriff's office and marched right in.

"Mornin', Ben," Kennedy said.

"The Shayes are in town, Adam," Carter said brusquely. "Have you seen them?"

"Saw them and spoke to them."

"What do they want?"

"To be left alone, I guess."

"No, I mean—"

"I know what you mean, Ben," the lawman said. "Why don't you sit down? I'll pour you a cup of coffee."

"I don't want to sit down," the mayor said and then promptly sat down. Kennedy went to the coffeepot, poured a cup, and handed it to the man.

"Ben," he said, "Dan Shaye and his boys have lived here for over a year. Don't you think it's time you gave them a break?"

"As soon as we let our guard down," Carter said, "somethin' will happen. Mark my words."

"They've been law-abidin' citizens since they got here."

"I know that," the mayor said, "but that don't mean trouble won't come huntin' them, does it?"

Kennedy sat himself back behind his desk.

"Tell me somethin'," he said. "How would you feel if they were wearin' badges?"

"Badges?" Carter asked. "What badges?"

"Deputy's badges."

"Deputy's—you mean here? In Winchester?"

"That's what I mean."

"Well..." Carter frowned, scratched his head. "If they were lawmen here, I guess that wouldn't be so bad. I mean, if folks knew they were on the side of the law, I guess that'd make 'em...less fearful, don't ya think?"

"I suppose so," Kennedy said. "I mean, if we endorsed them, that might put folks at ease..."

"Why don't you ask them?"

"You're the mayor," Kennedy said, "you ask 'em."

"Me? I—I can't."

"Have you ever talked with Dan Shaye at all since he and his boys arrived here?"

"Well...no..."

"With either of his sons?"

"No."

"Why not?"

Carter hesitated, then said, "That's always been your job."

"Well...it may not matter anyway."

"Why not?"

"They might be leavin'."

"Leavin'? When?"

"Probably tomorrow."

"For good?"

"I don't know," Kennedy said. "They didn't say anything about sellin' their property. Might just be a temporary thing."

"When will we know?"

"Later in the day, I guess," Kennedy replied. "Seems he sent out some telegrams and he's waitin' for some replies."

"Can we find out what those telegrams said?"

"Not legally."

"But you could—"

"I won't, Ben," Kennedy said. "We'll just have to wait and see what happens."

"Well... if they're leavin' town, even for a while... that should give us a breather..."

Kennedy knew the only one who needed a breather was the mayor. Carter had been as tense as a guitar string since the Shayes first arrived in Winchester.

"Okay... well, I'll leave you to it, then," Carter said. "We'll, uh, do like you said and wait and see." He went to the door, opened it, and turned back. "And let's talk about that... that badge thing, huh?"

"Sure."

"I mean, havin' them as lawmen here might even be good for the town."

"Right."

"Not that I want to replace you..."

"Of course not."

"Just... you could probably use the competent help, right?"

"Right."

"All right," Carter said, appearing calmer than when he'd entered, "okay. I'll, uh, wait to hear from you."

"I'll let you know what happens, Ben."

Carter nodded, looked as if he were going to say something else, then thought better of it and went out the door.

It must have been even more than the year they'd lived in Winchester since any of the Shayes had worn a badge. Sheriff Kennedy wondered if any of them were itchin' to put one back on. Even having one of them as a deputy would give him something he'd never had before—as Mayor Ben Carter had put it, a "competent" deputy.

Sheriff Harvey Dillon of Epitaph, Texas, had also sent Dan Shaye a telegram telling him he'd check Pearl River Junction to see if the girl still lived there. That meant that they didn't know anything they hadn't known before.

"When another response comes in," Shaye told the clerk, "one of us should be at the Golden Garter Saloon."

"Yes, sir."

Outside Shaye told Thomas and James the news, which was no news.

"So what do we do now?" James asked.

"We stay around town until we hear somethin'," Shaye said.

"And if we don't hear?"

"We'll leave in the morning," Shaye said. "Head for Pearl River Junction. Whatever happens happens."

"When's the Golden Garter open?" Thomas asked.

"Today," Shaye said, "when we get there. Come on..."

When they reached the Golden Garter Saloon, Dan Shaye banged on the door with his fist.

"What the hell—" The doors swung open and the owner of the saloon, Abner Moore, a black man in his sixties, appeared.

"Come on, you old geezer, open up. Me and the boys are thirsty."

"Dan Shaye, that you?" Moore asked, squinting against the sun. "When the hell did you start drinkin' early?"

"Today," Shaye said, "only we aren't gonna do much drinking unless you let us in."

Abner looked at Thomas.

"What's got into this man, boy?"

"He just found out he might be a grandpa," Thomas said.

"Well, hell's bells, man," Abner said, staring at Shaye. "Why didn't you say so?"

He stepped back, unlocked the batwing doors, and let the Shayes enter.

"Blessed events is somethin' that's got to be celebrated," Abner said. "What'll you boys have?"

"Three beers, Abner," Shaye said, "and make 'em cold ones."

If Dan Shaye had one friend in Winchester, it was Abner Moore. The two had hit it off from the moment they first met.

"My beers is always cold, goddamn it."

Abner drew four beers and set them on the bar.

"Why four?" Shaye asked.

"I'm celebratin' with ya," Abner said. "Which one of you boys made your pa a grandaddy?"

"Neither one of us," James said. "It might've been Matthew, our other brother."

"Might've been?"

"We're not sure," Thomas said, picking up his beer.

"Is there or is there ain't a baby?" Abner asked.

"There is," Shaye said," but we're not sure if it's family or not."

"So what the hell did I let you in my saloon early for?" the black saloon owner demanded.

"Gives you an excuse to have a cold beer early in the day, you old faker."

"Well," Abner said, picking his up, "there is that."

By the time the Golden Garter officially opened for business, the Shayes were into their second beer.

"Nurse this one, boys," Shaye said when Abner set them on the bar. "We might be here for a long time."

"If you gonna be here for a long time, you better be buyin' more'n two beers each," Abner complained. "Don't be takin' up no space at my bar if'n you ain't drinkin'."

"Abner," Shaye said, "you'll have plenty of men in here drinking in no time. We won't be getting in anybody's way. In fact, we'll just take these beers and go sit at a table."

With that the Shayes picked up their mugs and walked to a back table while one was still empty. The Golden Garter was the most popular saloon in town and usually started filling up the moment Abner opened the doors. There were so many regular customers that there was never any danger of Abner having a bad day. This was also the reason Abner always noticed a stranger—and today four of them came in and bellied up to the bar together. He reached under the bar and briefly touched the shotgun he kept there because he didn't like the way these four hombres looked—and he was usually a good judge of character.

Somebody at the bar wondered aloud what Dan

Shaye and his sons were doing in town and Abner noticed the four men look over at the Shaye table with interest.

"I help you boys?" Abner asked, stopping in front of the four men.

"Beer," one of them said, "four of 'em."

"Comin' up."

Abner drew four beers and set them in front of the men.

"Did we hear right?" one of them asked. "Those are Dan Shaye and his sons?"

"That's them," Abner said.

"What are they doin' here?" one of the other men asked.

"They live around here," Abner asked. "What's it to ya?"

"Hey, ol'-timer," a third man said, "take it easy. We're just curious, is all."

"You know what they say about curiosity, don't ya?" Abner asked.

"No," the fourth man asked, "what?"

Abner hesitated, then said, "If'n ya don't know, I sure ain't gonna tell ya."

The four men were on the run, but they weren't wanted in Wyoming. They'd come to Winchester to hide out for a while, but this opportunity was too good to pass up.

"I never heard of them," Paul Brocco said with a shrug.

"That's because you're stupid, Paul," George Griffiths said.

Paul sniffed, the way he always did when one of the other three men called him stupid.

"Don't gotta be smart to hear a name," he argued. "I ain't never heard of no Dan Shayne."

"It's Shaye, you moron," Lem Sanders said. "Dan Shaye and his two sons. They cleaned up the Langer gang."

"All of 'em," the fourth man, Ray Dolner, added. "I heard the pa, he got Aaron, and the oldest son, he got Ethan."

"Thomas," Griffiths said, "Thomas Shaye. I hear he's pretty good with that handgun."

"And the other one?" Paul asked. "He looks real young. Can't be all that tough."

"I tell you what, Paul," Griffiths said. "You can have the young one."

"Have him?" Paul asked. "For what?"

Dolner turned to face the others, who closed ranks so they couldn't easily be overheard.

"We're gonna take Shaye and his boys, are we?" he asked.

"Ain't they lawmen?" Sanders asked.

"I don't see no badges on them," Griffiths said. "I think they was lawmen, but they ain't no more."

"We come here to lie low, George," Dolner said.

"I know that, Ray," Griffiths said, "but we didn't know they was here. We take 'em fair and square and we're gonna have big reputations. A fair fight's a fair fight."

"You wanna take 'em fair?" Dolner asked.

"Hell, why not?" Griffiths asked. "There's four of us and three of them."

"That don't sound fair," Paul said.

"Shut up, Paul," the other three men said.

Brocco fell silent and pouted.

"Where do we do it?" Dolner asked. "In here?"

"No," Griffiths said. "That barkeep's got a shotgun behind the bar for sure. You see the way he was eyein' us?"

"Outside, then," Sanders said.

"Yeah," Griffiths said. "Outside."

"When?" Dolner asked.

"No time like the present," Griffiths said. "We finish our beers and wait outside. They gotta come out sooner or later."

"Okay, then," Dolner said.

"Fine with me," Sanders said.

"Me too," Paul chimed in.

"Shut up, Paul!" they all said.

* * *

Abner carried three fresh mugs of beer over to the table the Shayes were seated at.

"Fresh one," he said.

"We ain't done with these—" Thomas said, but Abner shushed him by slamming the mugs down on the table.

"Four men came in," he said. "They look like bad ones and they was interested in you."

With that he collected the other half-finished beers and took them back to the bar with him.

"Pa?" James asked.

"I saw them when they came in," Shaye said. "They're a wrong bunch, all right. See? This is why we stay out at the ranch most of the time."

"You think they know who we are?" James asked.

"If they didn't know, they heard it from somebody," Thomas said.

"Likely," Shaye said.

"What do we do?" James asked. "They're gonna be waitin' outside, ain't they?"

"Likely," Shaye said again.

"I could go out the back way and get the sheriff," James said.

"That might work," Thomas said, "except for one thing."

"What's that?" Shaye asked.

"Ain't no back way out of here, Pa."

10

"One of us could go out a window in the back," Thomas said.

"Which one of us were you thinkin' of?" James asked.

"Well... you."

"I ain't goin' out no window!"

"Well, I'm not—"

"That's enough," Shaye said. "Nobody's going out a window."

"So what are we gonna do?" James asked.

"Maybe," Shaye said, "they'll just get tired of waiting."

The four men at the bar filed outside. Facing the Shayes on the street would take the bartender and his shotgun out of the play.

Outside Paul asked, "Now what do we do?"

"We wait," Griffiths said. "We just wait."

When the four men left the saloon, Abner called over a man named Pete Winchell, who mopped up the saloon every night and got to sleep in the back room for the privilege.

"What'dya need, Abner?" Winchell asked.

"I need you to go to the sheriff's office and tell him there may be trouble," Abner said. "Big trouble."

"Sure, Ab," Winchell said. He ran his hand over his dry mouth and Abner could hear his dry flesh scraping over his gray stubble. "Can I get a drink first?"

"No," Abner said, "no drink until you get back."

"Aw, Ab—"

"Now move!"

Griffiths watched the old drunk stumble through the batwing doors. He righted himself briefly, rubbed his mouth, and squinted at the sun. On a hunch, he stepped into the man's way.

"Where ya goin', ol'-timer?"

"Who's askin'?"

"A man with money for a drink is askin'." Griffiths took some coins from his pocket and let them jingle in his hands.

Pete's eyes widened. "I—I got an errand to run for Abner."

"Who's Abner?"

"Fella runs the saloon," Pete said. "The bartender?"

"The nigger?"

"That's... uh, yeah, Abner."

"What's the errand, old man?" Ray Dolner asked, stepping up next to Pete.

"I, uh, I'm supposed to go and tell the sheriff that there's trouble brewin'."

"What kind of trouble?" Griffiths asked.

Still eyeing the hand that was holding his drink money, Pete said, "Uh, I dunno."

"Trouble where?" Dolner asked.

"Here, I guess."

"Tell you what," Griffiths said. "You go inside and

have a drink on us and we'll deliver the message to the sheriff."

"Ya will?"

"Sure."

"That's real nice of ya."

"We're friendly people," Dolner said.

"Here ya go, old man," Griffiths said, putting the coins into the old man's hands. "Ray, why don't you help our new friend back into the saloon?"

"Gotcha," Dolner said.

He walked Pete back to the batwing doors, then made a spectacle out of holding the doors open for him.

"Enjoy your drink, ol'-timer," Dolner said and left the batwings swinging in his wake as he left.

Abner saw one of the four strangers usher Pete back into the saloon.

"You deliver that message, Pete?" he asked when Pete got to the bar.

"Uh, no, but some new friends of mine said they'd do it, Ab," he replied. "I got money for a drink now."

Abner knew he should have put a back door in a long time ago. He also knew that Pete might break his neck trying to climb out a window.

"Yeah, okay, Pete," Abner said. "One drink."

He poured the old man a shot of whiskey, then stopped Pete's hand as he tried to bring it to his lips.

"Go slow," Abner said, "I ain't givin' you another one."

"I can pay!" Pete said indignantly.

"You keep that money in your pocket, Pete," Abner said, "and nurse that there drink."

Abner released Pete's hand and walked to the end of

the bar so he could look out the front window. Sure enough, the four men were milling around out there. He knew they were waiting for the Shayes to come out and the Shayes knew it too. Folks had been leaving the three men alone during their infrequent visits to town. Now Dan Shaye was in town for the second day in a row and trouble was already dogging him.

There was going to be trouble. Even though it wouldn't be their fault, Abner knew the Shayes would get the blame.

That's just the way it was.

11

"Just sit tight, boys," Shaye said to his sons. He got up and walked to the bar to talk to Abner.

"They still outside?"

"Jest waitin'," Abner said. "I tried to send Pete for the sheriff, but they sent him back in."

"Looks like they've got their minds made up."

"Looks like," the black man said. "You goin' out there?"

"Got to, eventually," Shaye said.

"Want me and my shotgun to go wit' ya?"

"No, Abner," Shaye said, "I want you and your shotgun to stay behind the bar, where you belong."

Abner looked around at his customers, then said, "Ain't nobody else gonna stand wit' ya, Dan."

"I've got my boys," Shaye said. "Should be enough to handle those four."

"When you gonna do it?"

Shaye shrugged.

"I'm not in a hurry to leave. Haven't got my telegram yet. Maybe they'll get tired of waiting."

Abner doubted that, but remained silent.

"Don't worry, Abner," Shaye said.

"Ain't fair."

"What?"

"I said it ain't fair," the barkeep said. "Folks been leavin' you alone up ta now. Ain't right some strangers come through town and cause trouble."

"Fair's got nothing to do with it, Abner," Shaye said. "Nothing at all."

He turned and went back to the table.

"What are we gonna do, Pa?" James asked.

"We're going to wait for our telegram, James," Shaye said.

"What about those men?"

Shaye looked toward the batwing doors. "Might as well let them wait too."

An hour later Paul Brocco started to fidget impatiently, then Lem Sanders joined in.

"Can't the two of you stand still?" Ray Dolner complained.

"How long we gonna wait?" Paul asked.

"As long as it takes," Griffiths said.

Some men had left the saloon and others had entered during the past hour, but apparently no one had gone for the sheriff. There was no lawman in sight. Paul still wondered how Griffiths knew that the drunk had been heading for the sheriff's office.

"Somebody comin'," Dolner said.

They all turned to take a look. Griffiths recognized the white shirt and sleeve garters of some kind of clerk. The visor on his head meant he was probably from the telegraph office.

"Interestin'," Griffiths said. "He's in a hurry."

The clerk hurried to the front of the saloon, but as he prepared to enter, Griffiths blocked his path.

"In a bit of a hurry, ain'tcha?"

"I got a telegram to deliver," the clerk said.

"Who to?"

The clerk was not going to answer the question, but the other three men closed rank around him.

"Uh, it's for Mr. Shaye."

"Which one?" Griffiths asked.

"Uh, Daniel Shaye."

"I'll take it."

Before the clerk could move or say a word, Griffiths had grabbed the telegram from his hand.

"Hey... well, uh, you'll give it to him?"

"No," Griffiths said. "You go inside and tell him I have it. Tell him he'll have to come out and get it."

"Um... if I do that, he'll be mad."

"I'm countin' on it."

The other men moved out of his way and the confused clerk entered the saloon.

"What's the telegram say?" Paul asked.

"Who cares?" Griffiths said and put it in his shirt pocket, unread.

"Finally," Shaye said as the telegraph clerk entered the saloon. The man stopped just inside, looked around, spotted their table, and hesitated. "Something's wrong. James, get him."

James reacted immediately, got to the clerk before the man could make a move. He grabbed his arm and walked him across the room to the table. The other patrons and Abner all watched, but Shaye didn't care anymore that they were the center of attention.

"Do you have my telegram?" Shaye asked.

"Well..."

"Come on, man, speak up!"

"Some men outside took it from me," the clerk said.

"They told me to tell you that if you want it you have to go and get it." Hurriedly, he added, "It wasn't my fault, Mr. Shaye—"

"I know that," Shaye said. He took some money out and handed it to the man without looking to see how much it was. "You can go."

"I—I don't wanna go back out there..."

"Go to the bar and have a drink."

"Yessir."

As the man left, James sat back down.

"Now what?"

"They're not leaving us any choice," Shaye said. "I want that telegram."

"Well," Thomas said, "I guess we better just go out and get it."

12

As they stepped outside, Shaye said to his sons, “Thomas, I want you to stand to my right and James, you stand to his right.”

“There’s four of ’em, Pa,” James reminded him.

“You’re right,” Shaye said. “Thomas, you’re the fastest. You stand center and take the two in the middle. Remember, son, pick out the leader and kill him first.”

“I got you, Pa.”

“Are we gonna try to do this first without guns, Pa?” James asked.

“We are, James,” Shaye said. “I’ll do the talking, but keep an eye on their hands and their eyes. Remember, use all of your vision. We’ll know real quick if we’re gonna need our guns.”

“Okay, Pa.”

Shaye looked at his sons. Thomas looked rock steady, James nervous. That was only natural. James was the youngest, Thomas—bigger, older, more confident—he had gunplay in his blood. Shaye wasn’t proud of that fact, but he had to admit it had come in handy in the past—and would come in handy now.

“Okay,” Shaye said, “Thomas goes out the door first and we follow right close behind. Are we ready?”

"Ready, Pa," James said.

Thomas just nodded and stepped through the batwing doors.

When Giffiths saw Thomas Shaye exit the saloon, followed by his father and brother, he pushed his partners and said, "Spread out. I'll take the middle one, Thomas Shaye."

"Who do I take?" Paul hissed.

"Shut up and spread out!"

The other three men obeyed. Shaye, Thomas, and James remained on the boardwalk in front of the saloon.

"One of you has something of mine," Shaye said.

Griffiths reached into his pocket with his left hand and came out with the telegram.

"Do you mean this?"'

"That's it," Shaye said. "Hand it over and you and your friends can leave."

Griffiths laughed and put it back in his pocket.

"If you want it, you're gonna have to take it...if you can."

"Oh, I can," Shaye said. "My only problem will be taking it without getting blood on it. Thomas?"

"Yes, Pa?"

"When you kill that man, make sure you don't shoot him in the heart," Shaye instructed. "That would soak the telegram with his blood."

"Yes, Pa."

"You're Thomas Shaye?" Griffiths asked.

"That's right."

"You killed Seth Langer?"

Thomas flinched. It was a sore point between him and his father that he had not killed Seth Langer.

"I brought him to justice," Thomas said. "He's in prison... and a cripple."

"My name is Griffiths, George Griffiths."

"Never heard of you."

"Some people have," Griffiths said. "More will, after I kill you."

Thomas laughed.

"You think killing me will give you a big rep?"

"We've heard of you—and your father," Griffiths said.

"I feel insulted," James said.

"And your brother," Griffiths added.

"Gee, thanks," James muttered.

"Enough talking," Shaye said. "Hand over the telegram or we'll take it."

"Take it, the—"

Before Griffiths could finish his sentence, Thomas drew his weapon and fired. George Griffiths never knew what hit him. The bullet plowed into his chest dead center, missing the telegram. Griffiths was knocked off his feet and onto his back in the street.

The other men, stunned by Thomas's speed, turned out to be easy pickings for Shaye and James, who both drew very deliberately—not sharing the speed Thomas possessed—and fired accurately. Only one of the other men even cleared leather and his gun ended up in the street next to his body.

All three of the Shaye men ejected the spent shells from their guns, replaced them with live loads, and holstered their weapons. Even though he knew they were dead, Shaye stepped down into the street and walked among the fallen men to make sure. He nudged each one with his boot, then picked up their weapons and tossed them away from him.

"Hold it!"

He turned and saw Sheriff Adam Kennedy approaching him, gun in hand.

"Take it easy, Sheriff," Shaye said. "It's all over."

"What the hell happened here?" Kennedy asked, looking down at the dead men.

"We didn't have a choice," Thomas said, stepping down into the street.

Kennedy turned, trained his gun on Thomas. Shaye took two quick steps and placed his hand on the lawman's gun.

"Holster it," he said.

Kennedy hesitated, looked around, and then obeyed. Slowly, men began to leave the saloon to have a look. People came from other directions as well and stared.

"We stayed in town too long," Shaye said. "That's what happened."

"And are you staying any longer?" Kennedy asked.

"I don't know. I guess that depends on what my telegram says."

"What telegram?"

Shaye leaned over the dead Griffiths, reached into his pocket, and removed the telegram. There was a bit of blood on one corner, but that was it.

"This one."

"What does it say?" Kennedy asked.

Shaye unfolded it, read it, and looked at the lawman.

"It says we're leaving town tomorrow."

13

The guard opened the door to allow Jeb Collier to leave Yuma Prison.

"Thanks," Jeb said.

"I got three months," the guard said.

"What?"

"The guards are all bettin' on when we'll see you in here again. I got three months. I mean, I figure you gotta get caught, then tried, and then they'll ship you over here...yeah, three months is about right."

"You got it wrong, Lane," Jeb said. "I ain't never comin' back here."

"Well," Lane said, "don't tell me you're goin' straight?"

"Straight?" Jeb frowned, as if he didn't know what that word meant.

"Yeah," Lane said, scratching his grizzled gray cheek, "like I figured. I been a prison guard for a lot of years...nigh on to thirty, I think, here and other prisons, and you're the worst I've seen."

Jeb looked back at the prison, and then at Lane. "I been in worse places, Lane."

"You got this place wired, that's for sure," Lane said.

"Everybody doin' your work for you...guards workin' for you..."

"Not you, though, huh?"

"No," Lane said, "not me. Like I tol' you. I been at this too long. You'll be back, Jeb."

"I don't think so, Lane."

Lane laughed.

"I'll keep your cell clean."

Jeb tried to think of a good response, but then decided that the best response would simply be to never return there.

He walked out the door.

Ben Collier watched as his brother walked out the front gate of Yuma Prison, a free man after two years.

"There he is," Clark Wilson said.

"I see him," Ben said.

Wilson and Dave Roberts exchanged a glance, but remained silent. They were both glad to see Jeb Collier leaving Yuma Prison. The past two years had been lean ones under Ben Collier. Jeb was always the brains of the two brothers.

However, Ben was the mean one, so they kept quiet.

Ben Collier moved forward to meet his brother with open arms.

"Hey, Ben!"

Jeb grabbed his larger, though younger, brother and hugged him tightly. Ben put his older brother in a bear hug and lifted him off his feet.

"Jesus, you're killin' me!" Jeb shouted. "Put me down, you big ox."

Ben put Jeb back on his feet and backed away.

"I'm just so damn glad to see you, Jeb."

Jeb looked past his brother to where Roberts and Wilson were standing with four horses.

"Boys," he said.

"Boss," Wilson said. Roberts nodded.

"You got my gun?"

"Right here." Ben turned. "Dave."

Roberts moved to one of the horse and fetched a gun belt from the saddlebags. He handed it to Ben, who turned and presented it to his brother.

Jeb took the gun belt and strapped it on.

"You don't know how naked I've felt without this," he said, adjusting it on his hip.

"You think you should be puttin' that on right in front of the prison?" Ben asked.

"Why not?" Jeb asked. "I'm out, ain't I? I'm a free man."

"Why don't we get away from here before they change their minds?" Ben asked.

Jeb smiled and patted Ben on the shoulder.

"That's not such a bad idea, brother," he said. "I've also been itchin' to be on a horse again."

Wilson walked the fourth horse over to Jeb.

"This horse any good?" he asked.

"I picked it out myself," Ben said.

"Clark?" Jeb asked, looking at Wilson.

"It's a good animal, boss."

Jeb nodded. Wilson was a much better judge of horseflesh than his brother Ben was.

"Okay, then," Jeb said. "Let's ride."

They rode for half a day and then camped, still in Arizona.

"Sorry we don't got better than beans for ya, Jeb," Ben said.

"Hey," Jeb said, "I'm eatin' them under the open sky. This is the best meal I've had in two years."

"Well," Clark Wilson said, reaching into his saddlebag, "you probably ain't had none of this in two years."

He came out with a bottle of whiskey.

Jeb's eyes lit up. "Give that here."

"It ain't the best stuff—" Wilson started, handing it over.

"It's whiskey," Jeb said. "That's all that matters."

He uncorked the bottle, lifted it to his lips, and took several big swallows. The rotgut burned its way down to his stomach, where it started a fire.

"Goddamn!" he said, lowering the bottle, his eyes watering. "That was good. So was them beans."

He stoppered the bottle and passed it back to Wilson.

"Now," he said, "tell me about Belinda."

"Aw, Jeb," Ben said, "why you wanna bother with her—"

"You know where she is, don't you?" Jeb asked. "Ben, you're supposed to know where she is."

"We know where she is, Jeb," Wilson said.

"And the kid?" Jeb asked. "She's got the kid?"

"She's got 'im," Ben said.

"Him? It's a boy, right?"

"It's a boy."

"What'd she name him?"

"We don't know that," Ben said.

"That's okay," Jeb said. "We'll find out."

"How we gonna do that, Jeb?" Ben asked.

"Easy," Jeb said. "We're gonna ask her."

Later, when Ben and Dave Roberts were asleep, Jeb and Clark Wilson sat around the fire together.

"We're sure glad you're out, Jeb," Wilson said.

"You been givin' Ben a hard time, Clark?" Jeb asked.

"No," Wilson said. "We did like you wanted, made him think he was in charge, but Jeb...he was always makin' the wrong decision, ya know?"

"I know, Clark," Jeb said, "but I knew I could count on you to keep him from gettin' killed."

"Believe me, there were times we all almost got killed."

"Well, things'll change now that I'm out."

"Maybe we can make some money?"

"We're gonna make plenty of money."

"You been makin' plans while you was inside?"

"Plenty of plans."

"What're we gonna hit first? A bank? A train?"

"First," Jeb said, "we're gonna go and see Belinda."

Wilson shook his head. "Jeb."

"This is somethin' I gotta do, Clark," Jeb said. "Where is she?"

"A town called Pearl River Junction," Wilson said, "in Texas."

"So that's where we're headed," Jeb said. "Pearl River Junction."

Wilson poured himself another cup of coffee and leaned back.

"What?"

"We need money, Jeb," Wilson said. "We're broke."

"Broke?"

"All we got," Wilson said, "is what you got in your pocket."

Which wasn't much. They'd given him a few coins when he left Yuma and the clothes he'd been wearing when he first arrived.

"Okay, Clark," Jeb said. "Okay. Does Pearl River Junction have a bank?"

"It does."

"Then we'll kill two birds with one stone," Jeb said. "We'll go there and see Belinda and we'll hit the bank."

"That's okay," Wilson said, "but we're gonna need some money to get there."

"Clark," Jeb asked. "you got somethin' in mind, don't ya?"

"Yep," Wilson said, "I got somethin' in mind."

"Okay, then," Jeb said, "pour me some more coffee and tell me what you got."

14

By the time Dan, Thomas, and James Shaye rode into Pearl River Junction, it had been almost four months since the letter had been sent from Belinda Davis.

Pearl River Junction was a good-sized town, one that was still growing. As they rode down the main street, the Shayes could see that many of the buildings were newly erected. In fact, they could still smell the new wood that had been used to build them. In the center of town was a new two-story building built of brick that was the town's City Hall.

The streets were bustling with traffic at midday: horses and buckboards in the street and a lot of pedestrian traffic on the boardwalks.

"Looks like a lively town," James said.

"Yeah," Dan said, "the kind that harvests trouble."

Thomas remained silent, but his eyes took in everything. He noticed that he, his father, and his brother were attracting some curious looks, most notably from a group of men in front of one of the saloons and from a deputy as they rode past the new brick sheriff's office, which was right next to City Hall.

"Pa..."

"I see 'em, Thomas."

"See who?" James asked, looking around.

"Lawman, givin' us the eye," Thomas said.

"So what? We ain't doin' anything wrong."

"We're strangers," Shaye said. "That's enough to make people curious. Wait a minute."

Thomas and James reined in their horses while Shaye turned his horse and rode over to where the deputy was standing, watching them.

"Hello, Deputy."

"Howdy," the young badge toter said. "Just passin' through?"

"Actually, no," Shaye said. "We're looking for a livery that'll take our horses for a few days."

"All the way to the end of the street, then go left, not right," the deputy said. "You'll see it."

"Thanks."

"When you're done, come by the office," the man added. "The sheriff's gonna want to talk to you."

"We'll do it," Shaye said. "Thanks."

He turned his horse and rode back to his sons.

"He didn't ask many questions," he told them. "I guess he's going to leave that to his boss. Come on, we'll take care of the horses and then talk to the sheriff."

"We're not gonna get a hotel first?" James asked.

"After," Shaye said.

"Why are we so eager to report to the local law?" James asked.

"Sheriff might be able to tell us where to find Belinda Davis," Shaye said. "Besides, it's better than having him come looking for us."

They found the livery with no problem and arranged for their mounts to be taken care of. That done they grabbed their rifles and saddlebags and walked back to the sheriff's office. Walking together, the Shayes continued to attract attention from the citizens on the boardwalks.

Dan Shaye knocked on the door to the sheriff's office and then walked in. A wooden shingle next to the door said: SHERIFF RILEY COTTON.

When they walked in Shaye was immediately struck by the fact that the office had two stories. Glancing up, he saw that the cell block was on the second level. Downstairs was filled with furniture—several desks—the sheriff's and, presumably, one each for two or more deputies to share. There were also chairs, filing cabinets, a pot-bellied stove, and two gun racks on opposite walls. In one corner was a safe worthy of a bank.

"Very impressive," Shaye said.

"Glad you think so," Sheriff Riley Cotton said. He stood up behind his desk. "My deputy told me we had three strangers in town. That'd be you three?"

"That's us," Shaye said. He approached the desk. "Dan Shaye. These are my sons, Thomas and James."

"The Epitaph bank job Shayes?" the lawman asked.

"That what they're calling us?" Shaye asked.

"Sorry," Cotton said. He was a tall man in his forties, bearded, wearing a clean shirt, tie, and trousers. He was dressed more like a schoolteacher than a lawman, but Shaye could tell more from the way the man stood than the way he was dressed. There was a gun belt hanging on a hook on the wall right behind him. The leather and the pistol itself were well cared for.

"Word gets around," Cotton said. "I notice you're not wearing badges."

"That's because we're not lawmen anymore."

Cotton raised his eyebrows.

"That by choice?"

"Yes."

"Too bad. From what I heard, you were good at it."

"How long have you been sheriff?" James asked.

"Been wearin' a badge for fifteen or sixteen years. I've been sheriff here for the last five. You fellas wouldn't be, uh, workin' in some, um, related capacity, would you?"

"What?" Thomas asked.

"He wants to know if we're bounty hunters," Shaye said. "The answer is no."

"So then what brings you to Pearl River Junction?"

"We're looking for someone," Shaye said.

"Who?"

"A girl named Belinda Davis."

The sheriff didn't react.

"Do you know her?"

"Why do you want this girl?"

"So you do know her?"

"Answer my question first, please."

"She sent me a letter asking for my help."

"Do you have that letter on you?"

Shaye hesitated, then shifted his saddlebags from his right shoulder to his left so he could dig into his shirt pocket and come out with the letter. He held it up, but did not offer it to the sheriff.

"Can I see it?" Cotton asked.

"Answer my question now," Shaye said. "Do you know her?"

"Yes, I know her."

"And you can tell us where to find her?"

"I can," the lawman said. "The question is: Will I?"

Shaye hesitated, then handed the letter over.

"I tell you what," the sheriff said. "You fellas wait around your hotel or one of the saloons and I'll get back to you."

15

After they left the sheriff's office, they went across the street to a hotel Cotton recommended to them. They got two rooms, with Thomas and James sharing one. After they stowed their gear in their rooms, they met in the lobby to go and get something to eat. Again, the restaurant they went to was recommended by the sheriff.

Once they were seated and had ordered their food, James asked, "Why did you let him get away with that, Pa?"

"Get away with what?"

The diners surrounding them stared curiously at the strangers, but went back to their meals fairly quickly. The Shayes simply ignored the stares.

"He knows the girl, but he ain't tellin' us where she is."

"He wants to check with her first," Thomas said. "I don't have a problem with that."

"But he has the letter," James said. "He knows she wrote to Pa askin' for help."

"Months ago," Shaye said. "Maybe she's changed her mind."

"That would mean we came all this way for nothin'."

"Not for nothing," Shaye said. "Even if she doesn't want our help anymore, I still want to find out if her child is Matthew's."

"So how long do we wait?" James asked.

"Don't be in such a rush, James," Shaye said. "We're here and the sheriff knows we're not going anywhere."

The waiter came over carrying three plates laden with huge steaks and generous portions of vegetables.

"Eat your food," Shaye told James. "When the sheriff knows what to tell us, we'll hear from him."

James hesitated, but when his father and brother bent to the task of consuming their meal, he followed.

Sheriff Riley Cotton lived in a small white house at the northern end of town. He could tell by the delicious smells filling the house that his wife was hard at work in the kitchen, baking and probably preparing supper. He found her there, wearing one of her many handmade aprons.

"Smells great," he said as he entered the kitchen, "but then everything you make smells great."

She turned her head so he could kiss her and said, "Peach cobbler for dessert."

He kissed his wife, who he loved dearly even after twenty years of marriage. Marion Cotton had always been supportive of his chosen career and had moved from town to town without complaint—until they'd arrived in Pearl River Junction five years ago. She told him after only a year of living there that she never wanted to move again.

"What brings you home two hours early?" she asked. "I wasn't expecting you until supper."

"Dan Shaye and his sons rode into town today," he told her.

She stopped what she was doing and turned to face him, wiping her hands on her apron.

"Have you told Belinda?"

"That's what I came home to do," he said. "Is she around?"

"I think she's out back with Little Matt."

"I better talk to her and see if she still wants to see him—and his sons," he said.

She grabbed his arm before he could leave the kitchen. "Why did they come, Riley?"

"Well, they say they came to help her," he answered, "that is, if she still needs help."

"Will they take her away?" she asked. "And the baby?"

"I don't know, Marion," he said. "I guess we'll all find that out at the same time."

"I couldn't bear it if—" she started, but then stopped abruptly and released his arm.

"I know," he said. "Believe me, I know."

16

By the time Dan Shaye and his sons reached Pearl River Junction, Jeb Collier and his men were still about a week away. They were making camp for the night while the Shayes were eating supper.

"We got enough money now, Jeb?" Ben asked as they sat around the fire.

"We got enough, Ben," Jeb said. "We're headin' straight for Pearl River Junction, come mornin'."

"You still gonna go after that gal?" Ben asked. "That ain't smart, Jeb—"

"Next time I need you to tell me what's smart, Ben," Jeb said, "I'll go back to Yuma."

"Aw, Jeb—"

"Go and get some more wood for the fire."

"Jeb—"

"Git!"

Muttering, Ben got up and went out into the woods to look for wood.

"We could hit another bank on the way, Jeb," Clark Wilson said. "I know of one—"

"Clark, you picked out two sweet banks for us and we hit 'em," Jeb said. "We got enough money to outfit ourselves and head for Texas, and that's what we're gonna do now."

"This bank I'm thinkin' of is on the way."

"In Texas?"

"Yeah."

Jeb shook his head.

"Ain't gonna hit no Texas banks until we're done in Pearl River Junction," he said. "Once we're done, we'll hit that bank and light out for Mexico." They had already hit one bank in Arizona and one in New Mexico. Wilson had chosen the banks, but it was Jeb's planning that enabled them to pull those jobs off successfully—without killing or injuring anyone.

"We gonna be takin' the woman and child with us?" Wilson asked.

"I don't know that, Clark," Jeb said.

Dave Roberts sat across the fire from them, but did not take part in the conversation. Wilson and Jeb Collier had been friends—or partners—for a lot longer than Roberts had known either one of them. He didn't feel he had anything to add to their discussion.

"I got to find out if this kid is mine before I decide somethin' like that," Jeb added.

"Well... he's the right age," Wilson said.

"I'll know," Jeb said. "As soon as I look at the boy, I'll know if he's mine or not."

Wilson looked across the fire at Roberts, who just shrugged.

"Okay, then," Wilson said. "You're the boss."

"Pearl River Junction," Jeb said. "We head there tomorrow."

17

Shaye and his sons left the café and stopped just outside the door.

"What now, Pa?" James asked.

"Let's split up and walk around the town," Shaye said. "If we're going to be here for a few days, I want to know what's going on."

Shaye split the town in three parts and they each went their separate ways. There was a saloon a few doors down from the café, small and quiet at the moment. They agreed to meet there in two hours. After that they'd check back with the sheriff.

Shaye kept the middle part of town—where most of the businesses were—for himself and sent James north and Thomas south.

It was nearing five o'clock, the time when many of the merchants would be closing their stores, and Shaye was surprised to find that many of them were still full of customers. The word "bustling" wasn't strong enough to describe the feeling he got walking around Pearl River Junction.

Shaye had been the lawman in many towns, but none of them had ever had the feeling of energy this one had.

It made him wonder what it would be like to wear a badge here and have an office that looked like Sheriff Cotton's.

On the trail to Pearl River Junction from Winchester with his boys, the subject of wearing a badge again had not come up. This was actually the first time in months Shaye felt like he missed it.

James walked north as far as he could go. The last building he came to was a schoolhouse. It was empty now, but it was the building itself that interested him. It was obviously new and it was the largest schoolhouse he'd ever seen. He walked up to it, around it, then stepped in to peer through a window. He was surprised to see someone inside. A pretty young woman was shuffling papers at the desk, stuffing them into a leather case. It looked as if she was preparing to leave. James decided to walk around to the front of the building and wait for her. It was the classic curse of every young man: Just a brief glimpse of her blonde hair and smooth skin and he was smitten.

Thomas walked south and eventually found himself at the fork in the road they had come to earlier when they first rode into town. Going right would take him to the livery where they'd left their horses, so he decided to go left. He thought it was strange that, given the name of the town, there was no river, and this was the only junction he had seen since arriving.

He kept walking and came to a collection of small houses. A few of them were aged, but most of them seemed new. He didn't recall having ever been in a town that was in this stage of growth. Even growing up in Epitaph, Texas, it seemed as if the town had reached a certain stage of growth and stalled. No one in Epitaph had seemed to even care. As for Winchester, that town seemed very happy with the way it was.

Pearl River Junction was a different story. He could feel that people liked it here and could see and smell the growth. He found himself wondering what it would be like to wear a badge in such a town.

Unlike his father, Thomas had often thought about wearing a badge again. Now the urge seemed to swell inside of him. Whatever happened with Belinda Davis, whether her baby turned out to be Matthew's or not, Thomas decided that he would not return to Wyoming with his father and brother. He was going to move on from here, not go back.

As Elizabeth Newland came out the front door of the schoolhouse, she saw a man loitering there.

"Can I help you?" she asked. He didn't look old enough to be the father of one of the students. He looked barely old enough to be out of school himself, but then she knew the same was true of herself. He was probably her age—or even a year or so older. "All the children have gone home."

"Oh, I'm not a parent," James Shaye said. "I'm, uh, a stranger in town. I was just...taking a walk and I saw the schoolhouse. It's...the biggest I've ever seen."

"Yes," she said, coming down the steps. She was clutching her leather case to her breast. It was filled to bursting with papers. "We're very proud of it."

As she approached him, coming down the walkway, James moved to intercept her.

"Are you going home?" he asked.

"Yes, I am."

"May I help you?" he asked.

"I really don't need—"

"I could carry those for you," he said. "Maybe you can tell me a little bit about the town?"

She hesitated, but the young man looked harmless enough. And he was not unattractive.

"Very well," she said, surrendering her burden to him. "I have to walk this way."

He fell in next to her as she led him back toward town.

"I actually live all the way on the other end of town," she told him apologetically.

"I don't mind the walk."

"I'm Elizabeth," she said. "What's your name?"

"I'm James," he said, "James Shaye..."

As James started walking with Elizabeth, he turned his head and saw the sheriff in the backyard of a small house. He was with a young woman and a small boy.

"Is that the sheriff?" he asked Elizabeth.

"Yes, it is," she said. "He lives there with his wife."

"Is that his daughter?"

"No, that's a girl who he and his wife took in to live with them," she said. "Her name is Belinda."

"And the child?"

"Her son," Elizabeth said, then lowered her voice. "She had him out of wedlock. It's something of a scandalous situation."

"Really?" he asked. "Her having the baby? Or living with the sheriff and his wife?"

"Well... both, actually."

"How long has she lived in town?"

"I'm not sure," she said. "I've only been here myself for a year, and she was living here when I arrived. I came from back East to teach here."

James filed away the information about the sheriff and Belinda Davis and turned his attention back to the pretty schoolteacher.

"So where back East did you come from?" he asked her as they continued on.

18

Thomas was the first one to arrive at the small saloon they'd chosen as their meeting place. Above the door was a handwritten sign that said: BO HART'S SALOON. Good, simple, straightforward name, he thought.

He went inside, found the place quiet, in spite of the fact that it was pretty full. A quick look around told him there was no piano, no stage, no gambling equipment. There was one barmaid moving through the room, carrying a tray. Seems Bo Hart's Saloon was simply a place a man could get a drink—and not much more. Well, at least there won't be any trouble here, he thought.

He walked to the bar and leaned on it. The bartender was a man who had the misfortune to possess both a barrel chest and bandy legs. Gave him an odd appearance and, as he moved about behind the bar, an odd gait as well. Thomas waited until the man finished loading the barmaid's tray with drinks before waving his hand at him.

"What can I get ya?" the man asked.

"Just a beer."

"Comin' up."

The man filled a mug with a frosty brew and set it down in front of Thomas.

"Mind if I start a tab?" Thomas asked. "I'm waitin' for two more fellas and they'll also be drinkin'."

"Sure," the man said, "why not?"

Thomas grabbed his beer, turned his back to the bar, and leaned against it. There were only about ten tables in the place and eight of them were full. There were two empties toward the back of the room. He waved at the bartender again.

"Another one already?"

"No, just a question," Thomas said. "Them two empty tables in the back, they reserved for anythin' special?"

"Poker games," the man said. "We usually have a couple goin', but they won't start for a few hours yet."

"Mind if I sit at one, then?"

"Uh...well, we usually keep them open," the bartender said, looking confused.

"Where's the harm if I sit at one for a little while?"

"Well...no harm, I guess—"

"Much obliged."

Thomas left the bar, walked to the back of the room, and sat at one of the tables. He sat facing the batwing doors so he'd see his brother and father when they entered.

The men seated at the other tables—seated by twos and threes—all turned to look at him as if he'd just dropped a turd in the middle of the room. He simply raised his beer to them, nodding his head.

It took a few moments, but finally several of the men—two from one table, a third from another—slowly stood up and walked over to him.

"You can't sit there," one of them said.

"You're not supposed to sit there," another said.

The third simply stood there, staring at him.

"I'm just waiting for my father and brother," he said. "When they get here they'll each have a beer and we'll be on our way."

"Can't sit there," the third man said.

"We'll be gone before your poker game is supposed to start," Thomas said. "I guarantee it."

A fourth man got up and came over.

"You gotta get up."

Now, Thomas knew that the simple thing, the easy thing, to do was get up—just get up and walk out. He could have waited for his father and brother right out front. But he also knew that once you let a man cow you, move you, tell you what to do... well, once you did that men tended to try to do that to you all the time.

"I'm not finished with my beer," he said, swirling what was left of it at the bottom of the mug. "There's no harm in me sitting here long enough to finish my beer and then I'll go. I'll wait for my brother and my pa outside."

A fifth man stood up.

"You gotta get up now."

"What is it with you people?" Thomas demanded.

"Them's the tables for poker games," a sixth man said.

"Well, maybe today they ain't," Thomas said stubbornly. "What do you think of that? Maybe today that's one of the poker tables." He pointed to the table two of the men had stood up from. "That one—and that one." He pointed to the other empty table, which was always used for poker. "If the game had to be played at another table, what would that mean?"

Nobody answered.

"Would the world end?"

No answer.

"Goddamn it!" Thomas said.

"That's one of the poker tables," the first man said. "Always has been."

"That's the way it is," anther man said. Thomas had lost count of how many men had spoken.

"Shit!" Thomas said.

He wasn't afraid. He was outnumbered, but he wasn't afraid. That wasn't why he was mad enough to cuss. These weren't gunmen, they were townsmen who did things the same way every day. If a day came when they had to do things differently, they wouldn't know how to react.

But if he let them make him move...

"Shit," he said and drank the rest of his beer.

James walked the teacher home, then handed her the armload of papers at the front door of her house.

"Thank you," she said.

"Thank you for tellin' me somethin' about this town."

"It's a town, like a lot of others," she said. "Folks around here get into a routine. If something changes that routine—"

"Like some strangers ridin' into town?"

"—they get curious. Wary. Don't let it bother you if you get stared at."

"All right."

She stepped through the door of her house, then turned and said, "Maybe, if you stay in town a few days, I'll see you again."

"Maybe," he said. "I'd like that."

She smiled a dazzling smile that made his heart skip a beat and then closed the door.

* * *

Dan Shaye was impressed by Pearl River Junction and its people. They stared at him as he went by, but he didn't let that bother him. They were just curious. He understood that.

One by one the businesses closed up as the last customer left and the merchants locked their doors. People went home for supper.

He found a wooden bench in front of the mercantile store and sat in it for a while, just watching folks walk by, listening to the locks being turned on doors. Finally, the owner of the mercantile store came out and looked at him.

"Can I help you?" Shaye asked.

"The chair," the man said. He was an older man, balding, pot-bellied, wearing an apron. "I got to put it away."

Shaye stared at the man for a few moments and could tell it would be useless to ask him to leave the chair out just this once. He stood up and the man took the chair and carried it into the store without a word. Seconds later Shaye heard the door lock.

Suddenly the streets were kind of quiet and empty. Occasionally someone rode by on a horse or a buckboard went by, but the amount of foot traffic on the boardwalks had dropped significantly.

It was time to meet the boys, so Shaye stepped into the street and headed for the saloon.

19

When Shaye reached the front of the saloon, he saw James coming toward him from the south end of town.

"I thought you had the north end," he said when his youngest son reached him.

"I did," James said. "I'll tell you about it inside."

Shaye nodded and they entered through the batwing doors. They became immediately aware that something was going on. Most of the men in the place were standing and they were all facing the same way.

"What do you want to bet your brother's somewhere in the middle of that?" Shaye asked.

"No bet," James said.

"'Scuse us," Shaye said and he and James started to make their way through the crowd.

Thomas had just about made up his mind that there were better things to fight over than a table when he saw his father and brother break through the crowd of men who were fronting him.

"Are you having a problem, Thomas?" Shaye asked.

"Not really, Pa," Thomas said, standing up, "but I think we better pick someplace else to have a drink."

"Oh sure," James said, pointing to his brother's

empty mug, "now that you've already had one."

"Believe me, brother," Thomas said, "you don't want to have a beer in here. Take my word for it."

"Let's get going, then," Shaye said. "That is, if none of your new friends has any objection."

Amazingly, the men had already started to sit back down at their tables now that Thomas had stood up.

"I don't think anybody minds, Pa," Thomas said and led the way out of the saloon.

"What was that all about?" James asked when they were outside.

"Well, supposedly, a table," Thomas said, "but to tell you the truth, I ain't really sure."

"I spotted another saloon down the street," Shaye said. "Let's go there and then we can compare notes."

"You were really gonna fight all those men over a table?" James asked as they started walking.

"It was the strangest thing..." Thomas started.

When they got themselves a table at the Wagon Wheel Saloon and nobody objected, Thomas breathed a sigh of relief.

"Why didn't you just get up and walk out?" Shaye asked. "Wait for us outside?"

"I was about to when you both arrived," Thomas said. "I'm still not sure what the hell was goin' on in there."

"You were tryin' to change their routine," James said. "According to Elizabeth, folks hereabouts don't want to change their routines."

"Elizabeth?" Thomas asked.

"I met this schoolteacher..." James started and continued on to explain how he'd walked her home.

"I almost got in a bar fight over a table and you're

walkin' a pretty school marm home?" Thomas said in disbelief.

"Took me all the way to the south end of town too," James said.

"Which I already checked," Thomas replied. "Nothin' but houses there."

"I know," James said, "she lives in one. But here's somethin' else. We passed the sheriff's house."

"At the south end of town?" Shaye asked.

"No," James said, "the north end, near the schoolhouse. He and his wife have got Belinda Davis livin' with them."

"What?"

"They took her in, I guess," James said. "Elizabeth really ain't sure of the details."

"Is she related to the sheriff?" Thomas asked.

"I don't think so."

"And the child?" Shaye asked.

"He's there too," James said. "I saw him."

"Does he look like Matthew?" Thomas asked, anxiously.

"I couldn't tell," James said. "I only got a glimpse. They were in the sheriff's backyard."

"Well," Shaye said, sitting back, "maybe that explains the sheriff's reluctance to talk to us."

"What do you think he'll say when we go and see him?" James asked.

"I guess that'll depend on what this Belinda says," Shaye answered. "If she don't want to talk to us—"

"She's got to at least talk to us, Pa," Thomas said. "Maybe now that she's livin' with the sheriff, she won't want our help anymore, but she's got to at least talk withus."

"I think so too, Thomas," Shaye said. "I just hope she feels that way."

20

The Shayes finished their beer at the Wagon Wheel and then left to walk over to the sheriff's office. They stopped just outside.

"Some office, huh?" Thomas asked.

"I wonder what it would be like to come to work here every day?" James said.

"Let's just get inside," Shaye said gruffly. His sons gave him an odd look, then followed him into the office.

Sheriff Cotton was seated behind his desk, waiting for them.

"Come on in, gents. Did you have supper?"

"Yes," Shaye said, "we went to the place you suggested."

"Good, good," Cotton said. "Just got back from having supper myself. Come on, have a seat. Can I get you some coffee?"

"No," Shaye said, answering for the three of them. "We're fine."

Shaye sat in a chair opposite the lawman and Thomas and James remained standing.

"We'd like to know what Belinda said about seeing us," Shaye said. "We know that she's living with you and your wife."

"Somebody talked, huh?"

"James saw you with her out behind your house," Shaye said, deciding to play it straight. "And with the child."

"Matthew," Cotton said.

"What?" James asked.

"His name is Matthew," Cotton said. "We call him Little Matt."

Shaye exchanged glances with his sons.

"Yes, I know," Cotton said. "Your other son's name was Matthew."

"Sheriff—"

"Okay, here it is," Cotton said. "She'll see you, Mr. Shaye, and only you, and the meeting will take place at my house."

"Wait," Thomas said, "why not us?"

"Maybe later," Cotton said. "All three of you at once would be overwhelming." He looked directly at Shaye. "Surely you can see that."

Shaye hesitated, then said, "Yes, I can. All right, I agree."

"Pa—"

"Don't worry, Thomas," Shaye said. "After all, it was to me she sent the letter." He looked at Cotton. "What other conditions?"

"Either I or my wife also has to be present," Cotton said. "But not the boy. Not yet."

"I want to see the boy," Shaye said. "I'll be able to tell if he's Matthew's."

Again, Cotton said, "Maybe later. Belinda wants to see you first, Mr. Shaye."

"When?"

"Tomorrow, around noon."

"Why not tonight?" James asked.

Cotton looked at James. "I'm doin' this the way Belinda wants to do it, sir."

"What's her relation to you, Sheriff?" Thomas asked.

"None."

"Then why does she live with you and your missus?"

"She needed help," Cotton said. "And she had a child. My wife is not the sort of person who could ignore that."

"She sounds like a fine woman," Shaye said.

"Thank you for sayin' that," Cotton replied. "She is."

"All right, Sheriff," Shaye said, getting to his feet. "We'll do this your way—the girl's way."

"Come by here tomorrow at eleven forty-five and I'll walk you over to my house," Cotton said.

"I'll be here."

"Meanwhile," Cotton said, also standing, "I'd appreciate it if you and your boys could stay out of trouble while you're in town."

"We always do our best to avoid trouble, Sheriff," Shaye said. "It's just not always our choice."

"Just your word on behalf of you and your boys that you'll try is fine with me," Cotton said.

"You have it."

"Good enough. See you tomorrow, then."

Shaye nodded and led his sons out on to the street.

21

They spent the evening drinking in the Wagon Wheel and trying to stay out of trouble. Thomas got a deck of cards from the bartender and they played three-handed poker for pennies, turning away any who wanted to join them.

"Family game," Shaye told them.

While playing, they talked over the day's events and what tomorrow might bring.

"I think we should go together to see her," James said. "We're all entitled."

"Maybe we are," Shaye said, "but the sheriff has a point. Facing the three of us at once would be too overwhelming for her."

"What if she's not so easily overwhelmed?" Thomas asked. "I'll take two cards."

"What?" James asked.

"What if she's puttin' on an act," Thomas said. "Conning us."

"You think she's a con woman?" James asked. "That her child is not really Matthew's?"

Thomas shrugged.

James said, "One card."

"And is she foolin' the sheriff too?" Shaye asked. "Dealer takes one."

"Maybe."

"Let me ask you this, Thomas," Shaye said. "If she wanted to con someone, why not pick a family with more money? Why us?"

"Our name?"

"Our name?" Shaye asked. "Up until two years ago, no one outside of Epitaph knew who we were."

"They knew who you were," James said. "In Missouri."

"Knew who I was," Shaye said. "But no one knew who the Shayes were."

"Until we tracked down the Langer gang and made a name for ourselves," Thomas said.

"Why would she want to be a part of that kind of name?" Shaye asked.

Thomas and James didn't have an answer.

"Well," Shaye said, "I guess I'll find out tomorrow." He slapped his cards down. "I've got aces full."

Shaye turned in before his sons. They chose to stay at the Wagon Wheel until closing.

"Remember what the sheriff said, boys," Shaye told them. "Stay out of trouble."

"We will, Pa," James promised.

Shaye returned to the hotel while Thomas and James continued to play penny-ante poker, two-handed.

About an hour before closing, three men came into the saloon and stopped just inside the door, looking around. Thomas noticed them, James did not. Eventually, they walked to the bar and ordered three beers.

"Thomas?"

"What?"

"How many cards?"

"Oh," Thomas said. "Uh, one."

"What's wrong with you?"

"We're bein' watched."

"By who?" James was smart enough not to turn around immediately.

"Three men, at the bar."

"Are they from that other saloon?" James asked.

Thomas hadn't thought of that.

"I don't know," he said. "I don't remember everyone from this afternoon."

"Well, what are they doin'?"

"Drinkin' beer, watchin' us," Thomas said.

"They wearin' guns?"

"Yes."

"What should we do?"

"I know what I'm gonna do," Thomas said.

"What?"

Thomas smiled. "I'm gonna bet three cents."

"Three more," one of the men at the bar said.

"We're gonna be closin' soon," the barman said.

"We'll drink 'em fast," the man said. "Three more."

The bartender shook his head and served them three more beers. Aside from these three men and the Shaye brothers, there were only a couple of other men in the place and they both had their heads down: one on a table, and one on the bar.

"Them those Shaye boys?" the man asked.

"Why do you want to know?" the bartender asked.

"We're just curious."

The bartender looked at the three men. He knew them. They worked for one of the larger ranches in the area, the Bar-K. He didn't know their names, but he recognized their faces. They came into the saloon a few times a month, usually to start trouble. The spokesman was named Cobb and the other two were...Martin and... Franks, he thought. Or was it Frank something?

"We just heard they was in town," Joe Cobb said. "Wanted to take a look, didn't we, boys?"

"Sure did," Harley Franks said and Kel Martin just nodded.

"You boys better finish your beers and move on," the bartender said. "I don't want no trouble here."

"We'll leave when we're ready," Cobb said. "Why don't you go back to work?"

The bartender stood there for a moment, then moved down the bar to wake up a sleeping drunk.

22

"They don't look like so much," Cobb said to his buddies.

"Wonder where the ol' man is?" Franks said.

"We better finish these beers," Martin said.

The other two men looked at him.

"The bartender's gotta close up."

"Shut up, Kel," Cobb said. "He'll close up after we drink up and leave."

"What are we gonna do, Joe?" Franks said.

"I dunno," Cobb said.

"We just wanted to get a look at them," Franks said. "We done that. Let's get back to the ranch."

They'd been drinking at several of the other saloons in town, then heard from somebody that Dan Shaye and his sons were in town and in the Wagon Wheel. Franks was right. The only plan they'd had was to get a look at the Shayes.

"But what fun would that be?" Cobb asked.

Thomas watched the bartender wake the two sleeping drunks and get rid of them. That left only him and James—and the three men at the bar.

"Closin' up, you fellas," the barman said, coming over to their table.

"Fine," James said. "We'll leave."

The bartender didn't move.

"What is it?" Thomas asked.

"Them three are troublemakers," he said. "They was askin' about you."

"You know 'em?" Thomas asked.

"Yeah, they work at the Bar-K."

"What kind of trouble are they lookin' for?" Thomas asked.

"The kind of trouble you fellas must be used to by now."

"Okay," Thomas said. "Thanks."

"Can you take it outside?" the bartender asked. "I gotta close up."

"Don't worry," Thomas said. "We're not lookin' for trouble."

Somehow that didn't ease the bartender's mind. He went back behind the bar.

"What do you wanna do, Thomas?" James asked.

"I'd like to get out of here and back to our hotel without trouble," Thomas said, "but my guess is that's not gonna be up to us."

James turned for the first time and looked at the three men.

"They look like ranch hands, Thomas," he said. "Not gun hands."

"But they're wearin' guns, James," Thomas said. "They're wearin' guns."

"Let's try 'em." Cobb said.

"What?" Franks asked.

Cobb turned and looked at his two compadres.

"Come on, they don't look like much. One of them's hardly old enough to shave. Let's brace 'em, see how tough they are."

"B-but...ain't they lawmen?" Martin asked.

"Not no more, they ain't," Cobb said. "Besides, them two ain't wearin' no badges."

"I don't know—" Martin said. "I think we better get back to the ranch, Cobb."

"Nobody cares what you think, Kel," Cobb said. He looked at Franks. "Whataya say, Harley? Wanna have some fun?"

Harley Franks had just enough beer and whiskey in him from a whole night of drinking that the idea appealed to him. They worked hard punching cows all the time. Where was the harm in having some fun?

"Why not?" he said. "What do we do?"

Cobb turned as he heard chairs scraping the floor and saw the two Shayes standing up, getting ready to leave.

"You two just follow my lead," he said to Franks and Martin. "We make them back down and we'll be the ones with a rep, not them."

"I'm a cowhand," Martin said, confused. "I don't want a rep."

Nobody was listening.

23

"Let's just leave, James," Thomas said. "There's nothin' else we can do."

"All right."

They pushed their chairs back and stood up. The bartender was behind the bar, watching all five men warily. There was a shotgun under the bar, but he wasn't going to get involved.

As they headed for the door, one of the men pushed away from the bar, followed by the other two, although Thomas could see one of them was moving reluctantly.

"Hold on, gents," the man said. "What's your hurry?"

"No hurry," Thomas said. "It's closin' time and we're leavin'."

"But we ain't even met yet," the man said. "My name's Cobb. What's yours?"

"It's a little late to be makin' new friends, don't you think?" Thomas asked. "Besides, I get the feelin' you and your partners already know our names."

"Shaye, right?" Cobb asked. "Dan Shaye's sons?"

"That's right," James said. "What about it?"

"I was just wonderin'," Cobb said, chuckling. "Didn't your daddy give you your own names?"

"Friend," Thomas said, "we don't have time for this. Move out of the way. We're leavin'."

"With your tails between your legs?" Cobb asked.

"What?" James asked. Thomas put a steadying hand on his little brother's arm.

"That's the only way you're leavin'," Cobb said. "With your tails between your legs... ain't that right, boys?"

"Uh, right," Franks said.

"Um..." Martin said.

Thomas looked at the other two men. One looked confused and the other simply looked drunk.

"You fellas gonna let your friend's mouth get you into all kinds of trouble?" he asked them. "Because that's what he's doin'. He's lookin' for trouble."

"And he's gonna find it," James added.

"You boys got guns on," Thomas said. "You ready to use 'em?"

"Hey..." Harley Franks said. "Hey... nobody said anything about no gunplay."

"Well," Thomas said, "your friend says we're leavin' here with our tails between our legs. The only way we're gonna do that is if you fellas know how to use those guns of yours."

"Cobb—" Martin said.

"Shut up, Kel. They're bluffin'."

"Bluffin'?" Thomas said. "What would we be bluffin' about, Cobb?"

"You ain't gonna use them guns."

"Why not?" Thomas asked. "You seem to know our reputation. What makes you think I won't kill you to get by you and then go back to my hotel and sleep like a baby?"

Cobb stared at Thomas. James looked at the other men, both of whom were shuffling their feet nervously.

"Time for you two to go," he said.

Martin and Franks exchanged a glance.

"Now!" James snapped. "Last chance."

Both men jumped, then turned and headed for the door.

"Sorry, Cobb," Franks said on his way out.

Both men went through the batwing doors so quickly that they swung back and forth violently in their wake. Cobb didn't turn his head or take his eyes off Thomas. It was as if he were afraid to, afraid that Thomas would shoot him down if he did.

"Now it's your turn," Thomas said. "Turn around and walk away."

"With my tail between my legs?"

"That's exactly—" James started, but Thomas cut him off.

"No," Thomas said. "You can leave with your…dignity, if you like. Let's just say this was all a mistake."

Cobb continued to stare at him.

"Back out if you want," Thomas said. "We'll wait."

Joe Cobb kept his hand away from his gun and started taking steps backward. Eventually, he had to turn his head to find the door, but he did it quickly. It wasn't until he had one foot out the door that he stopped and turned back.

"I can't do it," he said.

Thomas turned his head and looked at James.

"Step away," he said.

James obeyed.

"Bartender?" Thomas said. "You watchin' this?"

"Uh, y-yes, sir."

"Good." He turned back to Cobb. "Last chance."

"I can't," Cobb said and went for his gun.

Thomas's hand flashed down, drew his gun, and fired

before Cobb had a chance to clear leather. The impact of the shot to the man's chest tossed him through the batwing doors and off the boardwalk, where he landed on his back in the street.

"Jesus..." the bartender said.

"Yeah..." James said.

Thomas ejected the spent shell, replaced it, holstered the gun, and then said to James, "We'll have to wait here for the law."

24

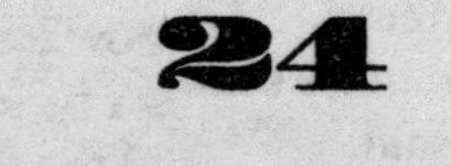

At breakfast the next morning, Thomas and James told their father what happened after he left the Wagon Wheel the night before.

"Did the sheriff come?" Shaye asked.

"He did," Thomas said. "The bartender backed my story that Cobb gave me no choice."

"And you still have your gun?" Shaye asked. "He's not holding you over for a hearing?"

"No," Thomas said. "I thought he was going to, but I think he let us go because of our names."

Shaye thought about that for a moment.

"I guess I hadn't realized what kind of reputation tracking the Langer gang down had given us," Shaye said.

"Not to mention Vengeance Creek," Thomas said.

Shaye rubbed his face with both hands.

"So our rep first got you into trouble—and then out."

"I guess so."

"Maybe my plan to hole up in Winchester at the ranch was the right one," he said.

"I don't know, Pa," Thomas said. "Don't that sort of sound like...hidin' out."

"Yep, it sounds a lot like hidin' out," Shaye agreed.

"Well, why should we?" Thomas asked, looking from his father to James and back. "It ain't like we're outlaws."

"We got nothin' to be ashamed of, Pa," James said.

"No, you're right, James," Shaye said. "We don't—but we'll have to think about all this later. Today we got something else to take care of."

"Matthew's kid," James said.

"If it is Matthew's," Thomas said. "Pa, what do we do if it is?"

"I don't know yet, Thomas," Shaye said. "I'm just trying to go one step at a time."

"Well," Thomas said, "I wanna talk to this girl. I wanna see this child."

"So do I," James said.

"You both will," Shaye said, "but we'll do it her way—for now."

"What if it ain't her way?" James asked. "What if she's doin' this because the sheriff's tellin' her to?"

"I'll find out, James," Shaye said. "I'll know a lot more after this afternoon."

The waiter came with their breakfast and they stopped talking and ate in silence, each man alone in his thoughts.

"Are you sure this is the right thing to do?" Marion Cotton asked her husband that morning.

"I don't see what else there is to do," Cotton said. "Belinda wants to see Shaye."

"But we've told her she can stay here with us."

"If Shaye is the boy's grandfather, he has a right to know and to see him, don't you think?"

"I suppose so," she said. "I've just come to love that little boy so much."

Cotton reached across the table and covered her hand with his.

"I know, honey. I know."

Dan Shaye and his sons killed the morning just sitting on chairs out in front of their hotel. Around eleven thirty-five Shaye got to his feet.

"Might as well mosey over to the sheriff's office," he said. "You boys going to wait right here?"

"Sure, Pa," James said.

"And you going to stay out of trouble?"

"Yes, Pa," Thomas said.

"Good. I'll be back soon."

They watched him cross the street and walk toward the sheriff's office.

"Are we gonna sit right here?" James asked.

"You bet we are," Thomas said. "We can't get into trouble doin' that...can we?"

25

As Shaye approached the sheriff's office, the door opened and Sheriff Cotton stepped out.

"Right on time, Shaye," the lawman said.

"Actually, I'm a little early."

"Five minutes or so," Cotton said. "I was just stepping outside to wait for you."

"Well, I'm here," Shaye said. "Can we go?'

"Sure," Cotton said. "This way."

"I know which way you live," Shaye said and the two men started walking north.

"Belinda is very nervous about meeting you, Shaye," Cotton said. "I hope you'll be...considerate."

"I'm not here to scare her, Sheriff," Shaye said. "I'm just here to find out the truth."

"Well, Belinda's no liar—if that's what you're implying."

"I'm not implying anything," Shaye said. "I'm just saying...Don't worry. I'm not going to attack her."

"Well, I'll be there while you talk to her, so I know you won't," Cotton said.

"What about your wife?"

"She'll stay with the boy."

"I want to see him too."

"In time, you will. Okay, here's my house."

They walked to the front door of the small one-story house. From the porch Shaye could see the schoolhouse James had told him about.

Cotton opened the door and allowed Shaye to precede him into the house. He showed him into a modestly furnished living room. From past experience Shaye knew that the house usually came with the job.

"Wait here and I'll fetch Belinda."

Shaye nodded and Cotton left the room. He surprised himself by feeling nervous about meeting the girl. Or maybe he was more nervous about possibly having a grandson.

Moments later Cotton came back into the room leading a young woman. Shaye saw immediately that she was the kind of woman a young man would find hard to resist. Or possibly even an old man. She was extremely lively, with long black hair, pale skin, and the kind of body he had seen on many young women in saloons, only she was wearing a plain gingham dress, not a revealing peasant blouse or gown.

"Dan Shaye," Riley Cotton said, "meet Belinda Davis. Belinda, this is Daniel Shaye."

"Belinda," Shaye said, removing his hat. "It's nice to meet you. I came in response to your letter."

"Mr. Shaye," she said very formally, "it's very nice to meet you."

She put out her hand and he shook it gently.

"I'm sorry it took so long to get here," Shaye said, "but your letter didn't reach us until—"

"I understand," she said, cutting him off. "I knew sending you that letter was a long shot. I'm just glad it finally reached you."

"Why don't we all sit down?" Sheriff Cotton suggested.

"Actually, Riley," Belinda said, "I'd love to have some coffee. Perhaps Mr. Shaye would as well?"

"But... Marion is with Little Matt."

Belinda smiled at him and said, "I thought maybe... well, could you get it... please?"

"Well..." The lawman looked confused. "All right."

From the looks of things, Belinda had Sheriff Cotton wrapped around her little finger. And from the look on Cotton's face, he didn't exactly think of her as a daughter.

She watched as Cotton left the living room to go to the kitchen, then turned back to Shaye with her arms folded across her breasts.

"You pretty much get your way here, don't you?" Shaye asked.

"They're nice people," Belinda said, "but they can't give me what I want... what I need."

"And I can?"

"You and your sons, yes."

"We don't have much money—"

"I'm not looking for money, Mr. Shaye," Belinda said.

"Then what is it?"

"I'm looking for protection."

"Protection? From who?"

"Do you know a man named Jeb Collier?"

"Collier?" Shaye thought for a moment. "No, can't say I do."

"He's an outlaw," Belinda said. "He also thinks he's my son's father."

"And you need protection from him?" Shaye asked. "What about the sheriff?"

"The sheriff and his wife have been wonderful to us," she said, "but there's no way he'd be able to handle Jeb and his gang."

"Gang? How big a gang?"

"I don't know," she said. "Four, maybe more. Jeb's brother Ben, Jeb's longtime friend Clark Wilson. Maybe one or two others."

"Well, if you're worried they're going to come to town, that would be the sheriff's job—"

"The sheriff isn't related to my son," Belinda said. "You are. You're his grandfather."

"Well... that remains to be seen," Shaye said. "I have to tell you, I have a hard time believing my son Matthew and you... well, especially after meeting you—"

"You don't think I was good enough for your son?" she demanded.

"Don't get all riled up," Shaye said. "Good's got nothing to do with it. I think my son was a little too... I don't think he could have handled a woman like you."

"Matthew was a handsome young man, Mr. Shaye."

"That may be," Shaye said, "but I don't think he could have carried on a... relationship with a woman without me or one of his brothers knowing about it."

Shaye could smell coffee from the kitchen and figured the sheriff would be returning any minute.

"What did you want to tell me that you didn't want the sheriff to hear?" he asked.

"I just don't want the sheriff thinking he's going to protect me and Little Matt," she said. "Jeb and his gang would kill him. I don't want to be the cause of Marion becoming a widow."

"The sheriff's got deputies—"

"Mr. Shaye," Belinda said, "you've been in this town long enough to get the feel of it. This is Texas, yes, but this is not the Wild West. This town is too damned civilized to withstand Jeb Collier and his men."

"What do you want my sons and I to do, Belinda?" he asked. "Stand up to them when they come here? Or take you away before they arrive?"

"Jeb Collier has spent the last two years in Yuma Prison," she told him. "By my reckoning, he either got out a few weeks ago or he'll get out a few weeks from now. I'm not dead sure he'll come here, but I believe he will. He believes that I'm his and that my son is his. I'm here to tell you that neither is true."

"Did you love my son, Belinda?"

"I can't say that I did, Mr. Shaye," she said. "I'm trying to be honest with you here. I liked Matthew and we...we have a son together."

"Let's say for a moment that's true," Shaye said. "Did Matthew know you were pregnant?"

"No, I never told him."

"Why not?"

"Truthfully, I thought Jeb would kill him."

"Jeb knew you were pregnant?"

"He found out just before he went to prison."

"Yuma is a long way from here," Shaye said. "How did he end up there instead of, say, Huntsville?"

"I'm not sure," she said. "He was wanted in Arizona for something, I don't know what, but I know he got two years."

"Belinda...this...relationship you had with my son, was it in Epitaph? Because I don't remember you from there and I don't remember anyone named Collier and his gang being there."

"You don't believe me," she said.

He didn't have time to answer because the sheriff came in carrying some cups and a pot precariously on a tray.

"I'm not used to this, so I'm hoping I don't drop it," Cotton said.

"I'll take it, Riley," she said, grabbing the tray from him with practiced hands. Shaye noticed the change in her demeanor as she once again showed more refinement than she had during their conversation. Her no-nonsense attitude disappeared.

"Mr. Shaye, do you take sugar?"

26

Thomas and James were wondering how the meeting with Belinda Davis and their father was going when the young deputy they'd met the day before came sauntering over.

Well, they hadn't actually met him, because they hadn't exchanged names, but they were sure he knew who they were.

"Heard you had some excitement last night," the deputy said, stopping in front of them. They were both seated in straight-backed wooden chairs, just sort of lounging. Thomas had his chair leaning back against the building, the front two legs off the ground, but when the deputy stopped in front of them he let the chair come down and shifted his weight in it.

"That so?" he asked. "Where'd you hear that?"

"From the sheriff."

"Well, it wasn't much," James said. "Just some cowhands who got a little too drunk. One of them drew and my brother planted him."

Thomas looked at James and said, "'Planted'?"

James shrugged.

"Uh-huh." The deputy said again.

"We ain't been properly introduced," Thomas said. "I'm Thomas Shaye. This here's my brother James."

The introduction caught the young deputy off guard.

"Oh, uh, my name's Thad Hagen," the young man said, "Deputy Thad Hagen."

"Glad to meet you, Deputy," Thomas said.

"Yeah, well...uh, yeah, glad to meet you fellas too. Where's your pa?"

"Dan Shaye's our pa," Thomas said. "He's with the sheriff right about now."

"Oh...well, okay, then," Hagen said. "I got to get on with my rounds."

"Thanks for askin' after us," Thomas said.

"Uh, sure," the man said. "I was just...uh, sure. Okay."

Slightly confused, the deputy walked away.

"Guess he didn't realize he was askin' after us," James said. "You sure took the starch outta him by introducin' us."

"Just tryin' to be neighborly, James," Thomas said. "Ain't that what Pa taught us?"

"That's it exactly," James said. "Neighborly."

"Wonder what's takin' Pa so long," Thomas said. "Sure do wanna get a look at this boy who's supposed to be Matthew's."

"Thomas," James said, "I don't think Matthew could've been with a girl without one of us knowin', do you?"

"No, sir, I sure don't, James," Thomas said. "He woulda been braggin' to one of us."

"Pa woulda knowed too."

"Or Ma," Thomas said.

James's eyes widened.

"You think it mighta happened while Ma was...was alive?"

"Could've, I reckon," Thomas said. "But she woulda known, James. Ma always knew when one of us was keepin' a secret from her."

"She was spooky that way."

James rocked in his chair for a few moments, then said, "I still miss her."

Thomas didn't reply, but he felt the same way.

Belinda's attitude was unaltered while Sheriff Cotton was in the room, but eventually she got him to take the tray of empty cups back into the kitchen. At that moment she turned to Shaye, her demeanor totally changed.

"What are you going to do, Mr. Shaye?" she asked. "Are you going to help me?"

"I assume you don't want me to discuss this with the sheriff."

"I prefer that you don't."

Shaye hesitated, then said, "I have to see the boy, Belinda."

"That's not a problem," she said, "but will you decide then?"

"Not today," he said. "After I see the boy, I'll have to talk to my sons. I'm sure they're going to want to meet both of you as well."

She looked exasperated.

"Jeb Collier and his men could come riding into town at any moment," she argued.

"That may be so," Shaye said, "but I won't be pushed into a decision before I'm ready. You won't be able to ride me or my boys the way you do the sheriff, Belinda."

She sat back in her chair and stared at him. The sheriff came walking back in and looked at them both.

"What did I miss?" he asked.

"Nothing, Riley," Belinda said with a false smile.

"I'm ready to meet the boy," Shaye said.

"Belinda?" Cotton asked.

"Yes," she said, "I'll go and bring him in. Please, Mr. Shaye, don't say or do anything to frighten him."

"I'm not a monster, Belinda," Shaye said. "I won't scare him."

She nodded and left the room.

27

Shaye was surprised to find that he was nervous to meet the boy who might be his grandson. When Belinda returned to the room, she was followed by the sheriff's wife, who was carrying the boy.

The first thing Shaye noticed was that the boy was big for his age, much the way Matthew had been. He also had brown hair and brown eyes. On the other hand, the boy seemed fairly alert, which had not been the case with the young Matthew.

"Mr. Shaye," Belinda said, "this is Marion Cotton, Sheriff Cotton's wife."

"Ma'am."

"Mr. Shaye."

"And this is Matthew," Belinda said. "We call him Little Matt."

Shaye wondered briefly why it was the sheriff's wife who was carrying the boy and not his mother.

Marion Cotton brought the boy toward Shaye, who took a few steps closer to get a good look at him.

"Hello, Little Matt," he said, reaching a hand out to the boy, who immediately grabbed one of his fingers. The child's grip on his finger was impressive.

"He's a strong boy," Shaye said.

"Yes, he is," the sheriff's wife agreed.

Shaye studied the boy, trying to see if he could find any trace of Matthew in there somewhere. Certainly this child had the size, but other than that Shaye couldn't see a resemblance between Little Matt and his own son. Neither did he see any of himself or his wife in the boy's face or eyes.

"Well?" Sheriff Cotton asked. "What do you think?"

"It's too soon to tell," Shaye said. "He's a fine-looking boy, but..."

"Why won't you accept him as your grandchild?" Marion asked.

"Ma'am," he said, "with all due respect, you didn't know my son. A relationship of this type between him and Belinda—or him and any girl—is hard to believe."

"I'm sorry that your son is dead, Mr. Shaye," Marion said, "but this boy needs his family."

"Marion!" Cotton said.

"No, it's okay," Shaye said. "She's right. The boy does need a family—I'm just not ready to say that my sons and I are that family." He directed himself to Belinda. "When can my sons meet you and the boy?"

"Any time, I suppose," she said. "Today, tomorrow."

"Tomorrow, I think, then," Shaye said. "I want some time to talk with my sons."

"Fine," Cotton said. "Should we do it here again?"

"Outside," Belinda said. "Maybe out back."

"Noon?" Shaye asked.

"Yes." He could tell Belinda was not satisfied with the outcome so far. "That's fine."

"Well..." Shaye said, not sure how to end this. "It was nice to meet you, Belinda."

"Yes, you too," she said, putting out her hand. Shaye doubted that the Cottons could see what he saw: the dissatisfied look on her face and in the set of her shoulders.

"I'll come out with you," Cotton said. "I have to go back to work."

They walked to the door together and stepped outside.

"Mind if I walk back to town with you?" the sheriff asked.

"No, sir."

They walked back together, but didn't talk very much, which suited Shaye. He wondered how the man would react if he told him how controlled he thought he was by Belinda Davis. He also wondered if Belinda was able to manipulate Mrs. Cotton in the same way?

When they reached the center of town, the sheriff said, "Well, I better get back to my office. I'll meet you there again tomorrow?"

"I know where your house is," Shaye said. "Why don't we just meet you there?"

"Fine," Cotton said. "I'll see you all then."

He broke away from Shaye, who continued on to the hotel, where his sons were waiting.

Thomas spotted his father first, walking up the street toward them.

"James."

James turned his head and saw his father. They both stood and waited for Shaye to reach them.

"Pa?" Thomas said.

"How did it go?" James asked, anxiously. "Is the boy Matthew's?"

"I can't tell, boys," Shaye said. "He's a big boy, all right, but there's no way to tell."

"Maybe we'll be able to tell," James suggested. "When can Thomas and me see him?"

"Tomorrow afternoon," Shaye said.

"Why then?" James asked. "Why not today?"

"Let's get some lunch, boys," Thomas said. "We can talk about it while we eat."

"But Pa—"

"Come on, James," Thomas said. "Pa's obviously got somethin' to talk to us about. Let's let him tell us."

"Pa?" James asked.

"Over lunch, James," Shaye said. "Over lunch."

28

"So she's puttin' on an act?" James asked.

"For the sheriff and his wife, yes," Shaye said. "Not for me."

"And the sheriff is buying it?"

"He is," Shaye said. "I don't know about his wife. She might be able to see through Belinda."

"So she's not the shy, helpless little thing she wants them to believe," Thomas said.

"I don't know if they would have taken her in otherwise," Shaye said.

He'd told both boys the entire story: what he saw and what Belinda Davis had told him.

"So she wants us to protect her from this Collier gang," Thomas said. "Do you plan to do that?"

"I don't plan to do anything until you boys have met her and her son," Shaye said. "We're in this together. You'll make your own decisions."

"Collier," James said. "I don't know that name, Pa. What was he in Yuma Prison for?"

"She doesn't know," Shaye said. "Maybe I can send some telegrams and find out."

"What about the sheriff?" Thomas asked. "Don't

you think he should be warned that there's a gang on its way?"

"Yes," Shaye said, "I do think he should be warned, even though Belinda doesn't want to tell him."

"That won't make him very happy with her," James said. "And she'll be mad at you for tellin' him."

"I can't worry about that," Shaye said. "I've been sheriff in enough towns to know that he needs to be told. I just wanted to talk to you boys first."

"How do you think he'll react?" Thomas asked. "Think he'll put her out of his house?"

"I think his wife will have something to say about that," Shaye said. "The way she was holding that boy, I know she loves him."

"Why do you think Belinda wasn't holdin' him, Pa?"

"I get the feeling Belinda's maternal instinct doesn't match the sheriff's wife's," Shaye said.

"They have any kids of their own?" James asked.

"Apparently not," Shaye said, "which would explain her attachment to...to Little Matt."

"If the boy is not Matthew's, Pa," Thomas asked, "why would she name him Little Matt?"

"I don't know. Maybe she was planning this that far back."

"Makes her kind of a schemer, don't it?" Thomas asked.

"Oh yeah," Shaye said, "I think that's a good word to describe her."

James pushed his plate away.

"When are you gonna tell the sheriff about this?"

"No time like the present, I thought," Shaye said. "We can go and tell him now."

"Then let's do it," Thomas said. "Maybe he'll know who Collier is."

"I just hope he believes you," James said.

"If he doesn't," Shaye said, "he just has to ask Belinda."

When Sheriff Cotton looked up from his desk and saw them entering his office, he looked surprised.

"Didn't expect to see you so soon," he said. "What's this about?"

"We've got something to tell you," Shaye said, "and I don't think it's going to make you real happy."

Cotton leaned back in his chair and stared at him. His gun was once again on a hook above his head. Shaye realized he was leaning back to get within reach of it.

"You won't need your gun," he told the lawman. "At least not now."

"What are you talking about?"

"Do you know the name Jeb Collier?" Shaye asked.

"Collier?" Cotton thought a moment. "Collier. I don't think so. Why?"

"Maybe you've got some paper on him," Shaye said. "He either just got out of Yuma or he's getting out soon."

"How long was he in?"

"Two years."

"Not wanted anymore, then, is he?"

"Maybe not," Shaye said, "but the word I get is that he might be on his way here with a gang."

"To do what?" Cotton asked. "What was he in for?"

"I don't know why he was in," Shaye said, "but maybe you should ask Belinda why he's coming here."

"Belinda? What's she got to do with it?"

"Sheriff," Shaye said, "she's the one who told me about Collier."

Cotton frowned.

"What would her connection be to a man like that?" he asked.

"Well," Shaye said, "for one thing, he apparently thinks he's Little Matt's father."

"What? What the hell are you talking about?" Cotton demanded. "When do you claim she told you this?"

"After she sent you into the kitchen to make coffee."

"She didn't send me—"

"She sent you, Sheriff," Shaye said. "That little gal has you wrapped around her little finger."

Cotton bristled at that.

"What are you saying?" he demanded angrily. "I never—"

"I'm not suggesting anything," Shaye said. "I'm just saying that Belinda hasn't shown you and your wife her real self. She's got you wrapped around her finger—maybe like a daughter might—and I'll bet that baby has won your wife's heart, hasn't he?"

Cotton calmed down a bit. "He has, yeah."

"Let me explain..."

Briefly, Shaye told the lawman everything Belinda had told him during the man's absence from the room.

"I'm finding this hard to believe," the lawman said when Shaye finished.

"Look, Sheriff," Shaye said. "All you have to do is ask her. If you do that, I think she'll tell you the truth."

"If she's afraid of this Collier and his gang, why wouldn't she just tell me?" he demanded. "Why send for you?"

"I guess you'd have to ask her that," Shaye said. He decided to leave the man his pride as long as he could.

"And why are you telling me this if she doesn't want you to?"

"Because I'm not wrapped around her finger," Shaye said. "And because I've been a lawman and I think you need to know if a gang of outlaws is on its way to your town so you can prepare."

Cotton thought about it for a moment, then pushed his chair back.

"I'm going to have to ask Belinda about this."

"I know you will," Shaye said, "but I'm asking you to put it off for a day."

"Why's that?"

"Give me and my boys time to settle our business with her," Shaye said. "After we meet with her tomorrow, you can confront her, but if you do it now she might not let my sons meet the boy."

"She wouldn't do that."

"Think about it, Sheriff," Shaye said. "Do you really know the girl?"

Cotton hesitated, then said, "I thought I did."

29

All four men left the sheriff's office together, but the Shayes stopped just outside and watched the sheriff walk off toward his house.

"Do you think he'll confront her now?" James asked.

"I hope not," Shaye said. "I hope he'll wait until tomorrow."

"And if he doesn't?" Thomas asked. "How can we leave without bein' dead sure if that kid is Matthew's?"

"I don't know if we'll ever be sure, Thomas," Shaye said.

"But Pa, if there's even the smallest chance that he's part of our family..." James said.

"I know, James," Shaye said, putting his hand on his youngest son's shoulder, "I know. We'll just have to wait and see."

Sheriff Cotton was halfway to his house before he made his decision. There was no harm in waiting one more day and giving Dan Shaye and his sons time to make up their minds about Little Matt.

When he reached the house, he found Marion still holding the baby and Belinda nowhere in evidence.

"What brings you back here so soon?" Marion asked.

"Just wanted to check and see if everyone was all right," Cotton said. "Where's Belinda?"

"She went out," Marion said, "right after you left."

"Did she say anything to you?"

"No," Marion said, rubbing the baby's back. "She just said she had to go out. I assumed she had some thinking to do."

"I think we all have some thinking to do," Cotton said.

"What do you mean?"

"I have something to tell you," Cotton said, "but we can't act on it right away."

"What are you talking about?" she asked.

"Sit down," he said, "and I'll tell you..."

When Belinda left the Cotton house, she hurried into town, hoping that she wouldn't run into either the sheriff or Dan Shaye. She made her way all the way to the south end of town and when she came to that Y junction in the street she went to the right. Before she reached the livery, she came to a hardware store and entered. The man behind the counter was busy with a customer, so she moved to one side and waited for the customer to finish his business and leave. Hurriedly, she ran to the door and flipped the OPEN side to the CLOSED side and locked the door.

"Belinda—"

The man came from behind the counter and they fell into an embrace, followed by a deep kiss.

"You're not supposed to come here during the day," Alvin Simon scolded her.

Simon was in his late twenties and had opened his hardware story only a year before. He and Belinda had met when he first came to town, flirted for a while, and then had become lovers six months ago. But they were determined to keep it a secret from the rest of the town—especially from Riley Cotton and his wife. To that end they rarely, if ever, met during the day, so Simon was surprised to see Belinda in his shop.

"I had to come," she said. "I just finished talking with Daniel Shaye."

"And? Has he accepted Little Matt as his grandson?"

"No, not yet," she said. She moved away from him and clasped her hands together. "He wants his sons to meet me and Matt first."

"So when will that happen?"

"Tomorrow."

"Did you tell him about Jeb Collier and his gang?"

"Yes."

"And?"

"He never heard of Jeb."

"I told you," Simon said. "Nobody has. He's not such a scary man." He walked over to her and took her hands. "I told you I can protect you if he shows up."

She pushed his hands away and said, "No, you can't. He'd kill you without a second thought."

"If I'm such a pathetic man," he complained, "why do you love me?"

"I never said you were pathetic," she replied, but like most men she'd known he was nearly pathetic and certainly easy to manipulate—every man but Daniel Shaye.

Alvin Simon was a young man with a bright future,

which meant that he had money and he had the means and the smarts to make more. That made him a good choice for Belinda. But if she could not convince Daniel Shaye and his sons to kill Jeb Collier for her, then Jeb was certainly going to kill Alvin Simon, Belinda's golden goose.

"But you're not a gunman. That's what it will take to kill Jeb," she finished.

"Gunmen like these Shaye men you keep talking about?" Simon asked. "I read about these men back East, Belinda. They are all killers... back shooters. How could you associate yourself with such... ruffians? First Jeb Collier and then Matthew Shaye?" He grabbed her arms. "You're so much better than that, my darling."

She allowed him to draw her into his arms and laid her head on his shoulder. "You're the only one who thinks so, Alvin."

"I don't think so, I know so," he said. "I'll protect you, dearest. I promise."

"I know you mean to," she said, but she knew that if she didn't do something, Alvin Simon and his money would be lost to her.

"That's not possible," Marion said when the sheriff finished his story. "Mr. Shaye must be wrong."

"Marion," Cotton said, "she gets her way all the time."

"That's because we love her," Marion said, "not because she manipulates us."

"Are you sure, Marion?" he asked. "Are you sure it isn't Little Matt that you love?"

"Well, of course I love him." She hugged the little boy close to her breast, kissing his forehead.

"What if it is true?" Cotton asked. "Then what?"

"You mean, that some desperados are on their way here and one of them thinks he's this child's father?"

"Yes."

"Well, you're the law...you'll tell them to leave town."

"Don't be naïve, Marion," he said. "You've been a lawman's wife long enough to know it doesn't work that way. It's more than likely I'd have to make them leave."

"Could you?"

"I don't know," he said honestly. "I really haven't had to deal with anything like this since taking this job. Drunken cowboys, yes. Gunmen, no."

"But...you have deputies."

"Two young deputies," he said. "They're not equipped for this."

Marion began to pace, bouncing the baby as she did.

"I can't believe this," she said. "If he's right...we can't let them take the baby, Riley. And if she's been using us, we should put her out."

"And keep the baby?" he asked. "Her baby?"

"Her baby?" She stopped pacing and faced him. "She never feeds him, I do. She never picks him up when he cries, I do." Her anger was sudden and fierce.

"Marion," he asked, "how long have you been this angry?"

"All right," she said, "all right, so I know she's using us. I see the way she wraps you around her little finger. But I love Little Matt." She hugged the baby tightly. "I was willing to put up with her to keep him here."

"Why didn't you tell me?"

She looked away.

"I didn't think you'd believe me," she said. "She's so young, so pretty...I see that way you look at her."

"Marion!" he said. "I never—"

"I know you never have, Riley," she said, "but sometimes I think...you want to."

"Marion," he said, putting his hand on her arm, "I love you."

"And I love you, Riley," she said. "What do we do?"

"Well, we'll let the Shayes make up their minds," he said. "If they decide that this baby is part of their family, they'll do whatever they can to protect him."

"You mean, they'll fight this Jeb Collier and his men? And kill them?"

"Yes."

"And then what?" she asked. "Will they want to take Belinda and the baby with them?"

"I don't think so," he said. "I think I could convince them to leave the baby with us. After all, they're three men living without a woman."

"But Belinda—"

"Belinda can't control Dan Shaye," Cotton said. "He sees right through her."

"But how do we get Belinda to leave him here if we put her out?" she asked.

"If what you say is true about her, then she won't want to take him with her. Or if she's the kind of girl Shaye thinks she is, maybe she'll sell the baby to us."

"*Sell* him? My God, would she do that? Could we have been that wrong about her?"

"I don't know," he said. He stroked Little Matt's chubby cheek with one finger. He had to admit he loved the child too. He also had to admit—to himself, but never to his wife—that he had, in the past, entertained the thought of being with Belinda. If she would leave, then that temptation would be removed forever.

"I think we'll have to wait and see what happens when Jeb Collier and his men get here, Marion."

"But if Dan Shaye and his sons won't face them, you'll have to," she said.

"It's my job."

"You could be killed."

"Maybe."

"I love this child, Riley," she said, "but I don't want to trade him for you."

He was thinking she wouldn't have to. If Jeb Collier killed him, he and his gang would probably take the child—and Belinda—away with them.

He didn't tell her that, though.

That night when Dan Shaye turned in he made sure Thomas and James did as well. He didn't want to take the chance of any more trouble with drunken ranch hands.

At breakfast they talked about what they would do if they were to decide that Little Matt was, indeed, Matthew's son.

"We could take both of them back with us to the ranch," James said.

Shaye and Thomas didn't comment.

"Are we goin' back to the ranch, Pa?"

"Well, we have to go back," Shaye said. "Even if we decide not to live there, we'd have to sell it."

"Without a ranch," Thomas said, "What would we do with a woman and a child?"

"It might not be up to us," Shaye said. "What if Belinda doesn't want to leave here?"

"But now that the sheriff knows she's not who she pretends to be, would they let her stay with them?" James asked.

"I don't know," Shaye said. "That would have to be between them. All we have to do right now is decide if the boy is Matthew's or not. The rest will come after that."

Thomas pushed his plate away.

"What if what she says about this gang is true?" he asked. "What if all she wants is for us to get rid of them? And the rest is a lie?"

"I get the feeling this girl has lied a lot," Shaye said. "Maybe the gang is a lie too. Today I'll send some telegrams to find out."

James finished his coffee and set his cup down.

"If we're all done," Shaye said, pushing his chair back, "we can go and do that right now."

At the telegraph office Shaye sent off three telegrams to lawmen he knew in the West.

"We'll be waiting outside for replies," he told the clerk.

"Yes, sir."

He joined his sons outside.

"Think we'll get an answer right away, Pa?" James asked.

"Maybe," Shaye said. "No harm in sitting right here and waiting until it's time to go."

"Well," Thomas said, sitting on one of three chairs, "Can't get into much trouble just sittin'."

"We hope," James said.

That morning Cotton asked Marion, "Can you resist confronting her until later?"

"I hope so," she said. "For the sake of Little Matt, I'll have to."

Cotton put his gun on, preparing to leave for his office.

"We'll have it out with her later, Marion," he promised. "After Dan Shaye's sons meet her and the boy."

"You go to work," she said, patting his arm. "I have to feed the baby and make breakfast for her. Don't worry. I'll be good."

Sheriff Cotton kissed his wife good-bye and left for his office.

On his way to open his office, Cotton passed the telegraph office and saw Shaye and his sons sitting out front. He crossed over and greeted them good morning.

"I sent some telegrams about Jeb Collier," Shaye told him. "Thought we should know for sure what his situation was."

"Good idea. Will you let me know when you find out?"

"Sure thing."

"Gonna wait here until noon?" the lawman asked.

"Why not?" Shaye asked with a shrug.

"Sure," Cotton agreed, "why not?"

"Did you tell your wife what I told you?"

"Yes, I did. She was upset."

"I'm sorry."

"Don't be. Turns out she's known more about Belinda's true character than I have."

"Is that a fact? And she was willing to put up with it?"

"For the baby's sake."

"He's two, ain't he?" James asked.

Cotton looked at him. "Yes."

"Not really a baby anymore, is he?"

"To my wife, he is."

"We'll see you around noon, Sheriff."

The sheriff gave a small wave and continued on to his office.

The telegram they were waiting for came at eleven-thirty. The clerk came out and handed it to Shaye.

"What's it say, Pa?" Thomas asked.

"Jeb Collier was sentenced to two years for a stage robbery in Arizona," he said. "He got out last month."

"And is he on his way here?" James asked.

"No way to know that."

"Well," Thomas said, "at least we know she told the truth about that."

"At least we know," Shaye said, "that she can tell the truth—when she wants to." Shaye folded the telegram and put it in his pocket. "Time to go."

31

It was all Marion Cotton could do to hold her tongue all morning. When she saw the three men walking toward her house, she was relieved. As they got closer, she recognized Daniel Shaye. When they reached her backyard, she saw that his two sons were quite handsome. One seemed barely a man and the other several years older—and bigger. They all wore guns. She hoped that the three of them would be a match for the Collier gang.

"Mrs. Cotton," Shaye said as they reached the fence surrounding the backyard. He removed his hat and his sons followed his example.

"This is my son James...and my son Thomas."

"Ma'am," Thomas said and James just nodded.

"I'm happy to meet you both," she said.

"Where are Belinda and the boy?" Shaye asked.

"They're inside," she said. "I'll go and fetch them."

"And your husband?"

"He hasn't come home yet," she said. "He must have been held up at his office. Please, come into the yard and wait."

She opened the gate and the three men entered while she went into the house.

* * *

In the house she told Belinda, "They're here."

Belinda went to the window to look out at Daniel Shaye's sons. She was impressed with the older one. He was tall, well built, and quite handsome. He reminded her of Matthew, but not as large.

"I'll get Little Matt," Marion said. If Belinda noticed the coldness in her tone, she gave no indication. "Why don't you go out and... talk to them?"

"All right," the younger woman said. "I'll see you outside."

She went out the back door while Marion went into the bedroom to get the child.

When Belinda appeared in the yard, wearing another simple gingham dress, both Thomas and James caught their breath. They could both see how she would be able to influence a man with her beauty. If she could do it to a mature man like Sheriff Cotton, then their brother Matthew would have had no chance against her.

Shaye could see the reaction both his sons were having to the lovely young woman. He gave James no chance against her charms, but hoped that Thomas was old enough and smart enough to resist.

"Boys, this is Belinda," Shaye said. "Belinda, Thomas and James."

"It's very nice to meet the two of you," she said. "I can see the resemblance between you and your brother Matthew."

Neither Thomas nor James commented on that remark.

"Where's the boy?" Thomas asked.

Belinda pouted, a gesture that annoyed Shaye.

"Aren't you interested in getting to know me first?" she asked.

"The boy is the one we might be related to," Thomas pointed out.

"And you?" she asked, directing her gaze at James now.

Shaye saw James swallow and hesitate. If they ever left him alone with her, he'd be lost.

At that moment the back door of the house opened and Marion Cotton came out carrying Little Matt.

"There he is," Shaye said.

While she walked toward them, Shaye noticed that Belinda had not removed her hot stare from James, who still seem mesmerized by her. Thomas must have noticed as well, because he stepped between the two of them, breaking the contact.

"Let's look at the boy, James," he said.

"His name is Matt," Marion said, stopping before them.

"We call him Little Matt," Belinda said, "because his father was so... big."

Thomas walked toward the boy for a closer look, but did not touch him. James followed, but when he reached the woman and the boy he stuck his finger out as Shaye had done the day before. The boy immediately reached for it.

"He's got a strong grip, Pa," James said.

"I know," Shaye said. "I felt it yesterday."

"It'll take more than a strong grip and a big ass to make him Matthew's son," Thomas pointed out.

Shaye noticed that the boy did, indeed, have a large behind. If nothing else, that reminded him of Matthew at the same age.

"We're never going to be able to find store-bought britches to fit him," Mary had lamented. "I'm going to have to hand-make them."

"We can't find store-brought clothes to fit him," Marion said then. "I hand-make his britches for him."

Shaye took a step back, as if she had slapped him, then shook his head to dispel the voice in his head.

"Hey, Pa," James said, "didn't Ma used to say—"

"Take a good long look, boys," Shaye said. "This is important. Is he part of our family, or isn't he?"

Thomas leaned in to examine the boy's face, but Little Matt turned his head then, to look at his mother. Shaye noticed that Belinda was not looking at the small boy, but at James. It was as if she had sensed the weak link in them.

Thomas moved around to get a look at the small face.

"I can't tell, Pa," he said finally. "He's a big one, that's for sure, and his eyes...his eyes are right, but..."

"James?" Shaye said sharply.

His tone startled James, who turned his head to look at his father.

"Pa?"

"What do you think?"

James looked at the boy.

"I don't honestly know, Pa," he said. "Could be."

"Could be ain't good enough," Shaye said. He looked at Marion, not Belinda, because it seemed to be the older woman who was the more responsible one. "We won't be able to decide today."

"I understand."

"But," Belinda said, "we don't have much time—"

"For what?" Marion asked, cutting her off. "What don't we have much time for, Belinda?"

"Nothing," the younger woman said, backing off.

"There's no hurry, Mr. Shaye," Marion said to Shaye. "No hurry at all. We'll be here."

"Yes, ma'am," Shaye said. "Tell the sheriff we're sorry we missed him."

"I will," she said. "I'm sure he was held up by something important."

"I'm sure he was," Shaye said. "Let's go, boys."

Sheriff Cotton stopped into the telegraph office and said to the clerk, "Hey, Beau."

"Mornin', Sheriff."

"You had a man in here this morning sending a telegram," the lawman said.

"Three," Beau said, "he sent three."

"Where to?"

"I ain't supposed to say, Sheriff."

"You can tell me, Beau," Cotton said. "I'm the law."

"Well...I guess you're right."

The clerk turned and retrieved the three handwritten slips that Shaye had written out.

"One to the sheriff of Epitaph, one to a lawman in New Mexico, and another to a lawman in Arizona, near Yuma.

"Did he get any replies?"

"One."

"What did that say?"

"I can tell you that by heart," Beau said, "'cause I remember. It was something about a feller who was in Yuma for two years and just got out last month. What was his name?"

"Collier?" the sheriff asked. "Jeb Collier?"

"That's the one," Beau said. "How'd you know that?"

Cotton smiled.

"Lucky guess."

The young clerk laughed and said, "Must be lucky guesses like that's the reason you're the sheriff."

"Yep," Cotton said, "must be. Thanks, Beau."

"Glad to help, Sheriff," the clerk said, "but, uh, you won't tell nobody where you got the information, right?"

"Don't worry," Cotton said, "it'll be our secret, Beau."

32

Jeb Collier stared across the table at his brother Ben, who was fidgeting in his chair.

"Ben," he said, "go to the bar and get us four more beers."

"Anythin's better than just sittin' here," Ben said.

As Ben left, Jeb said to Clark Wilson, "If he don't sit still, I'm gonna shoot him."

"Ben got like that when you got put away, Jeb," Wilson said. "Antsy. He can't never sit still. Maybe it'll change now that you're back."

"Yeah, maybe."

"So what're we doin' here?" Wilson asked.

They were about a week out of Pearl River Junction in a Texas town called Waco.

"We're waitin'," Jeb said.

"For what?"

"We takin' the bank here too?" Dave Roberts asked.

"No," Jeb said, "we ain't. You got any money left from the last two jobs we pulled, Dave?"

Roberts hesitated, then said, "Some."

"You're gonna have to learn not to spend it all on whores and booze so fast," Jeb said.

"And gamblin'," Wilson said.

"I can spend my money on what I want," Roberts said grudgingly.

"I ain't sayin' you can't," Jeb said, "just not so damn fast. You and my brother go through your money so fast...we ain't gonna pull a job every week, ya know?"

Ben came back with four beers, spilled a little out of each of them as he put them down.

"What're ya talkin' about?" he asked.

"Spendin' money," Wilson said. "And I asked your brother what we're doin' here."

"What are we doin' here?" Ben asked.

"He says waitin'."

"Waitin' for what?"

"And now you're all caught up, Ben," Wilson said.

"Just shut up and listen, all of you," Jeb said. "The last town we stopped in I sent a telegram."

"When'd you have time to do that?" Ben asked.

"When you were spending the last of your money on whores and booze," Jeb said.

"And gamblin'," Wilson added. He turned his attention to Jeb. "Who'd you send a telegram to?"

"Vic Delay." He pronounced the name *Dee-lay.*

"Delay?" Wilson asked. "He's a cold-blooded killer. Why'd you contact him?"

"I just want a little insurance when we go into Pearl River Junction after Belinda and my kid," Jeb said. "Struck me that the town—and the local law—might not take too kindly to us grabbin' a little kid and a woman."

"We don't know what kind of law they got there," Wilson said.

"All the more reason to have some insurance."

"Vic Delay," Wilson said, again, shaking his head.

"Vic's okay," Ben said. "I like Vic."

"And some of his boys," Jeb said. He was ignoring Ben's remark and responding to Wilson's.

"Jesus."

"Hey," Jeb said, sitting forward in his chair, "if the Pearl River Junction bank looks good, we'll probably take it while we're there. Vic and his men will come in handy."

"I never understood why you became friends with him," Wilson said. "We're thieves, not killers. That's why you only got two years in Yuma, 'cause we never killed anybody during a job."

"I killed people," Ben said. "I killed plenty of people."

Jeb and Wilson continued to ignore Ben, as did Dave Roberts, only he seemed to be ignoring everybody. He wasn't included in any decisions and was never asked any questions or opinion, so he generally just sort of wandered off in his head until his name was called.

"Dave!" Jeb said.

"Yeah? Huh?"

"Go out in the street and watch for Delay and his men," Jeb said. "Show 'em in here when they get here."

"Sure, Jeb."

"Ben, go with him," Jeb said. "You're drivin' me crazy in here."

"What am I doin'?" Ben complained.

"You can't sit still, damn it!" Jeb said. "You're makin' me feel like I'm in a stagecoach."

"Aw, Jeb—"

"Get up and git."

Both men stood up and walked out the batwing doors of the little saloon. Jeb picked it because there was no music, no gambling, and no women.

"They're probably gonna end up in another saloon," Wilson said, "or a whorehouse."

"Between 'em," Jeb said, "they ain't got the price of one whore."

"Jeb, you sure about Vic Delay?"

"I'm sure, Clark," Jeb Collier said. "A little bit of insurance never hurt nobody."

Vic Delay didn't like Jeb Collier, but he saw in Jeb something that Collier didn't even see in himself: a killer. In that way he felt that he and Jeb Collier were kindred spirits. So when he got the telegram from Jeb asking him to meet him in Waco, he agreed.

Delay knew a lot of killers, but in none of them did he sense what he did in Jeb Collier and he wanted to be there the day it came out.

"You know what this fella Delay looks like?" Dave Roberts asked Ben when they were outside.

"Yeah, I know."

Roberts waited for Ben to elaborate. When Ben didn't, Roberts asked, "So, what does he look like?"

"He's scary-lookin'," Ben said.

"Whataya mean, scary-lookin'?"

Ben shuddered.

"You'll know when you see him," he said. "It's somethin' in his eyes."

"How can somebody's eyes be scary?"

"Don't take my word for it," Ben said. "Take a look for yourself." Ben pushed off the pole he'd been leaning against. "Here he comes now."

* * *

Riding into Waco, down the main street, Delay spotted Ben Collier, who he disliked even more than his brother—but Ben had no redeeming qualities to make up for it. Delay thought Ben Collier was a waste of air and was surprised and disappointed that somebody hadn't killed him by now.

"That looks like the brother," Lou Tanner said.

"Yeah." Tanner was Delay's right hand and had been riding with him much longer than the other two men, Roy Leslie and Bill Samms.

"I could put a bullet into him from here," Tanner offered, knowing how Delay felt about Ben Collier.

"Forget it," Delay said. "Some day his own brother will probably do it."

The four men reined in their horses in front of Ben Collier.

"Jeb's in this little saloon, Mr. Delay," Ben said, nervously.

"Who's this?" Delay asked, indicating Roberts.

"Uh, this is Dave Roberts."

Delay stared at Roberts until the other man looked away, then dismounted, followed by his men.

"Want us to take care of your horses, Mr. Delay?" Ben asked.

"No," Delay said, "leave 'em. We don't know if we're stayin', do we?"

"No, I guess not."

"But I tell you what," Delay said, handing Ben his horse's reins. "You can stay out here and watch 'em for us."

"Sure, Mr. Delay, sure," Ben said.

Delay turned and walked into the saloon, followed by Tanner and the other two men.

* * *

Ben turned to Dave Roberts and looked at him expectantly.

"Jesus," the other man said.

"I told you."

"Them's are the deadest eyes I ever seen," Roberts said. "He'd just as soon kill ya as look at ya."

"Yeah," Ben said. "That's why I don't mind stayin' out here and watchin' his horse."

"Me neither."

Jeb Collier saw Vic Delay as soon as he entered the saloon, followed by Lou Tanner and two men he didn't know. He stood up as the man approached, because you never knew what to expect from a killer like Delay.

"Vic," he said.

"Jeb," Delay said.

"Beer?"

"Sure."

"Clark?" Jeb said. "Why don't you get Vic a beer and then take his men over to the bar. Hello, Tanner."

"Jeb," Lou Tanner said.

"Lou," Delay said, "take the boys over to the bar with Wilson."

"Sure, Vic."

Wilson brought a beer back to the table for Delay, another for Jeb, and then went to join Delay's boys at the bar.

"So," Delay asked Collier, "when did you get out?"

"A few weeks ago."

"Do anything worthwhile since then?"

Jeb Collier named the two banks he and his men had hit since his release from Yuma.

"Those were you?" Delay asked. "You didn't waste any time."

"I needed some traveling money."

"To travel where?"

"Pearl River Junction."

Vic Delay drank some beer and said, "Never heard of it. What's there? A bank?"

"They got a bank, sure," Collier said, "but I'm headed there for another reason."

"Like what?"

Jeb hesitated then asked, "You got any kids, Vic?"

"No," Delay said with a laugh. "What would I do with a kid?"

"Well, I might have one."

"Might?" Delay asked. "You mean you don't know?"

"That's what I'm goin' to Pearl River Junction to find out."

Delay sat back in his chair.

"That's why you asked me to meet you here?" he asked. "To go there with you?"

"Basically, yeah."

"You know, Jeb," Delay said, "there ain't a lot of things I do that ain't for money."

"I ain't askin' for a favor, Vic," Jeb said. "There's money there."

"How much?"

"I don't know," Jeb said, "but there's a bank, for sure. Once I'm done with my business there, we'll hit the bank and leave town."

"You're gonna pick up your kid?"

"I'm gonna talk to my gal, see if the kid she had while I was in Yuma is mine, and then..."

"And then what?"

"And then I don't know," Jeb said. "I'll have to make up my mind once I know for sure."

"Does this gal have a husband you're gonna have to deal with?"

"I don't know," Jeb said. "For all I know, we may have to deal with the whole town."

"The law?"

"That too."

Delay thought about it, then said, "Okay, it sounds like it might be interesting...might be fun."

Jeb Collier knew what Vic Delay thought of as fun. To Delay "fun" and "killing" usually had the same meaning.

"Yeah," he agreed, "it might be."

34

Shaye proposed to his sons that they go to the nearest saloon and discuss the events of the afternoon. They were all for it. They stopped into one they hadn't been to before called the Junction Saloon.

It was still early in the day, so there were not many other men in the place. Still, they chose to stand at the bar rather than take a table.

"All right," Shaye said once they all had a beer in hand, "let's hear it."

"She's very pretty," James said.

His father and brother stared at him.

"Belinda, I mean," James added. "Very pretty, don't you think?"

"That was fairly obvious, James," Thomas said, "but that's not what we're supposed to be talkin' about."

"James," Shaye said, "what did you think of the boy?"

"Well," James said slowly, "just from lookin' at him, I think he's Matthew's son."

"Thomas?" Shaye asked.

"I disagree," Thomas said, "and I think James has been influenced by Belinda Davis bein' so pretty."

"I have not."

"Come on, James," Thomas said, "if your tongue had been out any farther, you would have stepped on it."

"And you didn't think she was good-lookin'?" James demanded.

"Of course she's good-lookin', James," Thomas said, "but that's not the point."

"Thomas is right, James," Shaye said. "Our concern is the boy, not his mother."

"But if Matthew is the father," James said, "wouldn't he want us to help the mother as well as the boy?"

"He probably would," Shaye said.

"So we're back where we started," Thomas said. "Is this Matthew's son?"

"I say yes," James said.

"I say no," Thomas replied. "What about you, Pa?"

"I'm not sure."

"Pa," Thomas said, "if the Collier gang gets here and we haven't decided, what will we do? Stand up to them for her? Even though she might not be the mother of Matthew's son?"

"I think," Shaye said, "if the Collier gang arrives while we're still here and the sheriff needs help, we should probably give it to him."

"It's not our fight, Pa," Thomas said.

"It is if the boy is our blood," James said. "Our nephew, Pa's grandson."

"It's our fight if anyone needs help, isn't it, Thomas?" Shaye asked.

"It was when we were wearing badges, Pa," Thomas said. "I'm not so sure it is now."

"What about if she's just a woman who needs help?" James asked.

"I'm not so sure she'd need help against any man,"

Thomas said. "She'll probably be able to handle Jeb Collier as easily as she has the sheriff or as easily as she would you, James."

"Just because I think she's pretty doesn't mean—"

"That's enough about the girl," Shaye said, interrupting. "I need time to think, boys, to decide what to do."

"I think we should leave town," Thomas said. "Tomorrow... or even now."

"I think we should stay," James said.

"I know where you both stand," Shaye said. "I'll let you know what I decide to do. The two of you should make up your own minds."

"I'm gonna take a walk," Thomas said, "and do some thinkin'. I'll see you both back at the hotel."

With that he left the saloon, the batwing doors flapping in his wake.

"What's he got against the girl, Pa?"

"She's manipulative, James," Shaye said.

"Maybe not, Pa," James said. "Maybe you're wrong about her."

"I don't think so, James," Shaye said, "but like I said, you and your brother have to make up your own minds."

"I understand, Pa," James said. "I guess I should take a walk and do some thinkin' of my own."

"I'll see you at the hotel," Shaye said. "I'm going to have another beer."

James passed through the batwing doors with much less force than his brother had.

Just outside the saloon James ran into Sheriff Cotton.

"Where's your pa?" the lawman asked.

"Inside."

"And your brother?"

"I don't know."

"And where are you off to?"

"Just takin' a walk."

"Can I ask what you decided?"

"We haven't decided anything yet, Sheriff," James said. "We're still thinkin' it over."

"I see. Well, I think I'll go in and see your pa."

James nodded and walked away as the sheriff entered the saloon.

Shaye saw the lawman enter and called the bartender over.

"A beer for the sheriff."

"Comin' up."

Cotton joined Shaye at the bar.

"I saw your youngest boy outside," he said. "Sorry I missed you all at my house."

"That's okay."

The barman set a beer on the bar and Cotton picked it up.

"What did your boys think of Belinda?"

"They have different opinions. How about your wife?"

"She's afraid Belinda will leave and take Little Matt away with her," Cotton said.

"So you'll both just let her get away with playing you along all this time?" Shaye asked.

"Maybe she just did it to feel safe," Cotton said, "but then, she doesn't seem to think I can handle Jeb Collier."

"And his gang," Shaye reminded him.

"Yeah," Cotton said, taking a drink from his mug. "And maybe she just needed a woman to take care of the boy, because she couldn't."

"And now your wife loves him."

Cotton wiped his mouth with the back of his hand and said, "We both do, actually."

"So I guess we all have some thinking to do on the subject, don't we?" Shaye asked.

"Drink up, Mr. Shaye," Cotton said. "The next round will be on me."

"The name's Dan."

35

Eventually, Shaye and Cotton moved to a table in the back and the saloon began to fill up.

"I heard about Collier," Cotton said at one point.

"I thought you might check with the telegraph clerk."

"Why'd you think that?" the sheriff asked.

"It's what I would have done."

"How many men do you think he's coming here with?"

"I guess that would depend on how badly he wants Belinda and the boy," Shaye said. "And if I was him, I'd plan on taking the bank too."

Cotton rubbed his temples.

"All I've got are two young deputies."

"I've only seen one."

"The other one is part-time."

"And how much experience have you had with someone like Jeb Collier?" Shaye asked.

"Not much," Cotton said. "In fact, Belinda may be right about me. I may not be able to handle him."

Shaye shook his head.

"Oh, don't worry," Cotton said. "I'm not going to ask you and your boys to stay and help me. I mean, if you're convinced that Little Matt is not your grandson, you have no reason to stay."

"I haven't made my mind up about that yet."

"And your sons?"

"They have to make up their own minds."

Cotton thought a moment, then asked, "Do you think they'd hire on as deputies?"

"Maybe," Shaye said. "I can't speak for them."

"Are they both capable?"

"Very," Shaye said. "Thomas is the more capable of the two. He's older, a bit wiser, very good with a gun. He reminds me of me when I was younger."

"And James?"

"James is more like his mother," Shaye said. "She had hopes that he'd make something of himself—a doctor, a lawyer."

"Not a deputy?"

"No. Not a lawman, like his father."

"Do you miss it?" Cotton asked. "Wearing a badge?"

"That's something I'm not sure about as well," Shaye said. "You see? I've got a lot of thinking to do."

"I can imagine."

"But first," Shaye said, "there's the matter of helping you against Jeb Collier and his men."

"You'd do that? But why?"

Shaye shrugged.

"Once he's taken care of, my sons and I can take our time making up our minds about the boy," Shaye said. "This way we're under the gun—and I hate being under the gun."

36

Off on his own, Thomas was able to think better. His father had said that he and James had to make up their own minds. That meant he was free to decide what was best for him.

First, he knew his brother Matthew would never have stood a chance against a woman like Belinda—and she was more woman than girl, in his opinion, despite her youth. She was able to handle a man as young as James and a mature man like the sheriff. And, apparently, an outlaw like Jeb Collier. Belinda Davis was a lot wiser than her years.

But going back to Matthew, there was no way he'd father a child with her or have sex with her, not without first discussing it with one of his brothers or his father. Not with their mother, though. He'd never have been able to talk about that with his mother.

So, as far as Thomas was concerned, Belinda was lying in order to get the three Shayes to take care of Jeb Collier and his gang for her. But what was she getting out of it? If she did convince them that her son was Matthew's son and they protected her against Collier, what then? Would she want to stay with them? Or stay with the sheriff and his wife? Or go off on her own?

And did she have a plan that none of them knew about?

After walking and thinking for an hour, Thomas's vote was still that Belinda's baby was not Matthew's son—and therefore not part of their family. But if there really was a gang coming to Pearl River Junction after her, he didn't know if he could just leave Sheriff Cotton to handle them when it was clear he would not be able to.

He wished he could just ride out and forget about it, but he couldn't.

James was convinced that the baby had Shaye blood. He didn't think Belinda would lie about that. On the other hand was Thomas right about him? Was he influenced by the fact that Belinda was beautiful and his stomach sprouted butterflies whenever he looked at her or spoke to her? And if the baby was Matthew's, then he was having impure thoughts about the mother of his brother's child. What did that make him? Disloyal to Matthew's memory, to say the least.

He knew how Thomas was going to vote, because he knew his older brother stuck to it whenever he made up his mind. He didn't know how his father would vote, but he thought he knew one thing about both of them. Like him, they'd never be able to leave Pearl River Junction if the sheriff was going to have to deal with a gang of outlaws. James was young and his experience as a lawman was limited, but he knew after meeting the sheriff and talking to him that he'd never be able to stand up to them, not even with two deputies. Just riding out of town and leaving the man to be killed wasn't an option.

* * *

As the saloon filled up with customers, the sheriff decided he had to go back to his office. Shaye agreed to come and see the man there in the morning, to decide what their strategy would be to deal with a gang—if it showed up.

"I hope, when you come to my office, it's with your sons," Cotton said, before leaving.

"That'll be up to them," Shaye said, "but I'll see you in the morning."

After Cotton left, Shaye did some thinking on his own. Whether Belinda's boy was his grandson or not was going to have to be dealt with later. There was no way he could leave Sheriff Cotton on his own to face the gang, especially not after meeting the man's wife. So putting himself at the sheriff's disposal until the gang question got sorted out would give him more time to mull the question over. What he needed to find out now was what his boys were going to do. James, he felt, would stay. He was sweet on the girl. That would be enough to keep him there, but he also knew that James would feel as he did. They had to help the sheriff.

Thomas was a different story. Shaye had been waiting for the day Thomas would go off on his own. He was full grown, able to handle himself, and Shaye felt that his oldest son was a born lawman. Somewhere out there was a sheriff's badge waiting for him to find it.

He just wondered if today or tomorrow would be the day Thomas Shaye would finally strike out on his own?

James returned to the saloon to find it filled with the usual sounds—music, the clinking of glasses, men's voices raised in argument, discussion, or celebration. At a table in the back he saw his father, seated alone. He went to the bar, got himself a beer, and joined him.

"Where's Thomas?" he asked.

"I was about to ask you the same question," Shaye said. "I guess he's still walking around out there."

"Pa," James said, "I can't leave. I think these people need our help."

"These people?"

"Belinda, the boy," James said, "the sheriff and his wife. Hell, if there's a gang really on its way here, the whole town. I don't think Jeb Collier is gonna get his men to follow him here just so he can find his son. There is a bank in town, you know?"

"Yes, James, I know," Shaye said. "That's good thinking, son."

"You thought of it already, didn't you?"

"Yes, I did," Shaye said, "but I'm proud of you that you did too."

"Thanks, Pa."

"One thing."

"What's that?"

"Don't let the fact that you're sweet on that Belinda girl cloud your judgment."

James lowered his head. "You could tell that, huh?"

"Of course, James," Shaye said. "I been sweet on a girl or two in my time—and not just your mother."

"I feel bad about it."

"Why?"

"If her son really is Matthew's, then...I'm bein' disloyal to his memory"—he lowered his voice—"havin' thoughts about his woman."

"I don't think your brother would hold it against you, son," Shaye said.

"You don't?"

"Hell no, she's a fine-looking woman."

"Yeah, she is—"

"But remember what I said."

"Yes, Pa."

"You could get killed or get one of us killed, letting your mind wander at the wrong time."

"I know, Pa."

They sipped their drinks for a few moments and then James asked, "What do you think Thomas is gonna do, Pa?"

"I don't know," Shaye said. "I've had the feeling for a while that he's ready to strike out on his own."

"You really think he'd leave us?"

"Why not?" Shaye asked. "I expect you to go off on your own eventually too. Don't you?"

"I don't know," James said. "I...I ain't thought about it much."

"Would you like to wear a badge again?"

"I—I've thought about it," James said, "but I kinda thought we'd all do it together."

Shaye touched the front of his shirt where a badge would go. He was wearing one of his new shirts, without the old pin holes in it from the various badges he'd worn.

"I guess I thought that too."

"What do we do if he leaves?" James asked.

"We'll just have to stand with the sheriff and his deputy," Shaye said, "the two of us."

"Deputy?" James asked. "I thought he had two."

"One's part-time."

They fell silent again and then James said, "I don't guess there's any way we can find out how many there are."

"There's a couple of ways," Shaye said. "We'd just need the sheriff to send a few telegrams to some of his colleagues."

"Did you talk to him about it already?"

"No," Shaye said, "but I told him I'd see him in his office tomorrow."

"I'll be there, too."

"Good."

"But—"

"But what, son?" Shaye asked. "Come on, spit it out."

"We sure could use Thomas and his gun if Jeb Collier and his gang do show up here."

"I know, James," Shaye said. "We sure could."

Thomas appeared in the doorway of the saloon roughly a half an hour after James did. He spotted his brother and father at the table in the back, got himself a beer, and sat with them.

"Nice to see you, Thomas," his father said.

"Did you think I'd leave, Pa?"

"No," Shaye said and then added, "well, not tonight anyway."

"James," Thomas asked, "what have you decided to do?"

"I can't leave the sheriff to face Collier and his gang by himself, Thomas," he said.

"Sounds like that has nothing to do with Belinda and her son at all," Thomas said.

"It don't."

"Pa?"

"The question of whether or not the boy is Matthew's can be solved later, Thomas," Shaye said. "If there's a gang on the way here, everyone in this town is going to need help."

"So you're stayin'?"

"Your brother and I are stayin' to stand with the sheriff," Shaye said. "We hope you'll do the same, but we'll understand—"

"I'm stayin'," Thomas said, cutting Shaye off.

"Oh, thank God," James said and slapped his big brother on the shoulder. "I knew you would."

"You did, huh?"

"I'm gonna get Pa and me another beer and then we'll drink to it," James said. He got up and went to the bar.

"Pa, you know he's sweet on the girl."

"Yes, but it has nothing to do with his decision," Shaye said. "I'm confident of that. I believe you've both made the right decision because you're honorable men. I'm proud of you both."

"Have you talked to the sheriff yet?"

"Yes, he found me here," Shaye said. "I told him we'd be in his office in the morning."

"You were that sure of us both?"

"Well..." Shaye said rather sheepishly, "I told him I'd be there and I hoped you boys would be with me."

"And are we gonna wear badges?"

"If he offers them, I suppose so," Shaye said. "Is that all right with you?"

"Actually, Pa," Thomas said, "that's just fine with me."

38

The next morning all three Shaye men appeared at the sheriff's office. Both Sheriff Cotton and Thad Hagen, his deputy, were there.

"Sheriff," Shaye said. "I guess you got all three of us here, ready to help you."

"Well, that's fine," Cotton said. "That's just fine." He stood up, then opened a desk drawer. "I got three deputy badges here. I know you're used to being the sheriff, but I'd be honored if you'd wear them."

Shaye turned and looked at his sons, who both nodded.

"We'd be proud to."

Cotton brought the badges out, swore all three men in, and handed the tin stars over. Shaye made holes in his brand-new shirt pinning it on and knew they wouldn't be the last.

"I'm proud to serve with the three of ya," Deputy Hagen said and shook hands with all three men.

"Thank you, Deputy," Thomas said.

"What about your other man?" Shaye asked. "The part-time one?"

"I explained to him and Thad this morning that we

might be facing some desperados in the next few days and he turned his badge in."

"He was scared," Thad said.

"And you're not?" Shaye asked.

"Well..."

"It's all right to be scared, son," Shaye said. "Keeps you sharp."

"Yes, sir," Thad said. "I guess I just wasn't scared enough to quit on Sheriff Cotton."

"Sounds like you got yourself a good man here, Sheriff," Shaye said.

"Yep, I reckon I do," Cotton said and Thad Hagen's chest filled up until they thought it might burst.

"Well," Thomas said, "we were wonderin' what it would be like to work in a sheriff's office this grand."

"Now we know," James said.

"We might as well get our duties straight," Shaye said.

"Well," Cotton said, "I figure if we're waiting for a gang to show up and we don't know what size it'll be, that most of us should be on duty all day."

"Sounds right," Shaye said.

"Dan," Cotton said, "if you or your boys've got any suggestions, I'd be glad to hear them."

"Well," Shaye said, "if you've got a nice high building here in town, we can have one deputy up there all day. He might spot the gang from a ways off and give us some warning."

"That sounds good."

"We can set up shifts," Thomas said, "so no one is up there for too long a time."

"Good," Cotton said. "Anything else?"

"I'd say keep at least one of us on duty all night," James said, "in case they ride in after dark."

"Also good," Cotton said. "That can work by shifts as well."

"How many days we gotta do this?" Thad asked.

"I'd say they're getting here any day now," Shaye said, "if they're coming at all. But Sheriff, I have another suggestion."

"Let's hear it."

"If you could send some telegrams to some lawmen along the line, we might get some advance warning if the gang passes through one of their towns."

"Good thinking," Cotton said. "I'll take care of that today."

"Thomas, why don't you and James work with Thad setting up shifts for the roof and the night work?"

"Sure, Pa."

"I'll walk over to the telegraph office with the sheriff."

"We can all share this other desk over here," Thad said, "since we's all deputies now."

Thad walked Thomas and James over to the extra desk while Shaye followed Cotton out of the building.

"Seems like those three will get along," Shaye said outside. "Your deputy doesn't seem threatened."

"He ain't," Cotton said. "I explained the situation to him and he knows we need the help."

"And he's ready to use his gun—if he has to?"

"He says he is," Cotton said. "I believe he thinks he is. We won't know til the time comes, though."

They started for the telegraph office.

"Sheriff, you mind if I ask how often you've had to use your gun?"

"A time or two," Cotton said, "but if you're asking if

I've ever had to kill a man, the answer is no. That doesn't mean I won't, though."

"I'm just asking—"

"No need to explain," Cotton said. "I know your life depends on knowing who you're dealing with—on both sides of your gun. I'll watch your back, Dan—yours and your boys'."

"Okay," Shaye said, "that's good enough for me."

After they finished sending telegrams to sheriffs of other towns, Cotton asked Shaye to take a turn around town with him.

"Might as well let folks see you with the badge on," he said.

"Fine with me," Shaye said, "but what about your mayor? And the town council?"

"I'll introduce you and your boys to them later, but I've got the power to swear in deputies when I need to—especially in case of an emergency."

"Well," Shaye said, "this just may qualify."

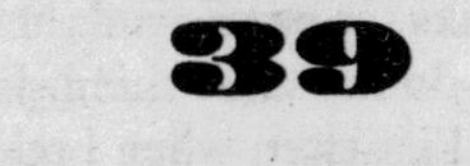

39

Once Thomas, James, and Thad had their shifts figured out, Thomas asked the deputy what the highest building in town was.

"That's easy," Thad said. "Right next door. City Hall."

"James," Thomas said, "you better get your ass up there, then. First shift's yours."

"Why don't we all go up?" Thad asked. "I can show you how to get up there."

"Good idea," Thomas said.

They followed Thad into City Hall and up two flights of stairs. Then he showed them how to pull a ladder down from the ceiling that led to a hatch. Once they were all on the roof, Thomas saw that they had a fine view of the entire town and the outskirts.

"Sure be able to see a passle of men ridin' up to town from here," James said. "What do we use as a signal?"

"I don't know," Thomas said. "A shot, I guess."

"Won't we need more'n one?" Thad asked.

"Not if we're all listenin' for one," Thomas said. "We'll hear it."

"Look there," James said, pointing to the street. "Pa and the sheriff."

They all looked and saw Shaye and the sheriff coming out of the telegraph office.

"Looks like they're gonna take a walk around town," Thomas said, "let folks see pa wearin' the deputy badge. Reckon we ought to do the same thing, James. I can do it now and you can do it later, when I relieve you."

James looked up at the sun.

"Reckon one of you boys can bring me a canteen?" James asked. "Might get hot up here."

"I'll bring one right back," Thad said.

"And each one of us who comes to relieve the other can bring a fresh one," Thomas said. "Good thinkin', James."

"Just don't wanna die of thirst up here and have one of you boys find me with my tongue all swole up."

Thomas slapped his brother on the back.

"I'll see you in a while."

He and Thad went back down through the hatch and James closed it behind them. He then took up a position at the front of the building. Before long he saw his brother and Thad leave the building and cross the street. He wished he had told Thomas to bring a rifle up with him, but made a bet with himself that his brother would think of that on his own.

He remained at the front of the building for a few moments, then decided it would be better to move around, make sure he could see on all sides. He started walking in a circle around the roof, found himself thinking about Belinda Davis, and shook his head to dispel thoughts of her. Like his pa said, that kind of thinking at the wrong time could get a man killed.

"What happened at your house last night?" Shaye asked. "I mean, between you and your wife and Belinda."

"My wife doesn't want to confront Belinda just yet," Cotton said.

"Why not?"

"She's afraid she might get mad and leave and take Little Matt with her," the lawman explained.

"Doesn't seem to me Belinda's all that loving toward the boy," Shaye said. "Every time I've seen him, it's your missus that's holding him."

"You're right about that," Cotton said. "Seems we never had any young ones of our own. My wife does everything for that boy, from dressing him and feeding him in the morning to putting him to bed at night."

"And what does Belinda do?"

"She goes out mostly. Does some shopping. Does...well, I don't know what she does."

"Where does she get money for shopping?"

Cotton hesitated, then said, "From my wife."

"Man," Shaye said, "that girl has been taking advantage of you and your wife long enough."

"I know it," Cotton said. "I see it now and so does my wife, but—"

"I know," Shaye said. "You don't have to try to explain."

They continued walking, nodding to men they passed, tipping their hats to ladies.

"Has Belinda got a man?"

"What?"

"A beau?" Shaye asked. "Somebody courting her?"

"Not that I know of."

"She can't be shopping all the time," Shaye said. "Where does she go when she goes out? She got friends in town? Other girls?"

"I don't think so."

"Sounds...doesn't sound right," Shaye said, shaking his head. "What if she's got a fella?"

"And?"

"She's using you and your wife to live off of, to take care of the baby while she goes and sees this fella, maybe on the sly. Maybe he's a married man."

"Well, most of the men in town are kinda stuck on her," Cotton said. "I see the way they watch her when she walks around town."

"Could be she wants you to take care of her baby, my boys and me to protect her from Jeb Collier, and then maybe she'll go off with this fella she's seeing."

"If she's seeing one."

"Right."

"I guess we'll find that all out in due time," Shaye said, "if we're not going to confront her now."

"I'll...talk to my missus about it."

"Fine," Shaye said. "It's your call, Sheriff."

They walked a bit more and then the sheriff said, "By the way, the town will be picking up the hotel bill for you and your boys while you're here. Won't cost you a cent."

"Well," Shaye said, "at least that's good news."

40

It was several days later when the newly formed Collier gang rode into a Texas town called Highbinder. It wasn't much of a town, really, but it had a lawman and a telegraph office. The lawman had received a message from the sheriff of Pearl River Junction to be on the lookout for a gang of men led by one Jeb Collier.

Sheriff Tate Coffey had no deputies and spent most of his days seated in front of his office, watching the street. Highbinder only had a few streets and there was rarely any trouble there. When this group of men rode in—eight in number—he knew it had to be the gang Sheriff Cotton had contacted him about.

Highbinder also had one hotel and one saloon and the eight men headed for the saloon first. If they went to the hotel next and checked in, he'd be able to take a look at their names. He decided to wait on sending a telegram to the sheriff of Pearl River Junction until he knew for sure that this was the gang in question.

Coffey was in his early thirties and had only been sheriff of Highbinder for a few months. It wasn't a position he had ever particularly aspired to, but he was new in town when the last sheriff accidentally shot himself in the head. When the job opened, he tossed his hat into the ring and got it. Highbinder was little more than a way station between towns and the town council—essentially, the mayor and his wife—didn't think they needed a man with special experience. All they needed was a chest to pin a star on.

Tate Coffey certainly qualified for that.

In the saloon the eight men spread out, most of them standing at the bar. Jeb Collier and Vic Delay sat at a table. The saloon was small, only five tables. Two of them had been occupied until Collier and his men entered. Their presence alone was enough to convince the others to leave. So at the moment only the eight members of the gang—and the bartender—were present.

"I tell you that sheriff was eyeballin' us," Delay said.

"So what?" Jeb asked. "That's his job."

"We stayin' here overnight?"

"Yeah," Jeb said. "Our next stop will be Pearl River Junction. I don't want us all ridin' in there at one time, but I ain't worked out what I wanna do yet."

"So we should get rooms at the hotel."

"Yes."

Lou Tanner came over and set a beer down in front of each man.

"Lou, send Leslie over to the hotel. We'll need..." He looked at Jeb.

"Four rooms," Jeb said. He and Delay would each have their own room and the others would share.

"Four," Delay told Tanner.

"Right, boss."

As Tanner sent Leslie out of the saloon, Delay asked Jeb, "What are you thinkin' of doin'?"

"We're too big a force to ride in together," Jeb said.

"I think we should ride into town in three groups, maybe four."

"You and me?"

"Separately," Jeb said, "in case someone recognizes us."

"I can ride in with Tanner," Delay said. "You can ride in with your brother. Then my two men and your two men."

"Sounds good," Jeb said. "And we'll stagger our times. Let's send the others in first, then you and Tanner, and then me and Ben."

"We don't know what kind of law they got there," Delay said. "Maybe we should take the sheriff out first."

Jeb put his beer down. "No, let's not start trouble as soon as we ride in. I'll need time to see Belinda and the boy."

"We really are goin' there so you can see if you have a son?" Delay asked.

"Well, yeah," Jeb said. "What's wrong with that?"

"I just thought there had to be more to it than that," Delay said. "I mean, I might have some kids here and there, but I don't really wanna know."

"Well, I do," Jeb said. "My ol' man left me when I was five. I know what it's like not to have a father."

"So do I," Delay said. "Big deal."

"Maybe it wasn't a big deal to you, Vic," Jeb said, "but it was to me."

"Fine," Delay said. "As long as there's a bank there."

"There's a bank in every town, Vic," Jeb said.

"This one?"

"Probably," Jeb said, "though I can't see that there'd be much money here."

Delay got a thoughtful look on his face.

"No," Jeb said, "I don't wanna hit a bank this close to Pearl River Junction. I noticed telegraph lines as we came in."

"Why's a town this size have a telegraph line?" Delay asked.

"I don't know," Jeb said. "What does it matter?"

"Yeah, you're right," Delay said. "What does it matter? I'm gonna freshen my beer."

Delay got up and left Jeb Collier to his thoughts. He walked to the bar, grabbed Tanner's arm, and pulled him to one side.

"Send Samms out to look around."

"For what?"

"This one-horse town has a telegraph line," Delay said. "I want to know why. See if it has a bank."

"A bank? This town? What kind of deposits would it have?"

"Lou?" Delay said, lowering his voice. "Why does this town have a telegraph line?"

"Okay," Tanner said, "I see your point. There's got to be something here to make it worth it."

"Right," Delay said. "Send Samms out."

"I'll go too."

"Fine," Delay said. "Just get me some answers."

41

Thomas climbed up through the hatch and tossed a fresh canteen to his brother.

"Thanks," James said. "I ran out a little while ago."

Thomas moved to the edge of the roof and looked around.

"Any sign of anythin' at all?" he asked.

"No," James said, putting the stopper in the canteen. He didn't want to drain his brother's supply of water. "Three days up here, Thomas, and nothing. You think Pa could be wrong?"

"Well, yeah, he could be wrong," Thomas said, "but I wouldn't want to bet against Pa, would you?"

"No," James said.

"Maybe," Thomas added, "it's not Pa who's wrong."

"Whataya mean?"

"Maybe it's Belinda."

"Why are you always pickin' on her?"

"James..."

"Okay, okay," James said, "never mind. All right, let's say she's wrong. Then what?"

"That means that there's not a gang comin' this way."

"So is that good news or bad news?"

"Both," Thomas said. "Good news that there's no gang, bad news 'cause we're still here."

"And no telegrams from any of the other lawmen?"

"No, nothing," Thomas said. "Why don't you head down, get somethin' to eat?"

"Okay," James said. "Thad'll relieve you in three."

"Good."

James handed his brother the rifle they were sharing while on "roof" duty and went down through the hatch.

"What if you're wrong?" Alvin Simon asked.

Belinda made sure the CLOSED sign was out and his shop door was locked. She pulled the shade down and turned to face him.

"What?"

"What if Jeb Collier is not on his way here with a gang?" he said.

Belinda crossed the floor and faced him.

"Even if Jeb comes alone, he'd kill you."

"I'm not helpless, you know."

"Against him, you would be."

"Belinda—"

"He's coming, Alvin," she said confidently, "and he'll have men with him."

"Well, at least you got Shaye and his sons to stay and help."

"They're not doing that for me," she said. "They're staying to help the sheriff."

"How are you doing with them?" Simon asked. "I mean, over at the sheriff's house."

"They're treating me different," she said. "They know something."

"About us?" Simon asked eagerly.

"No," she said, "and they're not going to find out."

Deflated, he asked, "About what, then?"

"Just about...well, me."

"You have been pullin' the wool over their eyes for a while now," he said. "Maybe they sense something."

"No," she said, "maybe it was Dan Shaye. He probably told them something."

"But you asked him not to," Simon said. "Don't tell me you couldn't control him?"

"Don't worry," she said, "I will. He's a man, after all."

"And you can control any man?"

Suddenly she realized she may have said too much. She came around the counter, then put her arms around his waist and her head against his chest.

"Most men, honey," she said, "but not you. You know the real me."

He put his arms around her and held her tightly to him.

"You see right through me," she lied.

"Yes," he said, "I do."

Riley Cotton and Dan Shaye were in the sheriff's backyard, smoking cigars and watching Cotton's wife play with Little Matt. They had become fairly good friends in the last few days.

"She really loves that kid," Shaye said.

"Yeah, she does," Cotton said. "I love watching them together. It would break her heart—and mine—if Belinda tried to take him away."

"I'm sure you'll be able to work something out, Riley."

"Whataya mean? Like buying him from her?"

"I get the feeling that once Belinda feels she's safe

from Jeb Collier, she'll want to be on her way. And I'm not all that convinced she wants to take a child with her."

"So you think she'll just leave him here?"

"Maybe."

"If she did that," Cotton said, "we could adopt him. Marion would love that."

"Sure, you could do that."

"But... what about you?"

"What about me?"

"What if he is your grandson?"

Shaye puffed on his cigar for a few moments, considering how he should reply to that.

"Riley," he finally said, "I don't know if there's any way we'll actually be able to know that. And even if he is, I don't see how my sons and I could ever give him the kind of home you and your wife could."

"So you mean... you'd just leave him with us?"

Shaye slapped the sheriff on the back and said, "Why the hell not?"

42

Sheriff Coffey watched as first one, then two of the men who had ridden into town left the saloon. One of them walked over to the hotel, went inside, and then came out. When the street was empty, Coffey left his chair and walked over to the hotel.

"Afternoon, Sheriff," the desk clerk said. His name was Norbert and he was also the owner.

"Norbert, that fella who just came in," Coffey said. "What did he want?"

"Wanted to give me a good day, that's what he wanted," the clerk said. "He took four rooms."

"Did he sign the book?"

"Sure did."

"Let me see it."

Norbert turned the book around for the lawman to look at. The four rooms had been taken in four different names and one of the names was Jeb Collier.

"Okay, thanks."

"Gonna be trouble, Sheriff?" the man asked, worried. "Should I collect in advance?"

"No, no," Coffey said. "Don't worry. You'll get your money."

Coffey left the hotel and walked back toward his

office and past it. He was on his way to the telegraph office, but he had to pass the bank to get there.

Lou Tanner and Bill Samms entered the bank and stopped just inside the door to look around. There was room for three teller windows, but only one was being used. Off to one side were three desks, but again, only one was in use. The others had been vacant for some time, as evidenced by the layer of dust covering them.

"Can I help you gents?" the teller asked.

Samms started forward, but Tanner put his hand on his arm to stop him. Instead, he walked to the window.

"We were just wonderin' about opening an account," he said, "but the bank looks... deserted."

"Well, yeah," the old clerk said, leaning on his elbows. The lone figure seated at the desk was an older woman who looked over at them and shook her head.

"That old woman hates when I talk to people," the old man said, "but I ain't only a teller, I'm the bank manager."

Now that he was standing at the teller's window, Tanner could see a large safe behind it—against a wall. Oddly, the safe was open.

"Is that a fact?"

"Sure is," the old man said.

"If you're the manager, how come you keep the safe open?"

The old man cackled and said, "That's 'cause there ain't no money in it."

"None at all?" Tanner asked. "What happened? You get robbed?"

The old man found that funny and started laughing so much he lost his breath and started to choke.

"Take it easy, old-timer," Tanner said. "It's just a question."

"I'm s-sorry," the old man said, wiping tears from his eyes with his palms. "It's just the idea of somebody robbin' this bank...there ain't nothin' for them ta get."

"Whataya mean?"

"There ain't been no money in this bank in years, mister," he said. "Oh, there was a time when we had plenty of money in the safe and the safe was always closed. We had a full staff here and a real bank manager. Those were the days."

"What days?"

"The days when most of the big ranches around here kept their money in this bank," the old man said. "Their operatin' expenses, their payrolls, they all came out of here."

"But not no more?"

"Not no more for a long time."

"But...you still got a telegraph line."

"We got that line because of the bank," the old man said, "but when the money got taken out of the bank, nobody came along ta take down the line. So we still got one, but ain't nobody got any more use for that than they do for this bank."

The old man cackled again and Tanner started to think that the man only had about half a brain left.

"Is this true?" Tanner asked, turning to the old woman at the desk.

"It's true," she said. "That old man tells the story to anyone who'll listen."

Tanner looked over at Samms, who just shrugged.

"Is he really the manager?"

"We ain't got much need for a manager anymore, mister," she said. "That there old fool is my husband

and, truth be told, the only reason we come in here every day is 'cause we don't got nowhere else ta go and we don't wanna stay home together."

Tanner looked over at the old man, who was smiling broadly, a yellow gap-toothed smile.

"Ain't no harm in lettin' him call hisself the manager, now, is there?" she asked.

"Lou," Samms said, "let's get outta here."

Samms turned and opened the door, but Lou Tanner had one more question.

"If the ranchers used to keep all their money here, where are they keepin' it now?"

"They're keepin' it in the bank that put us outta business," she said. "The bank that nearly killed this town."

"And where's that?"

"Why," she said, "that's in Pearl River Junction."

The sheriff took up a position across the street from the old bank. He knew Gladys Michaels and her crazy husband Henry were in there. They went in there every day. That meant that they were telling these men everything there was to know about the old bank.

After a while the door opened and the two men stepped outside. They never once glanced across the street, but headed straight back to the saloon, deep in thought the whole way.

He stepped from the doorway and turned to go to the telegraph office, but at the last minute crossed over to the bank.

"Gladys," he said, sticking his head in. "What'd you tell them fellers that was just in here?"

"Henry told them his story, Sheriff," she said, "after he told them he was the bank manager."

"And what else did you tell them?"

"Why, I told them where all the money went to," she said. "They seemed like nice enough fellas, no sense in lettin' them think they could open an account here. We told them to go to the Bank of Pearl River Junction, where the ranchers from miles around keep their money."

Sheriff Coffey closed the door and started walking quickly to the telegraph office.

43

Sheriff Cotton was in his office when the telegraph clerk found him.

"Thad, where's Dan Shaye?" he asked after the clerk left.

"I don't know, Sheriff."

"What are you doing now?"

"I gotta relieve Thomas on the roof of City Hall."

Cotton folded up the telegram and looked up at Thad.

"Go and get Thomas off the roof and both of you come down. One of you find Dan and the other James. I need all of you here as soon as possible."

"But we need somebody on watch—"

"Not today we don't," Cotton said. "Just do it."

"Sure, Sheriff."

As Thad left the office, Cotton unfolded the telegram and read it again.

"The Collier gang is in a town called Highbinder, Texas."

"How far is that from here?" Shaye asked.

"About two days' ride. I got a telegram from the sheriff there. They arrived today and checked out the bank."

"What's Highbinder's bank like?" Shaye asked.

"That's just it," Cotton said. "They don't have a bank there anymore. They used to, but all that's left is the building. See, before the Bank of Pearl River Junction opened, all the ranchers for miles around kept their money there. Now it's here."

"And the gang knows that now," Thomas said.

"Right. Sheriff Coffey says they took rooms and are going to stay overnight. If they leave town in the morning and head this way, he'll send us another telegram."

"So we've got a breather for a couple of days," James said. "No more roof watches."

"For now, no," Cotton said, "but now that they know how much money our bank keeps on deposit..."

"Makes sense that they'd hit it," Shaye said, "but probably not until after Jeb Collier meets with Belinda and sees the boy."

"Wait," Cotton said, "we can't let him see them."

"Why not?" Shaye said. "It's the reason he's coming here. Maybe if he sees her and she tells him to go away, he will."

"He's got seven men riding with him, according to this telegram," Cotton said. "You think they're going to come all this way and not try for the bank?"

"Probably not," Shaye said. "You got any names?"

"Four," Cotton said, consulting the telegram, "Leslie, Tanner, Jeb Collier, and Delay."

"Wait," Shaye said. "Vic Delay?"

"No first name," Cotton said. "Why? Who's Vic Delay?"

"A fast gun for hire," Shaye said. "A killer."

"Why would a killer be riding with Collier?" Cotton asked. "Isn't he a bank robber?"

"Bank robbers don't kill?" James asked.

"Well, yeah, they do," Shaye said, "but Vic Delay has never been known for robbing banks, just for killing."

"So then why's he riding with the Collier gang?" Thomas asked.

"Maybe Jeb Collier thought he'd have need for a fast gun when he came here."

"To find out if he has a son?" James asked.

"Collier's got something else on his mind besides that—obviously," Thomas said.

"Our bank," Cotton said, "now that he knows about it."

"How well is your bank protected?" Shaye asked.

"Two guards at all times," Cotton said. "The bank employs their own men."

"Well, we'll have to warn them," Shaye said.

"I'll have a talk with the manager," Cotton said, "and I guess I better talk to the mayor and the town council. We might be having some excitement in this town pretty soon."

"I'll go with you," Shaye said.

"And what do we do?" James asked.

"You can stop taking shifts on the roof," Cotton said. "In fact, you can take some time off, get some rest. We'll tell you when you should come back."

"We should probably keep one of them on duty, Riley," Shaye said, "just to make normal rounds."

"Okay," Cotton said, "decide among yourselves who'll make rounds tonight."

"I'll do it," Thad said immediately. "I'm used to it."

Sheriff Cotton got up, grabbed his gun belt from the peg behind him, and put it on.

"Let's go, Dan," he said, "we can still catch the bank during business hours. After that we'll come back to City Hall and talk to the others."

"You boys stay out of trouble during your time off," Shaye warned his sons.

"Hey, we're deputies now," James said. "Nobody's gonna want to start trouble with us."

"If you believe that..." Thomas said, shaking his head.

On the way to the bank Cotton let Shaye read the telegram for himself.

"How fast is Vic Delay?" Cotton asked.

"Fast, accurate, deadly."

"Have you ever seen him?"

"Once," Shaye said, "years ago, in Abilene." He handed the telegram back to Cotton.

"Maybe it's a different Delay," the sheriff said.

"Wishful thinking," Shaye said. "Let's just assume that Jeb Collier is on his way here with Vic Delay and six other men and go from there."

"Why would he need to bring a killer—unless he means to kill Belinda?"

"He probably just figures he doesn't know what to expect when he gets here," Shaye said.

"Eight men," Cotton said, shaking his head.

"Can you get any more deputies?" Shaye asked.

"Not with any experience."

"When this is all over," Shaye said, "you might consider getting the town council to let you bring in some experienced men—especially if your bank carries as much money as you say."

"The town was trying to keep a low profile about that," Cotton said. "They didn't want to overstaff my office and figured the bank had its own men inside."

"They gave you that big two-story office," Shaye said. "You might as well put it to good use."

"Well, if I come out of this alive, I'll take it up with the town council," Riley Cotton said.

"You'll come out of it alive, Riley," Shaye said. "We all will."

"How can you be so sure?"

Shaye shrugged and said, "Thinking about the alternative really doesn't appeal to me."

44

The bank manager's name was Edmund Brown and Shaye could see right from the first moment he met him that the man did not have much faith in the local law.

"We have enough men to handle any robbery attempt, gentlemen," he said to Shaye and Cotton. "Our men are especially trained."

"I realize that, Mr. Brown," Cotton said. "We just wanted to warn you and let you know we're on top of the situation."

"Well, we appreciate that, Sheriff," Brown said, "but rest assured, we can handle the situation ourselves. I'll just put two more men on duty and that should take care of it."

"How are they armed?" Shaye asked.

Brown looked at Shaye as if he was surprised that the deputy had spoken, instead of the sheriff.

"Our men have the newest Winchesters and the training to use them," the bank manager said.

"Have they ever killed a man?"

"W-what?"

"Have they ever killed a man before?" Shaye asked again.

"Sheriff," Brown said, "do you usually let your subordinates—"

"Mr. Shaye is no subordinate, Mr. Brown," Cotton informed the man. "He has volunteered to help the town on this. He's a well-known lawman in his own right."

"Well, that may be," Brown said, "but whether or not our men have killed before is not germane to the discussion."

"I'm not sure what 'germane' means, Mr. Brown," Shaye said, "but it sure is important whether or not your men have killed before, because they'll probably have to kill now. There can't be any hesitation on their part—"

"Not to worry, uh, Deputy Shaye," Brown said, "there will be no hesitation on the part of my men."

"I hope not, sir," Shaye said, "for all your sakes."

"What an ass!" Shaye said outside.

"That's true," Cotton said.

"He's going to end up getting a lot of people killed someday," Shaye said. "Maybe even some citizens."

"We'll talk to the mayor and the town council now," Cotton said, "but I got to warn you that Brown sits on the council."

"He's just one man," Shaye said. "Let's see if we can't convince the others to take some special precautions."

The mayor was an officious man named Walter Mann. He consented to see Cotton and Shaye without an appointment, but told the sheriff he had "five minutes."

"It's going to take longer than that, Mayor," Shaye said.

The mayor sported a mane of white hair that made him seem older than he was, which Shaye figured was about his own age.

"I don't know you," Mann said. "You're new."

"Mayor, this is Daniel Shaye. He and his two sons have volunteered to be deputies during this time."

"And what time is that, Sheriff?"

"We believe that a gang of outlaws is on its way here," Cotton said and went on to explain about the telegram from Sheriff Coffey on Highbinder. He did not, however, say anything about Belinda and her son.

"What makes you think these men are coming here, Sheriff?"

"They were told about our bank," Cotton said.

"Our bank is well protected."

"There's another man riding with the gang," Shaye said. "His name is Vic Delay."

Mann shook his head. "Should I know that name?"

"He has a reputation as a killer."

"And why would he be coming here?"

"We don't know that, Mayor," Cotton said. "We just want to alert you and the council to what we do know."

"Well," Mann said, "it doesn't sound to me like you know a lot, Riley, but I'll convene a meeting of the council tomorrow morning, nine A.M."

"Fine," Cotton said. "I'll be there."

He and Shaye turned to leave, but then he turned back.

"I forgot to tell you. We've already talked with Ed Brown at the bank. He's not taking our warning too seriously."

"I'll keep that in mind, Riley."

Cotton nodded and followed Shaye out the door.

* * *

"Two jackasses," Shaye said. "Why is it men like that hire men like us and then don't listen?"

"We do our jobs anyway, don't we?"

"This is the part of wearing the badge I always hated," Shaye said, "dealing with men like that."

"What can we do?" Cotton asked. "It's men like that who build towns and run things."

"Yeah," Shaye said.

"I could use some coffee," Cotton said. "How about you?"

"Sure."

"I know a place that serves a great cup."

"Not your house, I hope...no offense."

"None taken," Cotton said. "No, we can have coffee without having to see Belinda or Little Matt."

"Then lead the way..."

45

Jeb Collier was still seated in the saloon with Vic Delay when Lou Tanner returned. The other men had left in search of a meal or to check out their hotel rooms. Since they were sharing two or three to a room, they'd want to get first choice of a bed.

Lou Tanner got himself a beer from the bartender and sat down across from Jeb and Vic Delay.

"What'd you find out?" Jeb asked.

"What did you send him to find out?" Delay asked.

"Why this one-horse town has a telegraph key."

"What the hell—"

"Just listen," Jeb said. He looked at Tanner. "Go."

Tanner explained everything he and Samms had learned at the Highbinder bank—or what was left of it.

"That bank in Pearl River Junction has got to be busting with money, boss," he finished.

"Sure sounds like it," Jeb said.

"So what do we do?" Tanner asked.

"Go get yourself somethin' to eat, Lou," Jeb said. "Delay and I will be along in a while.

"Okay, Jeb."

"Ben's out there somewhere," Jeb reminded him. "Make sure he doesn't get into trouble."

When Tanner left, Jeb looked across the table at Delay.

"I knew there had to be a reason for this town to have a telegraph key."

"Whatever you say, Jeb," Delay replied. "You plan on hittin' that bank in Pearl River Junction now that you know it carries so much money?"

"It's too good to pass up," Jeb said. "You and your boys want to be in on it?"

"Why not?" Delay replied. "We'll be there, won't we?"

"But we can't do it until after I finish my other business."

"When do you want to leave?"

"Tomorrow," Jeb said, "and we'll still ride in the way I figured. We'll leave this town in four sets of twos, so we don't ride into Pearl River Junction too close together."

"Suits me," Delay said. "Whataya say we get somethin' to eat now? I'm starvin'."

As they pushed their chairs back and got up, Jeb asked, "Don't you want to talk about the split?"

"I figure you'll see I get a fair share from the bank, Jeb," Delay said, " 'cause you know I'd kill you, otherwise, and that brother of yours."

"I reckon I know that, Vic," Jeb said.

"All right, then," Delay said. "Let's go and find somethin' to eat."

Sheriff Coffey watched the last two men leave the hotel and walk over to the café. Some of the other men were inside already. When they were joined by the last two, Coffey crossed the street and peered in the window of the café. He counted and saw that seven of the men were inside, seated at two tables. They were all eating except for the two who had just entered, who were ordering from a scared-looking waitress.

He was trying to decide what to do next when he felt something hard poke him in the center of the back.

"Just stand fast, Sheriff," a voice said. "I'm gonna take your gun."

A hand plucked his gun from his holster.

"Okay," the voice said, "let's go inside."

Jeb Collier looked up as a man came stumbling into the café. The waitress gave a startled little scream.

"It's okay, darlin'," he said to her. "Just go and get us our steaks."

"Y-yes, sir."

Jeb turned his attention to the two men who had just entered. One was the sheriff and the other was Lou Tanner.

"Found the lawman peekin' in the window," Tanner said. "He's been watchin' us all day. Figured maybe he'd like a closer look."

"Good idea, Lou," Jeb said. "What's your name, lawman?"

"Coffey."

"You got any deputies?"

"No."

"Guess you don't need any in a town like this, huh?"

"Ain't much of a town," Ben Collier said.

"What's your interest in us, Sheriff?" Jeb asked.

"You're strangers," Coffey said. "It's my job to look out for strangers."

"Is that right?" Jeb asked. "You think maybe we're after your bank?"

"No, sir."

"'Sir'?" Jeb looked around at his men. "We got us a real polite lawman here, boys."

"Jeb, he was outside the bank when Samms and me were inside," Tanner said. He still had his gun in his hand, trained on Sheriff Coffey's back.

"Is that right?" Jeb asked. "I reckon you probably went in there to see what Lou here wanted, didn't you, lawman?"

"I'm just doin' my job."

"And does doin' your job mean you use the telegraph key?" Jeb asked.

"Use the key for what, Jeb?" Ben asked.

"I'm thinkin' he mighta warned Pearl River Junction that we're comin'," Jeb answered.

That made Vic Delay sit forward.

"How would he know we were headin' there?"

"I don't know," Jeb said. "Maybe the sheriff here can tell us."

"There's nothin' to tell," Coffey said, sweating. "Tol' you. I'm just doin' my job, keepin' an eye on you."

"We'll see, Sheriff," Jeb said. "We'll see. Lou, you and a couple of others make the lawman comfortable in one of these chairs. I want to eat before I talk to him some more."

"Sure, Jeb," Tanner said. "Samms, find some rope. We're gonna make the lawman real comfortable."

Sheriff Coffey watched the entire gang finish eating while tied to a chair that was shoved into a corner. It gave him time to wonder what they would do to him if he didn't tell them what they wanted to know. It also gave him time to regret he'd ever taken this damn job.

* * *

"What are we gonna do with him?" Delay asked Jeb while they ate. He kept his voice down so the sheriff couldn't hear him.

"We'll send one of the men over to the telegraph office, find out if he's sent or gotten any telegrams recently," Jeb explained. "I'm thinkin' maybe somebody in Pearl River Junction heard about me gettin' out of Yuma and figured I might be comin' to see 'em."

"Her, you mean," Delay said. "You're talkin' about your gal."

"Maybe."

"If she tol' them you're comin', then they'll be ready for us," Delay said. "And if this fella sent them a message tellin' them how many we are—"

"You're puttin' the horse before the cart, Vic," Jeb said. "Let's finish eatin', then find out what he knows and what he told people, before we panic."

"I ain't gonna panic, Jeb," Delay said. "That ain't what I do. See, this whole thing is your plan. You're gonna decide how we play it. I only know one thing."

"What's that, Vic?"

"This day's gonna end with me killin' a lawman."

Jeb forked a piece of steak into his mouth and said, "I got no problem with that."

46

Later that night Shaye entered the sheriff's office and found Cotton seated at his desk.

"You haven't gone home yet?"

"Nope."

"Anybody else around?"

"James is out doin' rounds," Cotton said.

Shaye came over and sat across from Cotton.

"Any more word from that sheriff in Highbinder?"

"No," Cotton said, "and I'm worried. That's a small town. Fact is, it can't hardly even be called a town anymore. If he gets too close to those men and they notice him..."

"I get your meaning," Shaye said. "If we don't hear from him again, we'll have to assume the worst."

"Yep," the other man said. "That he's dead and that Collier and his gang know that we know they're coming."

"That'd be the worst, all right."

"What do we do then?" Cotton asked. "I mean, if they come riding in here as bold as you please...if they come in peaceful and none of them is wanted for anything, there ain't much we can do."

"Not until they break the law anyway," Shaye said.

"Fact is, Jeb Collier'll probably want to finish his business with Belinda before he tries for the bank."

"What if she doesn't want to see him?" Cotton asked.

"Then we'll probably have a problem," Shaye said, "but I think she'll talk to him."

"What makes you say that?"

"It'll be the only way she can get rid of him," Shaye answered. "She'll have to convince him that he's not the father."

"And what if she has no better luck convincing him he's not the father than she did convincing you that you're the grandfather?"

Shaye stared at the lawman.

"Riley, I'm not even sure I understand that question, but why don't we just worry about it when the time comes?"

"Right, right."

"I've got a question for you, though."

"Okay."

"How long a ride is it from here to Highbinder?"

"Two days."

"So they'll have to camp overnight on the trail."

"Right," Cotton said. "What are you thinking?"

"I'm wondering what would happen if we met them on the trail?" Shaye said.

"And did what?" the lawman asked, carefully.

"Somehow persuaded them not to come to Pearl River Junction."

"And how would we do that without gunplay?"

"We probably couldn't," Shaye admitted.

"Dan, I don't think I could do that," Cotton said. "I mean... I'm the sheriff and—"

"That's okay," Shaye said, cutting him off. "I was

just trying it out on you. I know you can't do anything that's against the law."

"I'm sure there are some lawmen who stretch the law, Dan," Cotton went on. "Maybe it's a failing in me that I can't—"

"Riley," Shaye said, "it's okay. I understand."

They sat quietly for a few moments and then Cotton said, "You and your sons wouldn't ride out there and face them, would you?"

"No," Shaye said, "not without knowing exactly how many there are. Sheriff Coffey said eight, but we don't know if they'll be riding all together or not. I mean, if I was Collier I wouldn't want to ride in here with seven other men and attract attention."

"So you think they'll come in separately?"

"In three or four groups, probably," Shaye said. "We'll have to get a description of him from Belinda, just so we'll have a chance to recognize him when he rides in."

"That's a good idea."

"I think we're pretty safe in assuming they won't arrive until the day after tomorrow," Shaye said. "I just wish your sheriff friend would send us one more telegram."

"Maybe he will," Cotton said, "after they leave town."

"Yeah," Shaye said, "if he can. Given the size of that town, I also assume he has no deputies?"

"No," Cotton said, "and he hasn't had the job all that long either."

Shaye stared for a moment, not at anything in particular.

"You think he's in trouble, don't you?"

"Oh yes," Shaye said, "I do. And we're too far away to be of any help. All we can do is wait."

* * *

The blood from the wounds in Sheriff Coffey's face had run down his chest and soaked into the ropes that were binding him.

"That's enough," Jeb told Lou Tanner. Aside from Delay, Jeb had respect for Lou Tanner above all the other men and Tanner had proven him right by bringing the lawman in. Because of that he had allowed Tanner to don his leather gloves and "question" Sheriff Coffey.

When Jeb called him off, Tanner stepped back and stripped off his bloody leather gloves.

"We've got what we need," Jeb said. "One sheriff with one full-time and one part-time deputy in Pearl River Junction. That's all we need to know."

"So we don't need him anymore?" Vic Delay asked.

"No."

"I mean," Delay said, "we don't need him alive any—"

"No, Vic," Jeb said, "we don't need him. Do what you want."

All of the men except for Lou Tanner, who knew Delay well, were startled when the man simply drew his gun and fired a shot into the sheriff's chest, putting the bloody man out of his misery. The sheriff's chair hopped in the air and came down on its back with a *thud*.

Delay ejected the spent cartridge and inserted a live one before holstering his gun.

"Lou, take the men to the bar and get them a drink on me," Jeb said.

"Sure." Tanner kept himself from calling Jeb "boss." He didn't think it would sit right with Delay. The last thing he wanted to do was get Vic Delay mad at him. He knew better than anyone how unpredictable Delay was.

Once the six men were standing at the bar, effectively blocking the bartender's view, Jeb put his arm around Delay and said, "Vic, I don't think we need to leave the bartender or the telegraph operator behind when we leave either."

"I can take care of that right now."

"Do the bartender tonight and the telegraph operator tomorrow before we leave. For tonight we can put both bodies behind the bar and then close this place up when we go to the hotel."

"Okay," Delay said, "but maybe they'll be gone by mornin'."

"Not these people," Jeb said. "They got no place else to go."

"We should probably disable the key as well as the operator."

"No problem," Delay said. "And while we're checking out in the mornin' I could also do the desk clerk."

"Ah, why not?" Jeb said. "Then we at least get our rooms for free, right?"

Both men left and walked toward the bar, Delay drawing his gun again.

47

Jeb Collier came out of the hotel and found Ben waiting there with his horse. Behind him he heard a shot. He thought that must be Vic Delay taking care of the hotel bill.

The night before, when they had returned to the hotel, he'd heard Delay ask the clerk, "Say, how many people live in this town anyway?"

"Not very many anymore," the clerk said. "Probably a dozen or so of us left, is all."

Well, Jeb had thought, minus the sheriff and the bartender.

On the way up the stairs to their rooms, Jeb said, "You want to kill the whole town, Vic?"

"I'm thinkin' about it."

"Forget it," Jeb said. "Take care of the telegraph in the morning and the desk clerk, then we'll be on our way."

"You're callin' the shots," Delay had said.

Now it was morning and there was only the telegraph key and operator to take care of. Once the key was disabled, it didn't matter how many people they left behind.

Delay came out of the hotel, pulling on his black leather gloves.

"Paid the bill," he said.

"Okay, let's do the rest of it and get on the trail," Jeb said. He took the reins of his horse from his brother.

"Where's my horse?" Delay asked.

Nervously, Ben said, "Tanner's got it over to the saloon, Mr. Delay. That's where the rest of the boys are."

"Ben, I'm goin' to the telegraph office with Vic," Jeb said, mounting up. "Go get the rest of the boys ready to travel—and they better not be drunk."

"Sure, Jeb."

As Ben rode off toward the saloon, Delay said, "He's an idiot."

"But he's my brother," Jeb said. "Don't forget that, Vic."

The two matched stares, Jeb getting the upper hand because he was mounted and looking down at Delay.

"Like I said," Delay repeated, "you're callin' the shots," and then he added to himself—*for now.*

48

The next morning Shaye had breakfast with Thomas and James. He took them to the café Sheriff Cotton had taken him to for the good cup of coffee. Turned out they had the best food in town as well.

"Just don't tell my wife I come here," Cotton had said to Shaye. "This is the only place in town that makes better food than she does."

Shaye swore himself to secrecy and now did the same with his sons.

"I wouldn't want to get the sheriff in trouble," James said around a forkful of steak and eggs, "but he sure is right about the food. I don't know if it's better than his wife's, but it's the best I've had in a while."

"It's better than your cookin', I can tell you that much," Thomas said.

"Oh yeah? Well, when we get back to the ranch, you can do all the cookin' from now on."

They fell silent for a moment and then James added, "Uh, that is, if we go back to the ranch."

"I already told you both" Shaye said, "that we'll be going back to the ranch, even if it's just to sell it."

They ate in silence again for a few moments and

then James asked, "How do you feel wearin' a badge again, Pa?"

"Well, it's been a while," Shaye said. "I have to admit I really didn't like having to talk with the mayor yesterday and I'm not looking forward to talking to the town council half an hour from now. This is the political part of the job I have always hated."

"But..." James said.

"But it does feel good to have a star on my chest again, even if it is a deputy's star," Shaye said. "Been a while since I wore a shirt with the pin hole in it. What about you boys?"

"I like it," Thomas said without hesitation.

"I thought you would, Thomas," Shaye said.

"You didn't think I would, Pa?" James asked.

"I don't know, James," Shaye said. "You never seemed to take to the job the way Thomas did."

"You mean because he's better with a gun?"

"Not just that," Shaye said. "Your ma and I just always thought you'd get an education. You have the potential to be better than this—maybe a lawyer."

"A lawyer?" James asked. "Me? Really?"

"You never thought about it?" Shaye asked.

"Not really."

"You're smart enough for it, James," Shaye said.

"I agree with Pa," Thomas said. "I can see us both workin' for the law, James: me outside the courtroom and you inside. You are the smart one. You just haven't had a chance to use your smarts because you had to pick up a gun."

James stared at his big brother and asked, "You really feel that way?"

"Sure, why not? You took to book learnin' more than Matthew and me ever did. I don't mind admittin' that."

"You could still do it, James," Shaye said. "Think about it."

"I will, Pa," James promised.

"What are you gonna tell the town council, Pa?" Thomas asked, changing the subject to something more immediate.

"Nothing," Shaye said. "It's up to the sheriff, not me, to make them understand what's happening—or what might happen."

"Fellers like that," Thomas said, "they usually understand what's happenin' better than what might happen, don't they? I mean, I don't have that much experience, but that's what I've seen in the places we've worked in."

"You're right, Thomas," Shaye said. "They just don't have that much imagination."

It was very early and there were only a few more diners in the place, so when Riley Cotton appeared at the door, he attracted everyone's attention.

"Thought I might find you boys here," he said, taking a seat.

The waitress came hurrying over and asked, "Breakfast, Sheriff?"

"Uh, sure, Connie, why not? Steak and eggs."

"Comin' up."

"Something on your mind, Riley?" Shaye asked.

"Yeah," Cotton said. "I stopped by the telegraph office and asked the clerk to send a telegram to Highbinder."

"And? No answer yet?"

"No answer at all."

"Could be there's just nobody at the other end," Thomas suggested.

"I thought of that," the lawman said, "but the clerk says that his signal is not getting through."

"Oh," Shaye said.

"What's that mean?" James asked. "I mean, I know what it means for the signal not to get through, but what's it mean to us?"

"Well..." Cotton said. "your pa and I think that the gang may have killed Sheriff Coffey before they left Highbinder."

"And maybe they disabled the telegraph key?" James asked. "Or maybe that's all they did."

"I sure hope you're right, James," Cotton said.

"Whataya think, Pa?" James asked.

"If Jeb Collier's got Vic Delay riding with him," Shaye said, "that man just looks for reasons to kill people."

"Is he a fast gun, Pa?" James asked.

"More than a fast gun, James," Shaye said. "He's a killer. He likes it."

"I bet Thomas can take him," James said. He turned to Cotton and added, "Thomas is fast and he hits what he shoots at every time." There was pride in James's tone.

"Thanks, James," Thomas said, "but I ain't so high on tryin' my hand with a fella like that."

"Smart man," Shaye said. "You gotta look to avoid gunfights, not get into them."

"You ever avoid a gunfight, Pa?" James asked. "I mean, in your younger years?"

"Every chance I got, boy," Shaye said. "Every chance I got."

49

Shaye and Cotton left Thomas and James at the café and walked to City Hall.

"You know what these people are like, don't you?" Cotton asked.

"Oh yes," Shaye said. "They're the same in every town. They think because you have a badge on your chest you're used to being a target."

"They're paying you to do a job and you better do it without complaining," Cotton said.

"And don't ask for more help."

"Well," Cotton said, "today we're gonna ask. I don't know what good it will do, except that after the fact we might be able to say, 'I told you so.'"

They reached the building and entered.

"The bank manager, Brown," Shaye said, "he'll be against us already."

"There are four other people on the town council," Cotton said. "I'll have to talk directly to them."

They went up the stairs to the second floor and Cotton led the way to a closed door.

"This is where they meet," he said. "They should all be inside already."

"Want me to come in with you?" Shaye offered.

"Why don't we start with you out here?" Cotton asked. "This part is really my job, isn't it?"

Shaye nodded and said, "And you're welcome to it."

"What's this town council meetin' supposed to be about?" James asked Thomas as they left the café.

"Cotton wants to try to hire new deputies."

"I thought he had the power to do that?" James asked. "He gave us badges, didn't he?"

"Yeah, but we're not gettin' paid," Thomas said. "He needs more money to pay more deputies and that has to be approved by the town council."

"And why wouldn't they?"

"Because they're politicians," Thomas said. "It's their job to say no."

They crossed the street and started walking toward the sheriff's office and City Hall.

"The five of us can probably handle things," James said. "Don't you think, Thomas?"

"I think there's safety in numbers, James," Thomas said. "That's why Collier's comin' here with eight men and that's why we could always use more."

"But if we don't get them," James argued, "we can handle it. I know we can."

"Well," Thomas replied, "I did say you're the smart one, James, so I guess I'll take your word for it."

But there is smart, Thomas thought, and there is naïve. He thought James had a bit of each.

Occasionally, Shaye could hear raised voices from inside the meeting room, but he was never able to make out any words. Eventually, when the door to the meeting room opened, Shaye expected Cotton to ask him to come in. Instead, the sheriff stepped into the hall and pulled the door closed behind him.

"You look frustrated," Shaye said.

"Then I feel the way I look," Cotton said. "To a man—and the only woman on the council—they feel that the bank would be able to handle any robbery attempts."

"So no money for more deputies?"

"No money," Cotton said, "but they commended me for being able to get three new deputies for free."

"So what if we took off our badges?" Shaye asked. "Would they give you money to hire more deputies then?"

"No. They stood their ground and the mayor stood with them."

"And I'll bet bank manager Edmund Brown had a lot to do with it too," Shaye said.

"Oh yeah," Cotton said. "He had a lot to say. They also suggested that if I felt like I couldn't handle the job I should step down."

"Maybe you should," Shaye said.

"What would that accomplish?"

"They sure wouldn't be able to hire a new sheriff in time," Shaye said. "That would teach them a lesson."

Cotton shook his head.

"That would leave the town defenseless," he said. "I couldn't take my frustration out on the people of this town."

"Go around and try to recruit volunteers to stand with you, Riley," Shaye said, "and then decide whether or not you can take it out on them."

Cotton looked at the closed door and, for a moment, they could both hear laughter from behind it.

"Let's get out of here," Cotton said. "I can't think here."

"Can't blame you for that," Shaye said and followed the sheriff down the steps and out of the building.

"I guess it's up to us," Cotton said some time later as the two men leaned on the bar at Bo Hart's Saloon. "That is, if you're still willing to help."

"I can't very well leave town knowing that you and your deputy would have to face the gang alone."

"It's our job, not yours," Cotton said.

"That may be," Shaye said, "but my sons and I are here and we know what's going to happen. We can't just walk away."

"Integrity."

"What?"

"You have integrity, all three of you," Cotton said. "It's rare to find that, these days."

"If that's true, it's a shame," Shaye said, "but I don't think it's integrity... it's just common sense."

"I can't believe this is all going to happen because of Belinda."

"If that was the case, you could just send her out of town," Shaye said.

"You mean... run her out of town?"

"That's what I mean," Shaye said, "then when Collier gets here and realizes she's not here... but that's not the case, Riley. They know about the bank now. If they get here and Belinda's not here, they'll just hit the bank."

Cotton nursed a glass of whiskey, then asked the bartender for a second. Shaye was holding a half-finished beer.

"You got money in that bank?" he asked suddenly.

"What? Well, yeah, I do," Cotton said.

"Is there another bank in town?"

"Used to be, but eventually everyone just moved their money to this one."

"So anybody in this town or in the surrounding area who has money in a bank has it in *that* bank?"

"Yup."

"Well," Shaye said, "I guess there's one thing you could do right away."

"What's that?"

"Get your money out of that bank and stick in under your mattress."

50

Belinda Davis had heard Riley Cotton telling his wife how the deputies were going to split up their shifts to make their rounds of the town, and how the next day they were going to start taking turns on the roof of City Hall again. The only name she was really interested in was James Shaye's. She had seen the way the youngest of Dan Shaye's sons looked at her the day they met and she knew he was the weak link among the Shaye men. Thomas was the one she would have been interested in if she was simply looking for a man, but she didn't think she'd be able to control him any more than she would his father. Both of those men seemed immune to her charms, which was quite a new experience for her.

When Riley came home for supper, Belinda knew that James would be making rounds of the town. She told the Cottons she'd be having supper with a girlfriend in town and that she might be home late. With that she left the house in such a hurry that she slammed the front door behind her.

"What do you think she's up to?" Marion Cotton asked her husband.

"I don't know," Cotton said. "I don't know what goes on in that girl's head." He looked at Little Matt, who was sitting in Marion's lap, being fed. "Sure ain't you, is it, little fella?"

"I've been having some horrible thoughts, Riley," Marion said.

"What kind of thoughts?" Cotton couldn't imagine his wife having horrible thoughts of any kind.

"I was thinking that if those outlaws came here and they killed Belinda...I was thinking then Little Matt could be ours."

"Oh." Well, he thought, those were horrible thoughts, all right, but not any he hadn't already thought himself.

James came around the corner and ran right into somebody—someone soft and sweet smelling.

"Oh!" Belinda Davis said, staggering back from the impact.

"Oh God," James said. He reached out for her, grabbed her shoulders to steady her. "I'm real sorry, ma'am."

"'Ma'am'?" Belinda asked. "Don't you remember who I am, Mr. Shaye?"

"Oh," James said, releasing her. "Course I do, ma'am. You're Belinda."

"And there's no need to apologize," she said. "I believe I ran into you."

"Oh no, ma'am—"

"Please," she said, "call me Belinda."

"Uh, Belinda," he said. "I ran into you. I'm just...clumsy."

"Well, then," she said, "if you insist on taking the blame, then you must make it up to me."

"Ma'am?" he said. "I mean...Belinda?"

"You must let me treat you to supper."

"Oh, but I couldn't," he said, "I'm on duty."

"Aren't you to be relieved within the hour?" she asked. "Or have I memorized the wrong schedule?"

"Um, you memorized my schedule?"

"Shamelessly," she said, "I admit that I did. I heard the sheriff telling his wife."

"Why would you do that?"

"So that we could have supper together," she said. "You see, I must talk with you, James. I simply must!"

"Easy, ma—Belinda," he said, moved by her agitated tone. "Everythin's gonna be all right."

"I don't think so, James," she said, a single tear rolling down her smooth cheek. "I'm so afraid it won't. Can't you...please let me buy you supper and...and talk with me?"

"Well..."

"Oh, I knew you would," she said, "I knew I could count on you. Do you know the café down the street?"

"Yes," he said, "I was there this mornin'—"

"Please meet me there when you've been relieved."

"Well...all right."

She grabbed his arm, her strength surprising him.

"Please don't tell your brother or father," she said. "They don't like me or approve of me."

"That ain't so—"

"Oh, it is," she said, "but you're different. I could tell that from the moment we met."

"Belinda—"

"Please," she said, lowering her voice, "don't tell anyone. Promise!"

"All right," he said. "I promise."

She released his arm, said, "Thank you," and hurried off.

* * *

Belinda ran to the other side of the street, stepped into the shadows, and then covered her mouth with both hands and laughed. James Shaye would prove so easy to manipulate, indeed.

James watched her cross the street and lost her in the shadows. He knew he shouldn't have agreed to meet with her, but there was just no way he could refuse her.

Thomas was to relieve him soon. He thought about breaking his word to Belinda and telling his brother, but in the end decided not to. At least, not until he heard what she had to say.

51

Thomas found James checking doorways a few streets from the sheriff's office.

"Are you working your way toward or away from the office?" he asked his brother.

"Away," James said. "Sorry, but I did the other side of the street already."

"No problem," Thomas said. "I can use the walk. It's gettin' dark, brother. You better get somethin' to eat and head back to the hotel. You're gonna need a lot of rest for tomorrow."

"I was plannin' on eatin' anyway," James said. "I guess Thad'll be up all night?"

"Yep," Thomas said. "He says he don't mind stayin' up most of the night."

James was fidgety. He wanted to get over to the café before Belinda decided he wasn't coming and left.

"What's wrong with you?" Thomas asked, noticing. "You look antsy. You're not gettin' nervous, are you?"

"I'm not gettin' nervous," James said, slapping his big brother on the back. "I been nervous for a while."

"Pa would say that makes you a smart man," Thomas said, "but we already agreed on that, didn't we?"

"I'll see you in the mornin'," James said. "Try not to wake me when you come in."

"I'll walk soft," Thomas promised.

James entered the café. It was open late and Belinda was the only customer. She was talking with the waitress when he approached the table.

"This the fella?" the waitress asked.

"This is him, Connie," Belinda said, "and he looks hungry."

"You were in here this morning, weren't you?" the middle-aged woman asked. "With two others?"

"My father and brother."

"You had steak and eggs. Ready for a steak tonight?"

"Sure," James said. "Thanks."

"Sit down, I'll bring some coffee. Belinda?"

"Just coffee and a piece of pie, Connie."

Connie nodded and went to the kitchen. James sat down across from Belinda, placing his hat on an adjacent chair.

"Thank you for coming," she said.

"Somehow it didn't seem right not to."

"James," she asked, "do you believe that Little Matt is your brother Matthew's son?"

"I—I just ain't sure, Belinda. I'm sorry."

"That's all right," she said. "I knew it would be a hard sell if your pa didn't recognize the resemblance right off."

"The only resemblance any of us can see is the baby's size," James said. "He's a big boy."

"That he is."

"What about this other man, Jeb Collier?"

"What about him?" she asked. "He's no good. He's a thief and a liar. They should have kept him in Yuma Prison."

"What I meant was," James said, "was he a big man?"

"Are you asking me if Jeb Collier is really my son's father?" she asked.

"I guess I'm askin' if there's a chance."

She frowned and looked away.

"You're not sure, are you, Belinda?" James asked. "You're not sure who the father is."

Belinda looked across the table at James. Already this conversation was not going as planned. She didn't want to think of Jeb Collier as her baby's father. She wanted to steer the conversation in a direction that would benefit her.

Connie came out of the kitchen carrying a large plate and a smaller one. She set them down and then went back for the pot of coffee and two cups.

"Thank you," James said.

"You folks take your time eatin'," Connie said, "I'm just gonna close the kitchen down."

"Thanks, Connie."

She went back to the kitchen and James cut into his steak. Belinda thought that maybe Connie's interruption would help her get the conversation back on the right track.

"The only thing I know about Jeb Collier is that he's coming here and he's going to bring trouble. I need protection."

"My protection?"

"I was hoping it would be the protection of you, your father, and your brother," she said. "I was hoping you'd want to protect Little Matt."

"Belinda," James said, "my pa, my brother, and me—and the sheriff—we want to protect the whole town."

"That may be," she said, "but the whole town doesn't have as much to fear from Jeb as I do."

"And why's that?"

"Jeb loved me once," she said. "He's not going to let me go so easily."

"You think he's comin' 'cause he wants you back?"

"He wants to know if the baby's his," she said.

"How will he be able to tell any better than we can?"

"He won't," she said, "but if he decides it's his, he'll want it just because."

"And if he decides it isn't his?"

She sat back in her chair, stared at him, and hugged herself as if she'd just been overtaken by a chill.

"If he decides it's not his, he'll kill me for having a baby with another man."

James knew that his brother and father not only didn't believe Belinda when she said her son was Matthew's, they also didn't like her. But he didn't see how he could possibly leave her to her fears that Jeb Collier might kill her.

He reached across the table, placed his hand over hers, and said, "I'm not going to let anything happen to you, Belinda—whether you're the mother of my brother's child or not."

She turned her hand over and clasped his. "You have no idea how comforting that is to me, James."

Thomas stood across from the café and watched as his brother held hands with Belinda Davis. Initially, when he'd walked past the window and saw them sitting together in the empty café, his impulse was to rush in and interrupt them, find out what the hell James was doing. On second thought, however, he thought he might learn more by just watching. After all, James's intention was to eat and he might have run into the girl by accident.

So he melted into a dark doorway, folded his arms, and waited.

"I should be getting back," Belinda said after James had finished his steak. "Riley and Marion will be getting worried."

If his father and brother were right about her, she probably wouldn't have cared if they worried. He wondered why he saw a different woman than they did when they all looked at her.

"I'll walk you back," he said, standing up.

"That's not necessary—"

"Yes, it is," he said. "It's getting' dark."

"All right," she said, "but I'm paying for supper, remember?"

"But I can't—"

"Or I won't let you walk me home," she said playfully.

"Well...okay..."

Connie came out of the kitchen to collect the money for the meal, wished them both a good night, and locked the door behind them as they left.

Belinda linked her arm in James's and asked, "Do you mind?"

"No," he said, "not at all."

The girl had a good hold on James. Thomas could see that, physically and otherwise. As they started walking, he remained on his side of the street and kept pace. It soon became obvious that James was simply walking her home. Thomas decided to stay with them anyway, since James had been foolish enough to allow the girl to hang on to his gun arm.

"What will your father and brother think?" she asked as they walked.

"About what?"

She held his arm tightly, pressed herself against him so he could feel her firm young breast against him.

"About you becoming my protector?"

"I don't rightly know," he said. "I guess I'll find out, though."

"What if your pa tells you that you can't?"

"He's my pa," James said, "but I'm a full-grown man. He can't tell me what to do."

"I knew that would be your answer," she said. "I'm so glad we had this talk, James. I feel so much better."

"I'm glad too..."

* * *

Soon it became obvious to Thomas that he wasn't the only one trailing James and the girl. On their side of the street, about half a block back, he saw a shadowy figure following them as well. There was a full moon out, so when the figure crossed a street and moved away from the shelter of the buildings, Thomas was able to make out that it was a man and that he appeared to be unarmed. For that reason he did not move to intercept him...not yet anyway.

When they reached the house, Belinda released James's arm and said, "Don't come up to the porch. I don't want to get you into trouble before you're ready to tell everyone."

"I'll wait here until you get inside."

"James," she said warningly, "before he went to prison Jeb Collier was a hard man. I don't know what two years in Yuma Prison have done to him."

"Probably made him harder," James said. "Don't worry, Belinda. He's not gonna hurt you or your son. I promise."

"I believe you."

Impulsively, she kissed him quickly, right at the corner of the mouth, then turned and ran up the walk to the house and let herself in. James turned away, his hand to his face where she'd kissed him. Her sweet perfume was still in his nostrils and he thought he could taste her mouth on his. He was so enthralled that he was taken completely by surprise when he was grabbed from behind.

53

An arm snaked around James's neck from behind and was tightened with such strength that James could not breathe.

"You stay away from her!" a voice said urgently into his ear.

James couldn't make a sound and suddenly his feet were not touching the ground and it was as if he were hanging from a gallows. He grabbed at the arm that was strangling him, but it was too large and strong for him to dislodge. Finally, he started to reach for his gun when the man abruptly released him, letting him drop to the ground, and he became aware that someone was talking to him...

Thomas knew he should have stepped in sooner, but there was still no weapon being used. However, he eventually closed the distance between himself and the man who was strangling his brother and jammed his gun into the man's back.

"Let him go or I'll blow out your spine!" he hissed.

The man released James, who fell to the ground.

"Just stand still," he told the man. "James, you okay?"

"Jesus—" James said, getting to his knees. "I couldn't breathe."

"I saw that," Thomas said. "Get to your feet."

The other man was not making a sound, just standing there. He was a big man, as tall as Thomas, but with more girth. Not as big as their brother Matthew had been, though.

James staggered to his feet and turned to look at his brother and his attacker.

"What the hell—" he said to the man.

"You stay away from Belinda," the man said, again.

"Let's take this somewhere else so we don't attract attention from the house," Thomas said. "You live in town?"

"Yeah."

"Okay, you're gonna take us home with you."

"I ain't gonna—" the man started, but Thomas jabbed him in the back with his gun even harder.

"I'll take you to my shop."

"Okay," Thomas said, "get to walkin' then. James?"

"Right." James took one last look at the sheriff's house and fell into step behind his brother and the other man.

They had to walk all the way through town, almost to the livery, before they reached the man's hardware store. He used a key to open the front door and they all went in. James found a lamp and lit it.

"Let's find a seat for that gent that ain't near any hammers or pry bars," Thomas said.

James looked around and found a chair. He set it in the center of the floor and they made the man sit there, out of reach of any potential weapons.

"Now what's your name?" Thomas asked, still holding his gun.

"Alvin Simon," the man muttered.

Simon was in his late twenties, it looked, about Thomas's age. He had dirty blond hair and was powerful through the chest and shoulders. He also had very large hands. The size of his torso made his legs look too short for him.

"And you own this store?"

"Yes."

"Why were you tryin' to kill me?" James demanded.

"Wasn't tryin' to kill you."

"It sure felt like it."

"I was...mad," Simon said. "I lost my head."

"Why?"

"You were with Belinda."

"So?"

The man stuck out his jaw and said, "She's my woman."

"Is that right?" Thomas asked. "Does she know that?"

"Of course she does!" the man said. "We're in love."

Thomas and James exchanged a look.

"How long has this been goin' on?" Thomas asked.

"About six months."

So it wasn't possible that this man was the father of her baby.

"So you were followin' her tonight?"

"Yeah."

"And you saw her with my brother and got mad."

"Yeah."

"Why?" James asked. "We were only talkin'. We had supper and we talked."

"She kissed you!" the man accused.

"That was just...that was nothin'," James said angrily. "Sure wasn't enough for you to try to strangle me to death!"

"Settle down," Thomas said.

" 'Settle down'?" James repeated. "He damn near killed me. He woulda killed me if you hadn't...what were you doin' there?"

"I happened to see you two leavin' the café and him followin' behind you, so I followed too."

"So you were there the whole time, outside the house?"

"Yes."

"And it took you that long to get him to let me go?"

"He never woulda sneaked up on you if you didn't have your head in the clouds, James," Thomas said. He hadn't planned on berating his brother in front of Simon, but James opened the door. "And another thing. You let that gal hang on to your gun arm the whole time. You're double lucky you ain't dead right now!"

James glared at his brother, then switched his glare to the man that deserved it and kept quiet...because Thomas was right, damn him.

54

Thomas and James decided not to bicker in front of Alvin Simon. They told him not to move and went to the other end of the room, where they could still cover him.

"Okay, so he claims to be in love with Belinda," Thomas said. "I can believe that."

"So can I."

"Obviously."

"Whataya mea—"

"But," Thomas said, cutting James off, "is Belinda in love with him?"

"She could be."

"I don't think so," Thomas said. "I think he's just another fella she's tryin' to use. He's got his own business, so maybe he's got some money."

"Why do you have to think the worst of her?" James asked.

"Because," Thomas said, "she's tryin' to convince us that her son is Matthew's. Why do you think she's doin' that?"

"To get some help—"

"To use us, James," Thomas said, "just to use us."

"Thomas—" James started, but Thomas could see the argument coming and wanted to head it off.

"James, we could argue about this all night," he said. "What do you want to do about this fella?"

James looked over at Alvin Simon, who was staring at the floor glumly.

"Leave him alone," James said.

"He tried to choke you to death."

"We've got enough to worry about without adding him," James said. "Let's get back to what we're supposed to be doin'."

They both turned and walked back to the center of the room, Thomas holstering his gun.

"Mr. Simon, we're gonna leave now," Thomas said. "We're both deputies, as you can probably see, so if you should attack my brother again, we'll have to throw you in jail. Do you understand?"

"I understand very little, I fear," Simon said. He looked up at the two of them. "Why won't she look to me for protection? Why does she have to look elsewhere? The sheriff? Now you and your father?"

Thomas looked around the shop. Plenty of hardware, but there were no guns in sight.

"Mr. Simon, can you handle a gun?"

"Not very well."

"Well, that's your answer," Thomas said. "Against the likes of Jeb Collier you wouldn't stand a chance."

"That's what she said."

"Well, then," Thomas said, "for once I have to agree with her. Come on, James."

They started for the door, but Thomas stopped and turned to look back at Simon, who was still sitting slumped in the chair.

"Is this a thriving business, Mr. Simon?" he asked.

The man looked at him and said, "Why, yes. I do very well here."

"You've got money put away?"

"Quite a tidy sum, I think," Simon said. "I've told Belinda that I can care for her and Little Matt—at least, financially."

"Is that a fact?' Thomas asked, looking at James.

"Oh, come on," James said, opening the front door and barreling through.

Jeb Collier and his men were camped an hour outside of Pearl River Junction. He got them all situated around the fire with their beans and coffee and explained what was going to happen the next day.

"Clark, you and Dave will ride in first. Get yourselves a hotel room and then just hang around town. Don't go near the bank. Do you understand?"

"Got it, Jeb," Clark Wilson said and Dave Roberts nodded.

"Samms, you and Leslie will ride in next. Don't check into a hotel. Find a rooming house and get rooms. Then get somethin' to eat, walk around town, but stay away from the bank. Also, the four of you...stay out of the saloons. We'll all meet in a saloon later on in the evening."

"Which one?" Roy Leslie asked.

"I'll tell you in a minute." He looked across the fire at his brother. "Ben, you and Tanner will ride in next. Get rooms in a small hotel somewhere, have somethin' to eat and stay out of trouble."

"Sure, Jeb."

Jeb looked pointedly at Lou Tanner, a look that said: *Keep him out of trouble.* Tanner nodded that he understood.

"Vic and I will ride in last," Jeb said. "We're all gonna meet at dusk in the biggest saloon in town. That's so we won't stand out. But look... when you get to that saloon don't talk to each other until Vic and I get there. Don't sit or stand at the bar in a group. Two of you sit, two stand, or play some poker, whatever, but stay away from each other, stay out of trouble. Everybody understand?"

They all nodded except for Ben.

"So I ride in with Tanner, but I'm not supposed to talk to him?" he asked, looking confused.

Jeb took a breath, then said, "You can talk to the man you ride in with, but not to the others. Okay?"

"Okay," Ben said.

"Okay, then finish eating and get some shut-eye," Jeb instructed. "We're gettin' up at first light so the first two can ride in early."

Delay leaned over and asked Jeb, "We settin' watches tonight?"

"We don't need to be on watch," Jeb said. "Nobody's after us in Texas. Get some sleep."

"I don't sleep much anyway," Delay said. "I can keep an eye out."

"If that's what you wanna do, be my guest," Jeb said. "I'm goin' to sleep. Been a long time since I slept under the stars and I been enjoyin' it since I got out."

"Time enough to sleep when I die," Delay said and poured himself some more coffee.

55

Shaye had arranged to have breakfast not only with his sons the next morning, but with the sheriff and Thad as well.

Thomas and James had agreed not to tell their father about James's supper with Belinda the night before. For this reason James was hoping Connie the waitress would not say anything about it while she was serving them. Connie gave James a knowing smile, but did not say a word about him and Belinda being there the night before.

However, they did feel a need to tell him about Alvin Simon. At least, Thomas did. He went to his father's room that morning before breakfast...

"So this fella is in love with Belinda?"

"Right."

"And he says she's in love with him?"

"Yes."

"And the sheriff and his wife don't know anything about it?"

"No, they don't."

His father fixed him with a hard stare and asked, "And tell me again how you know about it?"

"I was makin' rounds and saw this fella outside of the sheriff's house," Thomas said, lying with as straight a face as he could. "I braced him and he told me the whole story."

"And he's got money?"

"Apparently."

"So it makes sense that Belinda would not want Jeb Collier to kill her golden goose."

"Right."

"So," Shaye said thoughtfully, "she sent for us to protect him from Jeb Collier, not her and the boy."

Thomas stared at his father. "I never thought of it that way."

Shaye stroked his jaw and said, "This probably means that the baby is not Matthew's—but the question remains: Why and how did Belinda pick us...how did she pick Matthew to claim as the father?"

"Maybe we should just ask her," Thomas said.

"That might not be a bad idea."

But the matter was not discussed at breakfast; they would bring it up with Sheriff Cotton later. After all, whatever the answer was, they were now committed to standing with the sheriff against Jeb Collier, Vic Delay, and their gang.

"You three," Shaye said to Thomas, James, and Thad, "go back on roof duty today."

"Yes, sir," Thad said as Thomas and James nodded. "We lookin' for eight men?"

"No, Thad," Cotton said, "Dan and I figure they'll come into town in groups of twos or threes, so be on the lookout for any strangers riding in."

"Yes, sir."

"And don't brace them," Shaye said. "Under no

circumstances are you to approach these men. Do you understand that?"

"Yes, sir, I do."

"Good."

"What do we do when we're not on the roof, Pa?" Thomas asked.

"Patrol the streets," Shaye said. "Keep an eye on the man on the roof because we don't want to use shots as signals. So you boys take something up there with you, something white like a towel, so you can wave it."

"I'll get one from my room," Thomas said.

"Now I have a question," Cotton said.

"What is it?"

"What do we do when Jeb Collier himself comes riding in?"

"I think we ought to make his acquaintance," Shaye said, "and take him to see Belinda and the boy."

"Pa," James said, "I thought we was supposed to be protecting her from him."

"James, I get the feeling Belinda can protect herself just fine from just about any man," Shaye said. "Our concern is the town and the bank."

"Why the bank?" Thomas asked. "They don't want our protection. They're happy with their own guards, ain't they?"

"Well," Shaye said, "the sheriff here has money in that bank and he refuses to take it out."

They all looked at the man.

"It wouldn't be fair," he explained. "What if they rob the bank and get everybody's money and the town finds out I took mine out?"

"You tell them you went to the bank and the town council and warned them," Thomas said.

"I can't do that to these people," Cotton said. "They're my neighbors."

"Well, then, get some of your neighbors to strap on a gun and help out," Thomas suggested.

"Thomas," Cotton said, "I just might approach some of them, but they're storekeepers, not lawmen and not gunmen."

"Okay," Shaye said, "are we clear on what we're going to do?"

"What are you gonna do, Pa?" James asked.

"I'll be on the street, James," Shaye said, "where you can all see me."

"And I'll be in front of my office," Cotton said.

Connie brought their breakfasts and they all started to eat, but Thad seemed to be real deep in thought and suddenly said, "I got fifty dollars in the bank...should I take it out?"

56

Jeb Collier had his brother Ben prepare breakfast for six of the eight men in camp.

"Not for you two," he told Wilson and Roberts.

"Why not?" Dave Roberts asked. "I'm hungry."

"You can get yourselves some breakfast after you get to town," Jeb said. "Have your horses taken care of, get a room, and then go find a place to have breakfast—and do it in that order."

"Why that order?" Roberts asked.

"Because I want you to follow my orders the way I give them to you," Jeb said. "Is that easy to understand?"

"I guess," Roberts said.

"Well, get mounted and study on it while you ride to town," Jeb said.

"Let's go," Clark said to Roberts.

While the others ate, Clark Wilson and Dave Roberts saddled their horses, mounted up and left camp.

"Clark's your *segundo*?" Delay asked.

"He was my second for a long time before I went inside," Jeb said, "but since I've been out I've been thinkin' about changin' that. I need somebody more like Tanner."

"Tanner and me have ridden together a long time," Delay said. "I never had somebody watch my back as good as him."

"I'm gonna have to give it some thought when we're done with all this," Jeb said. "That's for sure."

"I been noticin' somethin'," Dave Roberts said to Clark as they rode toward town.

"What's that?"

"Jeb's been leanin' a lot on Delay and Tanner," Roberts said. "You're supposed to be his right hand."

Clark frowned.

"Yeah," he said, "I noticed that too."

"So what are you gonna do about it?"

"I'm gonna think about it," Clark said. "Maybe I'll take my cut from this bank job and go my own way."

"You could get your own gang together."

"Yeah, I could."

"And if you do, you'll need a second."

Clark looked at Roberts.

"You volunteerin'?"

"You got any other takers?"

"I ain't even sure what I'm gonna do, Dave," Clark said, "but I'll keep this conversation in mind."

"That's all I ask."

They rode the rest of the way in silence, each alone with his own thoughts.

An hour later Jeb sent Samms and Leslie on their way to Pearl River Junction. James, on roof duty at City Hall, saw Wilson and Roberts ride down the town's main street. He'd spotted them farther out and had waved his white towel at Thomas, who was right across the street. Dan Shaye and Sheriff Cotton had also seen the signal from their vantage points, so as the first two robbers entered town, they were being well watched.

Shaye joined Cotton in front of his office as the two men rode by.

"Know them?" Cotton asked him.

"No, you?"

Cotton shook his head. "Never seen them before and neither one matches Belinda's description of Jeb Collier."

Shaye kept his eyes on the two men, who—if they were part of Jeb Collier's gang—were well trained and kept their eyes forward.

"I could brace them, as strangers in town," Cotton said. "Ask a few questions."

"I suggest you wait and see who else rides in today," Shaye said. "Could be they'll ride in at one- or two-hour intervals. Of course, it could also be they'll ride in on different days."

"And," Cotton said, "could also be these two men aren't even connected to Collier."

"If we have seven or eight strangers ride into town today," Shaye said, "I'm going to have a hard time believing that's a coincidence."

"Lawmen," Roberts said to Clark.

"I see 'em," Clark said. "Keep your eyes straight ahead. We ain't doin' nothin' but ridin' into town. Let's just find the livery stable and get the horses taken care of."

"How about a drink first?" Roberts asked. "There's a saloon right there."

"Let's do this the way we were told, Dave," Clark

said. "Besides, that saloon is right across the street from the sheriff's office. Let's just hope it ain't the biggest one in town."

"I just thought a cold beer would go down good right now."

"It might," Clark said, "but is this the way you'd carry out my orders if you were my *segundo*?"

Roberts had no answer for that.

"Besides which," Clark added, "it's too damn early and the saloons are still closed."

From his vantage point James was looking down at the two men and could not see their faces. He could, however, see his father and the sheriff. When he looked that way, Dan Shaye shook his head, indicating that neither of these men was Jeb Collier.

While Clark and Roberts took care of their horses and secured hotel rooms, the sheriff and his deputies remained where they were. The only one who had not seen the men ride in was Thad, as he was making rounds at the south end of town. Unfortunately, that meant that he saw Wilson and Roberts ride into the livery and recognized them as strangers. Contrary to the orders he had received not to brace strangers, he decided to go into the livery and talk to them. He felt this was a way he could prove his worth as a deputy.

Wilson and Roberts had turned their horses over to the livery owner and were turning to leave when Thad Hagen entered the stable.

"Mornin', gents."

Both men stopped short at the sign of the badge, but then noticed the youth of its wearer.

They were not impressed.

"Your momma buy you that badge, boy?" Wilson asked.

"I'm a duly appointed deputy."

"You?"

"I got some questions for you fellas."

Wilson made a rude noise with his mouth and he and Roberts started past Thad.

"Step aside, Deputy."

"Now hold on—" Thad said, grabbing Wilson's arm. The man turned quickly into Thad and hit him solidly on the jaw. The deputy staggered back, but didn't go down.

"Dave," Wilson said, "the deputy wants some trouble."

"Might as well give it to him," Roberts said and the two outlaws waded in, swinging their fists.

When Bill Samms and Roy Leslie rode in, they were also watched by all four men—Dan Shaye, Thomas, James, and Sheriff Cotton.

"Where's Thad?" Shaye asked Cotton as the two strangers rode by.

"I don't know," Cotton said. "Making rounds, I guess."

"The boy would like to prove himself, wouldn't he?" Shaye asked.

"I think so," Cotton said, "even more because you and your boys are here, though. Not just to me."

One of the riders turned his head and looked right at Shaye, then turned away.

"Neither of these men are Collier either," Shaye said. "I think I'm going to go and look for Thad."

"Why?" Cotton asked. "What are you worried about?"

"I'm just worried," Shaye said. "A young man like that, eager to prove himself, will not necessarily follow orders."

"All right," Cotton said. "I'll wait here. If you go to the south end of town, you might end up at the livery at the same time as these two riders who just came in."

"I'll do my best to stay out of trouble," Shaye said.

It was the liveryman who found Thad first. He was bending over him when the other two strangers reached the stable.

"Hey there!" Samms shouted.

Charlie Styles, who owned the livery, looked up at the two men.

"Be with ya in a minute, gents," he said. "Got me a unconscious deputy here."

"That a fact?" Leslie asked. "How'd that happen?"

"Don't rightly know," Styles said. "You leavin' your horses for the day?"

"Likely," Samms said.

"This fella's got him a few lumps, but he's still breathin'," Styles said. "Guess he won't mind if I take care of business first."

Styles left Thad in the stall where he was lying and went to take care of the two horses.

When Shaye reached the livery, the two strangers were just leaving.

"Deputy," one of them said by way of greeting.

Shaye touched his hat and nodded.

"Looks like one of your partners found some trouble," the other man said.

"What are you talking about?"

"You'll see," the man said and he and his partner kept walking, laughing together.

Shaye entered the livery and saw Charlie Styles leaning into one of the stalls.

"What's going on?" her asked.

Styles looked up and said, "Busy day in here. Got one of your young fellers in here."

Shaye walked over to the stall and saw Thad lying on the ground. His face was bruised and there was some blood coming from his nose. He'd obviously been beaten.

"Is he alive?"

"He's breathin'," Styles said.

"Get me a bucket of water."

"Sure thing."

As Styles went for the water, Shaye leaned over Thad, touching him, trying to determine if there were any other injuries that were not immediately evident, like a broken bone.

"Thad? Come on, boy." He slapped the young deputy's face. "Wake up, lad."

"Here's your water," Styles said, appearing with a bucket.

"Dump it on him," Shaye said. "Might be the only way to wake him up."

"Should I get the doctor, then?"

"Dump it on him and then we'll see."

"Here ya go, lad," Styles said and dumped the water on Thad, cackling all the while.

"Okay, old-timer," Shaye said to Styles as Thad came sputtering to life, "that'll do it."

Style went away, taking his empty bucket with him, still laughing.

"Jesus—" Thad said. "What the—"

"Easy, boy," Shaye said as Thad tried to jump to his feet. "Stay down a minute longer and tell me what happened."

Thad wiped his face and shook it to get water out of his eyes.

"Gimme a minute."

Shaye allowed him his minute and during that time noticed that Thad's gun was still in its holster.

"Two men," Thad said finally. "I saw them ride in, so I thought I'd check them out."

"You were told not to brace anyone."

"I just thought—"

"Tell me what happened."

"I wanted to question them," Thad said, "but they wouldn't answer any questions. They...laughed at me. Didn't think I was really a deputy. They...beat me up, left me in here, I guess."

"Can you get up?"

"I...I think so."

Shaye extended his hand and pulled Thad to his feet. The boy staggered a moment, then caught his balance.

"Find your hat," Shaye said.

He waited while Thad hunted up his hat, reshaped it, and placed it on his head.

"How do you feel?" Shaye asked.

"Okay."

"No permanent injury?"

Thad flexed his arms and hands, felt his face.

"No," Thad said, "just some lumps."

"Good. Now we can get back to work."

"Are we gonna arrest them?"

"The men who beat you up? No."

"What? Why not?"

"Why should we?"

"They beat me up! I'm a deputy."

"Not for long if you disobey an order again. You were told not to engage any of these men."

"I just thought—"

"It's the sheriff's job to think, Thad," Shaye said. "It's your job to follow his orders."

"So we're just gonna let them get away with it?"

"If we put them in a cell, they'd be out in no time," Shaye said. "That's not how we want them. When they make their move, we have to be ready. And you," Shaye said, pointing for emphasis, "have to do what you're told from now on. Understood?"

Thad looked down, shuffled his feet, and said, "Yeah, I understand, Mr. Shaye."

"Good," Shaye said, "we're going back to the office now."

As they started walking back, Thad asked, "Do you have to tell the sheriff about this?"

"What would you tell him about the bruises on your face? That you fell down? Would you rather he thinks you're clumsy?"

"No, I guess not."

A few moments later Thad said, "Mr. Shaye, do you think the sheriff will fire me?"

"For making a mistake?" Shaye asked. "And paying for it with a few lumps? Thad, if you admit to it and learn from it, I don't think you'll loose your job over it—unless I read Sheriff Cotton completely wrong."

"He's a decent man," Thad said. "I thought I could learn a lot from him, but now I think I could learn a lot more from you."

"I may be more experienced than Riley Cotton," Shaye said, "but there are a lot of things about being a man he can teach you that I can't."

"A man?" Thad asked. "Or a lawman?"

"Take your pick, Thad," Shaye said. "There are a lot of the same qualities in both."

58

Thad was inside the sheriff's office when Lou Tanner and Ben Collier rode in.

"What about them?" Cotton asked.

Shaye stared at the two men, who stared straight ahead as they rode by.

"That looks like Lou Tanner," Shaye said. "He rides with Vic Delay."

"And the other?"

"Don't know him."

By this time James and Thomas had changed places and Thomas was on the roof.

"Where are the other four?" Shaye asked.

"I took a walk while you were waking Thad up," Cotton said. "Two of them got rooms at the hotel over there."

"And the other two?"

"Don't know," Cotton said. "Not at the same hotel anyway. Now two of them are at Bo Hart's Saloon—his first customers of the day—and the other two are eating at the café."

Shaye started to laugh.

"What's funny?"

"They're riding in separate and staying in separate

places," Shaye said. "Sounds like a good plan—except for one thing."

"What's that?"

"They're all using the same livery," Shaye said. "Anybody could get a count from the liveryman."

"Charlie Styles."

They watched the two men ride to the far end of the street and disappear.

"Well, we know one thing, at least," Shaye said.

"What's that?"

"Where Lou Tanner is," he answered, "Vic Delay won't be far behind."

"So the next two will be Jeb Collier and Vic Delay."

"Unless they ride in separate."

Jeb emptied the remnants of the coffeepot onto the fire and then kicked the rest of it dead.

"We ridin' in together?" Delay asked.

"I been studying on that," Jeb said, tossing the coffeepot away instead of packing it. "I think we should go in separate."

"Why?'

"Because you and me are the only ones somebody might recognize," Jeb said. "We'll attract even more attention ridin' in together."

"Who goes first?"

"You."

"Why?"

"Okay, then," Jeb said. "Me. I thought you might want to get to a hot meal and a drink, but it's okay with me if you don't."

"Forget it, forget it," Delay said. "I'll ride in." He mounted up and looked down at Jeb. "How far behind me will you be?"

"Not far. I'll finish breakin' camp."

Delay nodded and rode off in the direction of town.

Jeb looked around, decided a lot of what was in camp could stay. After they hit the bank, they'd have plenty of money to buy new stuff. As far as sending Delay in ahead of him, he figured once the killer was recognized, it might take the attention away from him. Just one extra reason for having a man like Vic Delay ride along with him.

Jeb figured once he finished his business in Pearl River Junction—the girl and the bank—the only man he'd need would be his brother Ben. Not that he really needed him, but he was his brother. He couldn't very well sacrifice him the way he would the other men.

The only one he'd have to kill, though, was Delay. Once he realized that Jeb had no intention of sharing the bank money with him, he'd come looking for him for sure. Jeb didn't want to be looking over his shoulder while he was spending the proceeds of the Pearl River Junction bank job.

59

When Vic Delay rode into town, it was almost three. The outlaws had spread their arrivals out pretty good. Shaye was still in front of the sheriff's office with Cotton. They weren't going anywhere until all the men had ridden in.

Thad Hagen was on the roof and James and Thomas were at different ends of the main street, on different sides.

"That's Delay," Shaye said to Cotton.

"I could've guessed."

Delay was completely clad in black and was wearing his leather gloves. As he rode past the sheriff's office, he turned his head and looked at each man in turn.

"Think he recognized you?" Cotton asked.

"No reason why he should," Shaye said. "I've seen him before, but we haven't met."

Delay's face was expressionless and then he turned away, but instead of going to the livery he stopped abruptly in front of the café, as if he'd just noticed it or caught a whiff of the food.

"Stay here," Shaye said.

"Why?" Cotton asked. "What're you going to do?"

"I just thought I'd have a talk with Delay," Shaye said.

"Do you want me to come and watch your back?"

"No," Shaye said, "I don't want to spook him. I just want to have a talk. I'll be back."

Shaye stepped into the street and headed down to the café.

From the roof Thomas could not see that Delay had stopped at the café, but he did see his father crossing the street and he wondered what was going on. He waved at the sheriff, who looked up at him and shrugged helplessly.

Vic Delay entered the café and drew all eyes to him. The middle-aged waitress showed him to a table where he could sit with one shoulder against the wall. It was the next best thing to sitting with his back against one. Of course, Jeb Collier instructed everyone to board their horses and find a place to stay as soon as they entered town, but Delay didn't feel the instructions extended to him.

Nobody told Vic Delay what to do.

From his vantage point James thought that the lone man—who he assumed was Vic Delay, since he didn't match the description of Jeb Collier—was going to ride past him, but abruptly the man reined his horse in and entered the café. He wanted to go over and look in the window at the gunman, but suddenly his father appeared and actually went inside.

What was he doing?

* * *

Shaye stepped through the door of the café and became the center of attention. Most of the tables were taken, some by families. He hoped his appearance would not cause Vic Delay to do anything foolish. Briefly, he considered that he might be making a mistake, but once he entered the place he was committed. He walked over to Delay's table.

Delay's meal had not yet been delivered to him, but he did have a pot of coffee on the table and a couple of cups.

"Mind if I join you, Vic?"

Delay looked up at him calmly.

"Do I have a choice, Deputy?"

"Sure you do," Shaye said. "Everybody's got choices in life."

"Have a seat," Delay said. "Help yourself to some coffee."

"Thanks." Shaye sat across from the killer and poured himself a cup of coffee.

"What can I do for you, Deputy...what's your name?"

"Shaye. Dan Shaye."

"Shaye?" Delay frowned. "That name sounds familiar."

"I've worn a badge here and there—"

"No, further back than that," Delay said. "There used to be a fella named...what was it...Daniels, Shaye Daniels. Had him a rep around Missouri. He sort of...disappeared."

"That was a time in my life I'm not proud of," Shaye admitted. "That's what I mean about making decisions. I made some wrong ones back then and now I'm making right ones."

"Which name is the real one?"

"Daniel Shaye."

"Well, Daniel Shaye," Delay said, "changing sides may be the right decision for you, but I don't think it would work for me. Can't see myself drawing a deputy's pay, wearin' a badge...not for me."

"Well," Shaye said, "to each his own."

"I guess you want to know what I'm doin' in town."

"No, we already know," Shaye said.

"You do?"

"Your other men are already here," Shaye said. "Now we're just waiting for Jeb Collier to arrive. My guess is that after he takes care of his business with the woman and the child, you fellas are planning to hit the bank."

"What if all I'm doin' is passin' through?"

"That would be nice," Shaye said, "but we both know that's not the case."

"Wait a minute," Delay said. "You got some boys, don't you? I heard somethin' about you and the Langer gang."

"That was a couple of years ago," Shaye said.

"Grown sons as deputies, right?"

"Yes."

"They here with you too?"

"They are."

"Any other law? Got to be a sheriff, I reckon."

"There is and another deputy."

"Five of you?"

Shaye shrugged. "At least that."

"Well," Delay said, "I guess you feel that's enough."

"It'll do."

"Not that I care," Delay said, " 'cause I'm just passin' through, stopped here for a meal and a bed."

On cue Connie appeared with a plate of food for Delay.

"Somethin' for you, Deputy?" she asked.

"No thanks."

"Bring more coffee," Delay said. "The deputy is helpin' me drink it."

"Yes, sir."

"I won't be drinking much," Shaye said. "I just wanted to stop in and say hello, introduce myself."

"Well," Delay said, "if you see me around town, introduce me to your sons. They know about their father's past?"

"They know."

"Odd to find a man who changed his life and ended up with a reputation anyway."

"That's life," Shaye said, standing up. "We get to make our own decisions, and then we see how they play out. I'll see you around town, Vic."

"Glad to meet you, Shaye," Delay said. "Hope you have luck with that bank thing."

"Yeah," Shaye said, "so do I."

"What did that accomplish?" Cotton asked when Shaye returned.

"Not much, I guess," Shaye said. "Guess I just wanted to look him in the eye and let him know we knew who he was and why he was here."

"How did he react?"

"Calmly," Shaye replied. "Says he's just passing through."

"You gonna brace Collier that way?"

"I thought we both would," Shaye said. "I figured we'd take him to see Belinda, get that much out of the way. What do you think?"

"I think maybe I should check with her."

"Why?" Shaye asked. "She doesn't check with you about much that she does."

"That's true," Cotton said, "but I should talk to my wife, if I'm gonna bring someone like that to my home."

"Then let's not take him to your house," Shaye said. "Let's have them meet somewhere neutral."

"Like where?"

"Like whatever hotel Collier decides to stay in. They can meet right in the lobby."

"You think he'll go for that?"

"He will if we don't give him a choice," Shaye said. "You're the sheriff. This is your town. You call the shots."

The door of the office opened and Thad stepped in. His face looked swollen and had purplish bruises all over it. When he and Shaye returned from the livery, Shaye had not even had to speak to Cotton on the young deputy's behalf. The sheriff made up his own mind not to fire him.

"Maybe he'll learn from it," he'd said.

"We can hope so," Shaye replied.

"You feeling any better?" Cotton asked him.

"Yes, sir," Thad said. "Well enough to go back out on my rounds."

"You take a seat right in one of those chairs and stay where I can see you," Cotton said, pointing to three chairs out in front of the office. "You're lucky I'm not firing your ass after the stunt you pulled."

"Yes, sir."

Thad sat in one of the chairs, shoulders slumped.

"Okay," Cotton said then, "you're right. We won't give Collier any options. We'll go and get Belinda and bring her to him...and we won't give her any choice either."

"They've both put us in this position," Shaye said. "Why should they get a choice?"

Cotton nodded, his jaw firm.

While they continued to watch the street, the first two men who rode in walked over to the Wagon Wheel Saloon and entered. Shortly after that the second duo did the same, followed by the third. Finally, Vic Delay walked into that saloon as well.

"What's the Wagon Wheel got that the other saloons don't?" Shaye asked Cotton.

"Well... it's the biggest saloon in town."

"That's probably it," Shaye said. "They want to meet there and blend in."

"But... Collier's not here yet."

"He'll probably ride in any minute," Shaye predicted. "They're not all going to the Wagon Wheel for nothing."

"So what do we do?" Cotton asked. "Keep waiting out here?"

Shaye tried not to tell the sheriff what to do unless the man asked first.

"I think you and James and Thad can stay out here, while Thomas and I go inside."

"You gonna talk to them again?"

"We're just going to be seen," Shaye said. "That's all. Just to let them know they're being watched."

"Well, okay," Cotton said, "but if I hear a shot, I'm gonna come running in there."

"I can't ask for more than that," Shaye said. "I'll go and get Thomas."

"Be careful, Dan."

"I always am."

The Wagon Wheel had a back door. Shaye decided to send Thomas in that way, while he went in the front door. The saloon was in full swing, girls working the floor, gaming tables open and operating, and a piano player tickling the ivories in a corner.

It took Shaye a few moments to locate the outlaws. Two were standing at the bar, two were at a table drinking beer and grabbing for girls, and two were gambling: one playing poker and the other standing at the wheel of fortune. Vic Delay had managed to secure himself a table at the back of the room. He was sitting alone, nursing a beer. Shaye had no doubt they were waiting for Jeb Collier to arrive.

Farther back in the room he saw Thomas, standing with his back to a wall. Just a few feet to his left was Vic Delay's table. Shaye knew that Delay was aware of Thomas's presence.

Shaye was torn between staying in the saloon with Thomas or stepping outside and waiting in front of the place for Jeb Collier to arrive. In the end he decided to treat Thomas as if he was just another lawman and not his son. He would not have hesitated to leave another lawman in the room alone. That was the way Thomas would want to be treated.

Shaye turned and went back out through the batwing doors.

61

Delay watched Dan Shaye leave, then turned his head to look at the other deputy, the one who had come in through the back door. He attracted the attention of one of the girls, who came over in a swirl of skirts and red hair.

"You want some company?" she asked.

"Yeah," Delay said, "but not yours. Ask that deputy to come over and have a drink with me and then bring him what he wants."

"That handsome deputy?" she asked. "Maybe he'll want some company."

"Ask him after I finish talkin' to him."

"Yes, sir."

She turned and approached Thomas.

When Thomas saw his father step back out of the saloon, he knew what he had in mind: to wait in front for Collier to arrive. He was proud that his pa knew he could leave him in the saloon alone.

He saw the girl coming and was prepared to turn her advances away—temporarily, at least.

"Hey, handsome."

"Hey, yourself, pretty girl."

"Man over there wants to buy you a drink."

"Who? The man in black?"

"That's right," she said. "Unless you'd rather have one with me?"

"I'd much rather have one with you," Thomas said. "I like gals with red hair. But I'm afraid this is business."

"All right, then," she said. "Tell me what you're drinking and I'll bring it over."

"A beer will do," he said. "What's your name?"

"Shannon."

"Thanks for the message, Shannon."

"My pleasure, handsome."

Shannon went to the bar for Thomas's beer and Thomas walked over to Delay's table.

"Have a seat, Deputy," Delay said. "Is the gal bringin' you a drink?"

"She is."

"Then let's talk."

Thomas sat, but moved the chair so that he could see the rest of the room. He also sat with his hip cocked so he could get to his gun if he had to.

"You're a careful man," Delay said.

"I learned from the best."

"Your pa."

"That's right."

"He was a good man with a gun in his day."

"You know about that?"

"I do."

"Well, he still is good."

"How good are you?"

"Fair."

"And your brother?"

"Fair."

"Somehow I doubt that, in your case," Delay said. "I think you'd be...interestin'."

Shannon returned with Thomas's beer and set it down with a big smile.

"Later, handsome," she said.

"I'll look forward to it."

"You know," Delay said, "that's what you should do."

"What's that?"

"Get yourself a nice room," Delay said, "lay up with that red-haired gal for a while."

Thomas sipped his beer, holding it in his left hand, and asked, "And how long would you suggest I 'lay up?' "

"Couple of days ought to do it."

"And I suppose you'll pay the freight?"

Delay laughed. "The way that gal was lookin' at you, I don't think anybody will have to."

"Well," Thomas said, "is that why you bought me a drink? To tell me that?"

"Just some friendly advice, Deputy."

"It's my guess Jeb Collier will be arrivin' any minute," Thomas said. "I got to be at my post when he does, so"—Thomas drank half the beer down and stood up—"thanks for the drink."

"Think about what I said, Deputy," Delay said.

"You tryin' to save my life for a reason?"

"Maybe I'm just tryin' to save you for myself."

"Like you said before, Mr. Delay," Thomas replied, "that might be interestin'."

Thomas went back and resumed his position.

Shaye looked in the window of the saloon and saw Thomas sit down with Delay. He watched for the few moments they spoke and then Thomas got up and went back to his post, leaning against the back wall.

He turned away from the window and looked up and down the street. It was quiet, as if the town knew that something was amiss. It was so quiet, in fact, that he could hear a horse coming down the street. The *clip clop* of the horse's hooves came closer and closer and Shaye knew that, after waiting all day long, they were finally about to get a look at Jeb Collier.

62

Jeb Collier spotted the lawman in front of the sheriff's office right off as soon as he straightened out and started down the main street. Then he saw the man on the roof. Last, he saw there was a lawman standing right in front of the Wagon Wheel Saloon. Without seeing the other saloons in town, he pegged the Wagon Wheel as being the biggest. That meant that the rest of his men—and Vic Delay—had already attracted the attention of the law.

He rode by all three lawmen without turning his head and eventually found the livery stable at the far end of town.

"Sure is a busy day for strangers," the liveryman said.

"That a fact?"

"Not that I'm complainin', mind ya," Charlie Styles said. "I can always use the business."

"Saw some lawmen linin' the streets," Jeb said. "They expectin' trouble?"

"Already had some."

"Bad?"

"Naw," Styles said, "young deputy took a beatin' at the hands of two strangers. Difference of opinion, I think. He thought he was a deputy and they thought he was too young to tote the badge. Guess they was right."

"That land them in jail?"

"Beats me, mister," Styles said. "I ain't left here all day."

Jeb grabbed his rifle and saddlebags and readied himself to leave.

"I need a small, quiet hotel," he said to Styles. "Can you recommend one?"

"Just up the street, right after the junction, but before you get to the middle of town. It's pretty quiet. Ya can't hear all the noise from the Wagon Wheel there."

"The Wagon Wheel," Jeb said. "That the biggest saloon in town?"

"Sure is, biggest and noisiest."

"Sounds like it'll do, then," Jeb said. "Thanks."

He started out the door, then stopped and said, "Oh yeah, you know a gal named Belinda Davis?"

"Sure, that's the gal lives with the sheriff and his wife."

"Oh yeah? Where would that be?"

When Jeb Collier didn't reappear at the Wagon Wheel, Shaye figured he was boarding his horse and checking into a hotel first. When dusk passed and he still didn't appear, he thought they'd been had and went across the street to talk to the sheriff...

Tanner eventually made his way across the floor to Vic Delay's table and sat down.

"Past dusk, Vic," he said. "Reckon Jeb got held up?"

"I'm thinkin' he never meant to meet us here at dusk," Delay said. "He just wanted us to occupy the local law."

"While he goes to see his gal?"

"That's what I figure."

"So whatta we do?"

"We wait here," Delay said. "He'll be along when he's done."

"We got us a lot of attention from the law," Tanner said. "How we gonna hit that bank?"

"That's Jeb's lookout," Delay said. "He's the big bank job planner."

"So we still dependin' on him?"

"Lou," Delay said, "all I can say is he better come through for us or I will be pissed that he hung us out here to give him time to see his girlfriend."

"I seen the deputy come over and talk to you."

"I invited him," Delay said. "I also talked with his pa."

"His pa?" Tanner frowned.

"You ever heard the name Shay Daniels..."

"My house?" Riley Cotton asked.

"That's what I figure," Shaye said. "When he didn't come back, I thought, That sonofabitch. He's got us watching all the other men while he sneaks over to see Belinda and the baby."

"And Marion!" Cotton said. "I gotta get over there!"

"Slow down, Sheriff," Shaye said. "He's not going to hurt Marion. Let's just take a walk over there and see what's going on."

"What about Thomas?" Cotton asked. "He's inside."

"He'll be fine. Just let me wave James down from the roof. He can go inside and back Thomas up."

Shaye turned, caught James's attention, and waved for him to come down. Then he pointed, hoping James would understand that he wanted him to go inside the saloon.

"What about Thad?"

They both turned and looked at the young deputy, still seated in a chair in front of the office.

"Let's leave him here," Shaye said.

Cotton walked over to Thad and said, "You don't move from here unless you hear a shot, understand?"

"Yes, sir."

Cotton turned to Shaye and said, "Let's get the hell over to my house."

"Take it easy, sheriff," Shaye said. "Remember, we don't want to spook him."

63

When they came within sight of the sheriff's house, they saw three figures in the backyard. One was Belinda, one was obviously the boy, Little Matt. The third was Jeb Collier.

"Where's Marion?" Cotton said. "If he's done anything—"

Shaye grabbed Cotton before he could rush the yard.

"Let's go in the front," Shaye said. "We'll probably find Marion inside, safe and sound."

"But what about—"

"He's not going anywhere for a while. Come on."

Shaye practically dragged Cotton around to the front of the house, where the sheriff opened the front door and they went inside.

"Marion?"

"In the kitchen," she replied right away.

They went into the kitchen and found her sitting at the table, hands clasped in front of her.

"They're out back," she said.

"Did he force her to talk to him?"

"Not at all," she said. "He knocked on the door, I answered, he asked to speak to Belinda. He was very... gentlemanly. Belinda went out back with him willingly and carried Little Matt with her."

Shaye went to the back window and looked out. Jeb Collier was down on one knee, talking to the boy. Belinda was watching them and the look on her face was anything but frightened. She seemed calm, content, even. Shaye was suddenly dead sure that the boy was not Matthew's, but Jeb Collier's.

Cotton came up next to him and looked out.

"What are they doing?" he asked.

"Just talking," Shaye said. "She doesn't look like she needs any protecting."

"They're going to take the baby away, aren't they?" Marion asked, her hands clasped so tight the knuckles were white.

"We don't know that, Marion," Cotton said, turning to face her.

"I'm going to go out and talk to them," Shaye said. "Why don't the two of you wait here?"

"All right," Cotton said. "Since he might be your grandson... all right."

Shaye didn't bother pointing out that he had just decided the boy was not his grandson. Instead, he simply opened the door and stepped outside...

"Another deputy just came in," Tanner said.

"I see him," Delay said. "Looks like another brother."

Tanner looked over at the other men. They had also noticed the two tin stars in the room.

"The men are gonna get antsy."

"Go around and calm them down," Delay said. "Tell them nothin's gonna happen today. Tell them we're still gonna wait right here for Jeb to get here."

"Got it."

Tanner got up and started moving around the room.

When James entered he took a few steps sideways to get out of the doorway and remained there, his hands clasped in front of him. He saw Thomas standing calmly at the back of the room and they exchanged a nod. One by one he located the strangers who had ridden into town, starting with the man dressed in black, who was seated not far from where Thomas was standing.

He settled in, decided he'd take his cue from his brother.

When Shaye stepped out the back door, both adults in the yard looked over at him.

"Mr. Shaye," Belinda said, "this is Jeb Collier."

"I figured," Shaye said, approaching them.

"Yeah," Jeb said, "I saw you in front of the saloon."

"The rest of your men are inside the saloon," Shaye told him. "I guess that's where they're supposed to meet you, huh?"

"I got men?" Jeb asked. "That's news to me."

"I've already had a talk with Vic Delay."

Jeb didn't react.

"Don't know him," he said.

"We'll see." Shaye leaned down and said, "How are you doing, Matt?"

The little boy looked up at him with wide eyes, then looked at his feet.

"That's not his name," Jeb said.

"It's not?" Shaye asked, straightening.

"Well, it has been till now," Jeb said, "but it's gonna change."

Shaye looked at Belinda, who just shrugged.

"What gives you the right to change his name?"

"Didn't she tell you?" Jeb asked. "He's my boy."

"No," Shaye said, "she's been telling me that he's my grandson."

"Naw," Jeb said, "just look at him. Can't you tell? He's my son." He looked at Belinda.

"Ain't that right, sweetie?"

Again, all the young mother did was shrug.

"Well, if you're so sure he's yours," Shaye asked, "what are you going to do about it?"

"I'm gonna take my woman and my boy and leave town," Jeb said. "We're gonna go somewhere and live together."

"And would that be before or after you and your men hit the bank?" Shaye asked.

"The bank?" Jeb asked, looking puzzled. "Mr. Shaye—Deputy—if you know anythin' about me, you know I just got out of Yuma Prison. I ain't lookin' ta go back."

"Is that so?"

"Yeah, that's so."

"I'm glad to hear it, Collier," Shaye said. "That will put a lot of minds at ease."

"I only came here to see my woman and my boy," Jeb said. "You know what it's like to know you got a son and you ain't ever seen him?"

"No," Shaye said, "I don't. I raised my three sons."

"Then you're a lucky man, Mr. Shaye," Jeb said. He looked at Belinda. "Sweetie, I got to go and get myself settled in, but I'll come back to see the both of you."

"Tonight?" Belinda asked.

"The boy will be going to sleep soon," Shaye pointed out.

"Well," Jeb said, "I wouldn't wanna be a bad father and wake him up, would I?" He directed his attention back to Belinda. "How about I come and take you to breakfast in the mornin'? Huh? How would that be?"

"Fine," Belinda said, "that'd be fine, Jeb."

"Good," Jeb said, "good. Deputy, it was real nice to make your acquaintance."

"Same here," Shaye said.

Jeb left the yard and walked back toward town. Shaye looked at Belinda, who gave one last shrug before picking up the boy and going back inside.

64

The sheriff and his wife came out the back door and approached Shaye.

"She just walked past us without a word," Marion said, "took Little Matt upstairs. What happened?"

"Collier says the boy is his," Shaye said. "He says he's going to take them away with him."

"I knew it," Marion said, pressing her face against her husband's chest.

"What did Belinda say?" Cotton asked.

"Nothing," Shaye said. "She just shrugged."

"She's afraid of him."

"I don't think so, Riley," Shaye answered. "I didn't see any sign of fear in her."

"So... when did he say they're going to leave?"

"He didn't. He said he'll be back to take her out for breakfast in the morning."

"You think he's headed for the saloon now?" Cotton asked.

"That'd be my bet."

"Honey," Cotton said, "go back inside. We'll try to work this out, don't worry."

"We're going to lose the baby, Riley."

"Not if I can help it," he said. "Come on, come inside."

Cotton looked at Shaye, who motioned that he would wait out front while the sheriff took her inside.

When Jeb Collier entered the Wagon Wheel Saloon, he spotted James immediately.

"Hello, Deputy," he said, turning his head.

James just nodded.

"Nice town."

James nodded again.

Jeb walked to the bar, ordered a beer, and—when he had it in hand—turned his back to the bar and studied the room. He located each of his men and saw Thomas standing against the back wall. He'd picked Delay out as soon as he entered and now walked back to his table, where he was seated alone. It didn't matter to him that he had told the deputy that he didn't know him.

"You're late."

"I know."

"Went to see the woman first, didn't you?"

"That's right."

"The boy yours?"

"Yeah."

"So what are you gonna do?"

"When we leave, I'm takin' them with me."

"And when are we leavin'?"

"After we take the bank."

"You saw the deputies, right?"

"I see 'em."

"You hung us out here so you could see the woman without any interference."

"It didn't work," Jeb said unapologetically. "I met a deputy named Shaye at the sheriff's house."

"They're all named Shaye, near as I can figure," Delay said. "At least, these two are."

"Father and sons?"

"That's right."

Jeb frowned.

"Dan Shaye?"

"That ain't the half of it," Delay said and told Jeb about Shay Daniels. He also told Jeb about his conversation with Thomas Shaye.

"You been busy."

"I've had my mind on business, Jeb."

"Don't worry, Vic," Jeb said. "My mind is on business."

"With all this attention we're gettin', you still want to hit the bank?"

Jeb smiled and said, "More than ever. I got a family to support now."

65

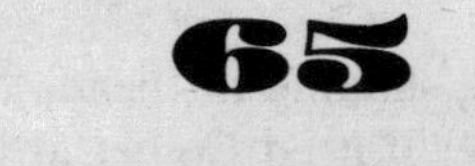

When Sheriff Cotton and Dan Shaye returned to the office, Thad was still seated out front, eager to do what he was told and make up for his mistake.

"I didn't hear no shots, Sheriff," he said.

"Good, Thad," Cotton said. "Just stay out until you do."

"Sure, Sheriff," Thad said, "but what do I do then?"

"You'll figure it out, son." He turned to Shaye. "Shall we go into the saloon, Dan?"

"I guess that's a likely next move," Shaye said.

"What other one could there be?"

"To wait for them to make a move for the bank."

"And leave them to the bank guards?"

"No, I don't think so," Shaye said. "I don't know the training of the bank guards, but I do know the reputations of Jeb Collier and Vic Delay. They've done what they do many times before."

"You don't think the guards would be able to handle them?" Riley Cotton asked.

"I doubt it."

"So if we just keep watching them," Cotton reasoned, "they won't be able to make a move."

"There are eight of them and five of us," Shaye said. "If they split up, three of them can hit the bank."

"But if we watch Collier and Delay, they'd have to do it without them."

"No," Shaye said, shaking his head, "they won't be able to do that. They'll need Collier at least. He's the brains. And they'll need Delay, because he's the killer. So they'll need both of them."

"So we're back where we started," Cotton said. "Why don't I just order them out of town? That'll force them into a move."

"Yeah, it would."

"So?"

Shaye turned and looked at Thad, at his bruised face.

"Maybe we got another way to force their hand," he said, "and change the odds at the same time."

"How?"

Shaye told him.

Cotton nodded and said, "Okay. Let's go do it."

"We'll take Thad too," Shaye said.

"Why?"

"He can identify them," Shaye said, "and he owes them."

Cotton turned to Thad.

"You wanna go in, boy?"

"Yes, sir!" Thad said eagerly.

"You gonna do what you're told?"

"Every step of the way, sir."

The sheriff looked at Shaye and said. "Let's go, then."

Cotton entered the saloon first, followed by Shaye and then Thad. James and Thomas both stood up straight at the sight of them, knowing something was about to happen.

From the back of the room Delay and Jeb saw the three extra lawman enter and also knew something was in the air.

"Jeb," Delay said, lacing his hand on his gun.

"Wait," Jeb said.

"We got a lot of cover in here," Delay told him. "Lots of people. The lawmen'll try not to hit innocent bystanders. We don't have that problem."

"Just wait, Vic," Jeb said. "Let's see what they're after before we go off half-cocked."

Delay sat back, moved his hand away from his gun.

"Pick 'em out, boy," Cotton said to Thad.

The place grew quiet as the lawmen moved among the patrons. At the bar Tanner looked over at Jeb, who shook his head. Ben Collier was standing next to him and also saw his brother shake his head.

Samms and Leslie were playing poker at the same table and didn't notice anything until the place grew quiet. Samms looked around, noticed all the lawmen in the room, and got nervous.

"Stay calm, boys," Jeb said under his breath.

It was Wilson and Roberts, though, who were the object of Thad Hagen's attention. They were seated at a table with drinks in their hands and girls in their laps when the place grew quiet. Now they watched as the lawmen approached them, the young deputy in the lead.

"These are them," Thad said.

"What is he talkin' about?" Wilson asked the two older lawmen.

"You ladies move along," Cotton said.

The two women got up and hurried to the bar, where they huddled together.

Roberts looked over his shoulder to where Jeb and Delay were sitting, but neither man moved or signaled.

"You men are under arrest," Cotton said.

"Arrest?" Wilson asked. "For what? We just got to your town today."

"And you couldn't even get out of the livery stable without getting into trouble," Shaye said.

"What are you talkin' about?" Roberts asked.

"You assaulted my deputy," Cotton said. "You're both comin' with me—with us." He turned to Thad. "Get 'em on their feet, Deputy."

"You heard the sheriff," Thad said. "Up."

Wilson and Roberts stared at the young deputy, then at Shaye and Cotton. Beyond them they could see James. When Roberts turned his head to look to Jeb for guidance, he saw Thomas standing behind them.

Thad produced his gun and said, "Up!"

Wilson and Roberts slid their chairs back and got to their feet.

"You young pup," Wilson said. "You didn't get enough—"

"Deputy Shaye," Thad said.

"Yep?" Shaye answered.

"Take their guns."

"Yes, sir," Shaye said, but it was Thomas who moved in behind Wilson and Roberts and plucked their guns from their holsters before they could make a move. He then tossed one to his father and the other across the room to James, who surprised himself and everyone in the room by catching it one-handed before it could sail through the window.

"Deputy Hagen," Cotton said, "take them over to the jail and lock their asses up."

"Yes, sir," Thad said. "You boys heard the sheriff. Get movin'."

Wilson and Roberts were still waiting for Jeb or Delay—or both—to make a move when Thomas put his hand against each of their backs and pushed.

"You heard the man!"

Both men staggered forward and then kept walking. Thad fell in behind them. When they went past James, he fell in behind Thad.

"We gonna let them do that?" Delay asked.

"You see that deputy's face?" Jeb asked.

"Yeah. So?"

"I told everybody to stay out of trouble," he said, "but those idiots couldn't do it. Let them sit in a cell for a while."

"But we're gonna need them for the bank."

Jeb turned his head to look at Delay and said, "No, we ain't."

* * *

"Those fellas have any friends in here that object to them being arrested?" Cotton asked.

He, Thomas, and Shaye looked around. Shaye's eyes fell on Jeb Collier and Vic Delay, but neither man made a move.

"Then I guess you folks better go back to having yourselves a good time," the sheriff said.

"Pa?" Thomas asked.

"You leave with us, Thomas."

"Yes, sir."

Cotton went out the door and both Shaye and Thomas backed out, watching his back. Slowly, activity started up again in the room and then the piano started and things were in full swing again.

Thad came down from the second floor, hung the cell keys on a wall peg, and told Cotton, "They're tucked away nice and safe."

"In the morning you'll bring them breakfast from the café."

"Yes, sir."

"And you'll stay here and guard them."

Thad hesitated a moment, then said, "Alone?"

"No," James said, "you won't have to stay alone. I'll stay with you tonight. We can take turns sleeping."

"That sounds good."

"All right," Cotton said. He looked at Shaye. "You think they'll come for these two?"

"They didn't look all that upset when we took them," Shaye said. "Collier will probably come and talk first."

"You think they'll try for the bank with six men?"

"Maybe," Shaye said. "We'll have to see."

"I can stay tonight too," Thomas said. "Just in case. James, will you make some coffee?"

"I will, just to keep you from making it," James said.

"Riley," Shaye said, "why don't we go and talk to Belinda? Maybe it's time she told the truth...all of it."

"Okay," Cotton said. "Then let's do it."

* * *

At the saloon Jeb and his men gave up the pretense of not knowing each other and congregated around one table.

"What do we do now?" Samms asked. "We're down to six men."

"You let me worry about that," Jeb said.

"But are we gonna leave Clark and Dave in jail?" Ben asked.

"At least for tonight, Ben," Jeb said. "The rest of you get some sleep and meet me back here in the morning."

"The place won't be open," Leslie said.

"Just meet me out front."

As the men started to get up to leave, Delay put his hand on Tanner's arm to stay him. Jeb allowed Ben to go back to the hotel. He'd talk to him later.

Once the men were gone, Tanner asked, "What's the deal?"

"You, me, Vic, and Ben are gonna take the bank tomorrow mornin'," Jeb said.

"The four of us?" Tanner asked. "We don't even know if they got guards or how many people work there."

"I do," Jeb said. "I know how many employees, how many guards, and where they're placed, and now I'm gonna tell it to the three of you, so listen up."

Bill Samms and Roy Leslie walked back to the rooming house they were staying in.

"We gonna leave Dave and Clark in jail overnight?" Samms asked as they approached the house.

"That's what we been told to do," Leslie said. "What's the difference? They ride with Collier, not with us."

"How long you reckon Vic is gonna let Collier call the shots?"

"Don't rightly know," Leslie said, "and I don't care, just as long as I don't have to call them."

"Amen to that, I guess," Samms said.

Cotton and Shaye entered the house and found Marion sitting on the sofa, holding the sleeping boy.

"Where's Belinda?" Shaye asked.

"She went out."

"You know where?"

"No," Marion said, "she didn't say, but she said she'd be back."

Cotton and Shaye exchanged a look.

"She either went to Jeb or to Alvin Simon."

"Simon?" Cotton asked. "The owner of the hardware store? Why would she go to see him."

"Well," Shaye said, "he's in love with her and he claims she's in love with him."

"What?" Marion asked.

"Where did you hear that hogwash?" Cotton asked.

"Thomas and James heard it from Simon," Shaye said. He went on to explain how.

"Why didn't you tell me that before?" Cotton asked.

"What difference does that make to what we're doing?"

"Well, it makes a difference now," Cotton said. "We don't know which man she went to see."

"Doesn't really matter," Shaye said. "We can just wait here for her to get back."

"Marion," Cotton said, "why don't you put the boy to bed and make some coffee?"

"I'll make the coffee," Shaye said.

"No," Marion said, "that's all right." She stood up.

"I'll put the baby down and then make coffee. It'll give me something to do until Belinda gets back." She started from the room, then turned back. "I assume we're going to get the truth out of her tonight?"

"We're gonna try," Shaye said.

68

Shaye and Cotton were sitting in the living room with coffee cups when the front door opened and Belinda came in.

"Well," she said, "nice of you to wait up for me. I'll be going to bed now."

"Don't you want to check on your son?" Shaye asked.

"I assume Marion has put him to bed. Good night, gentlemen."

"Sit down, Belinda," Cotton said.

She stopped short.

"We've got some talking to do, Belinda," Shaye said. "Do like the sheriff said and take a seat."

She turned, stared at them defiantly for a few moments, then dropped her shoulders and walked to a chair. She sat prim and properly, with her hands in her lap. She was wearing a dress Shaye had seen her wear once before.

"Where've you been?" Cotton asked.

"Out walking."

"All this time?"

"I had a lot to think about."

"I'm thinking," Shaye said, "that you went to talk to Collier or Simon. Which was it?"

"Simon?"

"Yeah, we know about Alvin," Cotton said. "He says he loves you. What do you say?"

She shrugged. "He's well fixed. He'd make a good husband."

"But you don't love him," Shaye said.

"No."

"How could you marry a man you don't love?" Marion asked, entering the room.

"It's not like I have a lot of choices, Marion."

"You're young," Marion said. "You've got your whole life ahead of you."

"Who's gonna want a girl with a child?" Belinda asked.

"What about the child's father?" Shaye asked. "It wasn't Matthew, was it?"

Belinda hesitated, looked away, then said, "No, it wasn't."

"Did you ever know my son?"

She smiled.

"I met him once," she said. "He was nice, gentle. We hardly spoke, but I remembered him, remembered his name and who is father was. So when I knew I needed help..."

"You lied to this man and his sons and made him come hundreds of miles?" Marion said. "To fight for you?"

Belinda lifted her chin and said, "Yes."

"And you're proud of it?"

"Well...I'm not sorry."

Marion stared at Belinda, shaking her head, and then said, "I don't know you at all, do I?"

"Nobody does, Marion," Belinda said. "Nobody ever

has. I've been on my own since I was fifteen. I have to look out for myself first."

"And what about your baby?" the sheriff's wife asked as Cotton and Shaye sat back to watch and listen. "Don't you think you should think of him first?"

"Why should I?" Belinda asked belligerently. "My mother never thought of me first. When is it my turn?"

"You give up your turn when you have a child!"

"How would you know?"

The two women were shouting at each other now, so Shaye got between them.

"Okay, that's enough," Shaye said. "Belinda, did you see Jeb Collier tonight?"

"No."

"What do you intend to do about him?" he asked.

"What do you mean?"

"Is he your baby's father?"

"I—I don't know."

"Apparently he thinks he is," Cotton said. "Are you willing to leave here with him—with your baby?"

"I don't know," she said. "I might be willing to leave with him, but I don't know if I should take the baby."

"Don't take him," Marion said. "Leave him here with us. We'll raise him right, Belinda."

"I don't even know if I'm going!" Belinda shouted. "Maybe I'll stay and marry Alvin—if Jeb doesn't kill him or me."

"Jeb's not going to kill anyone, Belinda," Shaye said. "We're not going to let him."

"That's what you say," Belinda said. "How do I know you can stop him?"

"You don't know," Shaye said. "None of us do, for sure."

"Can I go to bed now?" Belinda asked. "I'm tired."

"Are you having breakfast with Jeb in the morning?" Shaye asked.

"I think I should, don't you?" Belinda asked, getting to her feet. "I have some decisions to make."

"You wanted protection from Jeb Collier," Cotton said. "How could you even consider leaving with him?"

"I have a lot of thinking to do, Riley," she said. "I have to decide what's best for me."

"Go on to bed, Belinda," Shaye said. "We'll talk tomorrow—after your breakfast."

Belinda left the room without saying good night to anyone.

"I don't understand her," Marion said.

"And you're a woman," Shaye said. "If you don't understand her, how do you think we feel?"

69

Thomas was awake when the sun came up the next morning. James and Thad were both upstairs in empty cells, sleeping. He stood up from the desk, stretched, and walked to the front door. He opened it and took a deep breath, wondering what the day was going to bring. What he wanted was for this whole business to come to an end so he and his brother and father could get on with their lives. They all had decisions to make when they left Pearl River Junction, which couldn't happen soon enough to suit him.

Sunlight came through the cell window and a stripe of it struck James right in the eyes. He woke and sat up on the pallet, rubbing his face vigorously. In the next cell Thad was snoring. Across from them, in another cell, the two prisoners were also sawing wood.

James pulled his boots on and stood up. It was Thad's responsibility to go to the café and get breakfast for the prisoners, but James decided that since he was awake and Thad was not, he would do it. He could also bring back breakfast for everyone else.

He made his way out of the cell and down the stairs without waking anyone.

* * *

"Thad up?" Thomas asked as James came down.

"No," James said, "but that's okay. I'll take a walk to the café and bring back some breakfast for all of us."

James came up next to his brother at the open door and they stared out at the street together.

"What do you think is gonna happen today?" James asked.

"I can only tell you what I hope will happen."

"Yeah," James said, touching his brother's shoulder, "me too."

He stepped outside and headed for the café.

Belinda woke early for her breakfast with Jeb Collier. Nobody was going to tell her that she shouldn't think of herself first. She'd gone to bed with that thought and woke up with it also. It was time to make the final decision and everyone else could pay the consequences for her decision. She was tired of always paying. It was time for her to collect.

As she prepared to leave the house, she could hear that someone else was up, probably the sheriff. It was going to be a big day for him too.

A big day for everyone.

Shaye woke in his hotel room, stood up, and walked to the window. From there he could see the sheriff's office across the street, where his two sons had spent the night. He was proud of both boys, wondered what they'd decide when this was all over. Stay with him or go their own ways? There was no point in even thinking about it, though, until they were ready to leave Pearl River Junction.

He was about to turn away from the window when

the front door of the office opened and James stepped out. He crossed the street and walked out of sight. Shaye assumed he was on his way to the café to pick up breakfast.

This time he did leave the window. He walked to the dresser, where there was a pitcher and basin. He poured water from one into the other and began to wash, hands, face, neck, chest, armpits. When he was done with his whore's bath, he picked up a towel and walked back to the window. He saw Belinda walking down the street, past the sheriff's office, where she crossed over. She was probably also on her way to the café for an early breakfast and that meant that Jeb Collier would be there also.

Shaye hurriedly dressed, strapped on his gun, and left the room.

James was waiting for Connie to bring out the food when the door opened and Belinda walked in. She stopped short at the sight of him.

"Oh, James," she said.

"Good mornin', Belinda," he said, trying to ignore the usual flutter he felt in his stomach when he saw her. "I'm pickin' up breakfast for the jail."

"I see."

Connie came out of the kitchen with a tray she had covered with a towel.

"Oh, Belinda," she said. "Good morning. Take any table and I'll be with you in a minute."

"Thank you, Connie." The place was empty, so Belinda had her pick.

"This should feed all of you," Connie said, handing the tray to James.

"Thanks."

He tried balancing the tray with one hand, but

realized it would take two to get it across the street to the jail. At that moment the door opened again and Jeb Collier stepped in. Like Belinda, he stopped short when he saw the deputy.

"Well, Deputy," he said. "We ain't met."

"Jeb Collier," James said. "I know who you are."

"And you're Shaye," Jeb said, "or one of them."

"He's James," Belinda said.

"Thank you, honey."

The two men faced each other. James knew if Jeb Collier drew on him at that moment he'd have to drop the tray before he could go for his gun. He figured he'd be dead before the tray hit the ground.

Connie, sensing the tension, backed into the kitchen.

"Jeb..." Belinda said.

But it wasn't until the door opened again that the tension was broken. Dan Shaye stepped into the room, closing the door behind him.

"That the food for the jail, James?"

"Yeah, Pa."

"Better get it over there, then. I'm sure Mr. Collier wouldn't want his men to starve."

"My men?" Jeb asked, stepping aside to let James by, at the same time turning to look at Shaye. "I never said they were my men."

"You didn't have to," Shaye said. He opened the door for James without taking his eyes off of Collier. "Have a good breakfast."

"Thanks."

Shaye backed out, pulling the door closed.

Outside he caught up to James and walked alongside him.

"Don't ever have both hands occupied like that,

James." Shaye thought the world of his youngest son, thought he was very smart. If he went to college, he'd do very well in life, but wearing a badge, living by the gun...this just wasn't something James was as quick to take to as Thomas was.

"Pa...the tray..."

"You should have brought Thad with you."

"Yes, Pa."

"Collier wasn't going to draw on you anyway," Shaye said. "That would ruin his plan."

"What plan is that, Pa?"

"I don't know, James," Shaye said. "If I knew that, then we could ruin his plan."

After both Shayes left the café, Jeb turned and sat down with Belinda. Connie came back out of the kitchen nervously.

"Nothing to worry about, waitress," Jeb said. "My sweetie and I are hungry, though. We'd like to order."

"Yes, sir," Connie said. "What can I get for you?"

Alvin Simon woke, feeling excited and frightened. Belinda had come to see him the night before and he was supposed to meet her at the bank this morning when it opened. She'd told him that she was ready to marry him, but she had to be sure that he had the money he said he had.

"A girl has to make sure she's secure, Alvin," she'd told him.

"How do I do that, Belinda?" he'd asked. "How do I show you that I can make you secure?"

"That's easy," she said, putting one hand on his chest and kissing his cheek. Her lips were like velvet on his face, her scent heady enough to make him dizzy. She pressed her lips to his ear then and said, "Show me your money."

So that was what he was going to do this morning. Take her into the bank and prove to her that he had enough money to take care of her and her baby and keep them secure.

Samms and Leslie woke, but not well. Both had drank too much the night before.

"Come on," Samms said, "we got to meet in front of the saloon."

Leslie groaned. "I hope it's open. I'm gonna need a little hair of what bit me to get goin'."

"Just think about the money we're gonna take out of that bank," Samms replied. "That should get you going."

Samms started pulling his pants on.

"We got enough water to wash?" Leslie asked, pointing to the pitcher on the dresser.

"Never mind," Samms said. "There'll be plenty of time to wash later. Just get dressed and let's get going."

When Cotton arrived at the jail, Dan, Thomas, and James Shaye were all there and awake, as was Thad. There'd been enough food on the tray to feed the prisoners and the deputies, including Shaye.

"You fellas all look well-fed," Cotton said.

"There might be somethin' left on the tray for you," James offered.

"That's okay," Cotton said. "I had something before I left home. Belinda was gone when I left."

"She's in the café with Jeb Collier," Shaye said. "James and I saw them a little while ago."

"What about the rest?"

"No sign."

"Thad," Cotton said, "Why don't you and James take a turn around town, see if you spot them?"

"Yes, sir," Thad said.

James put down his empty coffee cup and followed Thad out the door.

Samms and Leslie sat on chairs in front of the saloon, waiting.

"Where's everybody else?" Leslie wondered.

"Overslept," Leslie said. "Relax, they'll be here."

Leslie put his head back, closed his eyes, and fell asleep.

It didn't take long for Thad and James to spot the two men seated in front of the saloon.

"I'll watch them," James said, "you go back and tell the sheriff about it."

"Think they're waitin' for the others?"

"Looks like it," James said. "Go ahead."

Thad nodded and headed back to the office.

Jeb and Belinda enjoyed a leisurely breakfast—at least, Jeb did. Belinda picked at her bacon and eggs until Jeb started eating from her plate. Picking at her bacon with his fingers.

"Nervous?"

"Yes."

"But this is what we've waited for," he said. "This is

what you wrote to me in Yuma about, taking this bank."

Belinda was a contradiction, even to herself. Yes, she'd written to him about the bank in Pearl River Junction, but she'd also written to Dan Shaye, to try to convince him to come to town and protect her—and Alvin Simon, for that matter. Once she met him, she thought his money was her way out and didn't want Jeb to kill him. As for Jeb himself, she really wasn't sure what he would do when he got there. It wasn't until he came to the house to see her and her son that she knew he wasn't going to kill her. That's when she decided to throw in her lot with him.

"We're gonna take that bank," he'd told her, "and then I'm takin' you and the boy away from here."

"Do we have to take the child?" she'd asked.

"He's mine, ain't he?"

"Yes."

"Then we're takin' him."

Now she watched Jeb put the last piece of her bacon into his mouth and said, "Do we really have to take Little Matt—"

"Don't call him that!" he snapped, slamming his first down on the table, startling her into silence. "You only named him that to try to convince Shaye he was his grandson, right? Because you wanted protection against me?"

"I didn't know..."

"Yes," Jeb said, reaching out and taking her hand, "you didn't know what I'd do when I got here. You thought I might kill you and take the boy. But you're the one who knows where all the guards are in the bank, honey. You're the one who can get in there with your new boyfriend."

"Jeb," she said, "you aren't going to kill..."

"Kill?" he asked. "Kill who? If I can help it, I'm not gonna kill anyone."

She seemed relieved by that, but of course he meant that he wasn't going to do the killing, Vic Delay was. That's what he was there for.

Jeb took his watch from his pocket and checked the time.

"The bank should be openin' soon, darlin'," he said. "Time for you to go."

"Yes," she said.

"I'll pay the bill here and be along."

She nodded, stood, and left the café. Connie came out and cautiously approached Jeb with the check.

"Thank you, sweetheart." Jeb took the bill, looked at the price, and paid the waitress, tipping her well. "Now, is there a back door out of here?"

Walking back to the sheriff's office, Thad noticed Alvin Simon, who owned the hardware store, standing in front of the bank. He also saw Belinda Davis rushing up the street and, eventually, joining Simon in front of the bank. It looked like the two of them were waiting for it to open. He turned his attention away from them and kept on to the sheriff's office.

"I thought you weren't coming," Simon said to Belinda.

"Of course I was coming, Alvin," she said. "This is important to me. I know you think I'm horrible to want to actually see your money, but—"

"I'll do whatever I have to do to get you to marry me, Belinda," Simon said. "To prove that I love you."

Belinda was about to reply when they heard the lock on the door of the bank *click*. Then one of the employees opened the door.

"Ah," the older woman said, "good morning, Mr. Simon. Early for you today, isn't it?"

"I—that is, we—have business with Mr. Brown, Miss Hastings."

"Well, he's in his office. Come in, come in."

As Simon and Belinda entered, the younger woman noticed the older woman giving her a look of distaste. It was the way most of the women in town regarded her and this morning it steeled her resolve to do what she had to do.

Jeb Collier had gone out the back door of the café, finding himself in an alley that ran the length of the street. He was able to use that back alley to get down the street without passing in front of the sheriff's office to the bank. Beyond the bank, he knew, was the Wagon Wheel Saloon. With any luck, Samms and Leslie were attracting some attention from the law. When he reached the bank, he used another alley to work his way around behind it, where he found Vic Delay and Lou Tanner waiting for him. Also there was Ben, holding the reins of five horses, one for each of them and another for Belinda.

"About time," Delay said. "You sure this is gonna work?"

"I told you," Jeb said. "She's the one who planned it. She said she knew that if I didn't kill her on sight, we'd be able to take this bank."

"Well, she better do her part."

"She'll do it," Jeb said.

"I don't like it that there's no guards behind the bank," Delay said. "I mean, if there's so much money in there—"

"Belinda says they keep most of the guards inside the bank, near the vault, and there's always one on the roof, but he's always watching the street."

"I don't like it," Delay said, "counting on a woman—"

"Just be ready, Vic," Jeb said. "If we have to take the guards out, we're gonna have to move fast to grab as much cash as we can."

"Don't worry," Delay said. He was wearing a leather vest today and he pulled it back to show two knives on each side. "I can take them out quietly."

"So they're just waiting in front of the saloon?" Cotton asked.

"That's right," Thad said.

"How many?" Shaye asked.

"Two."

"Where are the other four?" Thomas asked.

"That's what I'd like to know," Shaye said.

"James is watchin' them?" Thomas asked.

"Yeah, he sent me back."

"Pa, if they're waitin' for the others, I better go and stay with James."

"All right, son. Watch your back."

"I'll watch James's back," Thomas said, "and he'll watch mine, Pa."

Thomas left the office, leaving only Cotton, Thad, and Shaye.

"Thad," Cotton said, "you're gonna have to stay with the prisoners. If we leave the office empty, they might come and break them out."

"Okay, Sheriff."

"Take a shotgun from the rack and stay behind that desk until we get back," Cotton instructed.

"Yes, sir," Thad said, "but where are you goin'?"

"I don't know," Cotton said, looking at Shaye. "Where are we going?"

"Let's go back to the café," Shaye said. "That's where we left Belinda and Jeb. Maybe he's still there."

From behind the desk, loading the shotgun, Thad said, "He might be there, but she ain't."

"What do you mean?" Shaye asked.

Thad looked at him and said, "I just saw Belinda in front of the bank."

"What was she doing there?"

"She was with Alvin Simon," Thad said. "They looked like they're waitin' for the bank to open."

"What?"

"Alvin must have some business there," Cotton said.

"Riley, we better get over there. I think this may be it."

"May be what?"

"Collier and his men need a way into the bank. This is it!"

"You saying Alvin Simon is in on this?" Cotton asked. "That's just crazy, Dan. I can't see—"

"Riley, it's Belinda," Shaye said. "She's using Simon and Collier is using her! Thad, toss me that shotgun and get yourself another."

"Should I come—"

"No," Shaye said, catching the shotgun in both hands. "Stay here!"

Shaye ran for the front door. Cotton stopped long enough to grab a rifle from the rack and then followed.

72

"Good morning, good morning, Mr. Simon," the bank manager, Edmund Brown, greeted. "What can I do for you this morning?"

"I'd like to talk in your office, Mr. Brown," Simon said, "if you don't mind."

"Of course," Brown said. "This way." Since Alvin Simon was one of the larger depositors in the bank, the manager was willing to go out of his way for him. However, when he saw that Belinda was to accompany them, he stopped short. "Ah, is this charming young woman part of our business?"

"Miss Davis is my fiancé," Simon said. "She is very much part of my business."

"Very well," Brown said. "This way."

In order to get to his office, they had to pass the huge vault, which had three guards with rifles standing around it. There was a fourth guard by the front door and a fifth on the roof. They all wore blue uniforms. Belinda was happy to see that the number was what she had reported to Jeb.

They entered his office and as Brown crossed to the desk Belinda closed the door behind them.

"Oh, you can leave the door open, Miss—"

"I don't think so," Belinda said.

"I don't und—"

Belinda reached into her purse and came out with a nickel-plated .32 revolver. She pointed it at the bank manager and said, "Shut up."

"Belinda—" Simon said, aghast.

"I'm sorry, Alvin," she said. "I decided a whole bank is better than one man. Now move over there with him."

"But—what are you doing?"

"Just do it!" she said. "Don't make me shoot you."

"You better come over here, Alvin," Brown said. "She looks serious."

Slowly, Simon walked across the room and joined Brown behind the desk. The manager started to sit, but Belinda stopped him.

"Stay standing and put your hands on your head. Don't go for a gun in your drawer and don't press any buttons."

"Miss," Edmund Brown said with confidence, "you can't really think you're going to get away with this. There are guards—"

"Mr. Brown, if you don't shut up right this minute, I will shoot you."

Brown fell silent.

"Alvin, go to the window."

"What?"

"Go to the window—that one, at the back—and open it."

"The window?"

"Goddamn it, Alvin," she snapped, "don't keep repeating everything I say. Just do it!"

Alvin Simon walked to the window and opened it. In

seconds a leg appeared and he backed away to allow Jeb Collier to enter.

"Oh my God," Brown said.

The saloon was down the street, but on the other side of the bank. Shaye didn't feel he had time to go there and fetch Thomas and James. And even if the men waiting in front of the saloon were a decoy, they were still dangerous. As it stood now, there would be four bank robbers—five, if you counted Belinda—against the two of them and five bank guards, although he was pretty sure Jeb Collier had plans for the guards.

Delay and Tanner followed Collier through the window and they all brandished guns.

"Put him in a corner," Jeb said, pointing to Alvin.

Tanner pushed the shocked hardware store owner into a corner and said, "Stay there and keep quiet."

"You, Bank Manager."

"Yes?"

"You're gonna open the door and call two of the guards from the vault in here."

Brown, seeing this as his chance to alert the guards, started for the door quickly.

"Slow!" Jeb said. "If you try to warn them, you'll be the first one to die. I'll put a bullet in the back of your head. Do you understand?"

"Y-yes, I understand." For the first time Edmund Brown wished he had accepted the offer of help from the sheriff.

Shaye and Cotton reached the front of the bank.

"Now what?" Cotton asked. "Do we rush them?"

"We don't know what's going on inside the bank," Shaye said. "If we rush in, they might start shooting and somebody will get killed."

As they watched, a woman approached the front door and entered. She was obviously a customer.

"They're letting people in," Cotton said.

"Okay," Shaye said. "Let's take a chance, Riley."

"What do you mean?"

"One of us has to go inside, without a badge on, as if we're just another customer. The badge would attract immediate attention. This way maybe we buy a valuable second or two."

"And the other one?"

"Around back."

"Which one of us will they recognize easier?"

"Doesn't matter," Shaye said. "They've seen us both. I'll go inside, you go around back."

"Maybe I should—"

"We don't have time to draw straws, Riley," Shaye said. "Let's just do it."

"All right," Cotton said. "All right. Let's do it."

73

"I need two of you gentlemen in here, please," Edmund Brown said from the doorway of his office.

"Sir?" one of the guards said.

"Two of you," Brown said, "in here."

The guards all exchanged glances.

"Sir, we're not supposed to leave the—"

"I have an important depositor in my office and I need two of you in here...now!" Brown snapped.

"Yes, sir."

The three men exchanged another glance and then two of them broke away from the vault and moved toward the office. Brown backed away so they could come through the doorway.

"What's the prob—" one of them started, but he was literally cut off. Vic Delay grabbed him from behind and, using one of his knives, cut the man's throat.

The other guard got a gun barrel shoved up in his nose by Lou Tanner, who growled, "Don't move." He relieved the guard of his rifle.

Belinda stifled a scream by placing both hands over her mouth as a torrent of blood ran down the guard's chest. Delay caught the man beneath the arms and lowered him to the floor.

"That's to let you know we mean business," Jeb Collier said, pointing down at the dead man.

"W-what do you want?" Brown asked, finding his voice with difficulty.

"Money," Jeb said, "and lots of it."

"There are still two guards outside," Tanner said.

"I know," Jeb said. "We're goin' out there in a minute."

"How are we gonna play it?" Delay asked.

"You take the manager," Jeb said, "and I'll take the girl."

"What?" Belinda asked, surprised.

Jeb smiled and said, "Relax, sweetie. You're gonna be a hostage."

Before entering the bank Shaye relinquished the shotgun to Sheriff Cotton. Next he took off his badge and put it in his shirt pocket. Hoping he wouldn't garner too much attention, he opened the door and entered.

Everything looked quiet inside. Three of the five teller cages were manned. The woman who had entered before him was standing at one of them. To his left was one security guard, who gave him a hard once-over, his gaze lingering on Shaye's gun.

But nobody else was looking at him, so he sidled over to the guard, removed his badge from his pocket, palmed it, and showed it to the guard.

"There may be a robbery going on," Shaye said.

"What?" The man took a good look at Shaye's badge. "What are you talkin' 'bout, Deputy. It's quiet in here."

Shaye looked around again. Belinda and her beau, Alvin Simon, were nowhere in sight.

"You know Belinda Davis? Alvin Simon?"

"Yeah, they came in a little while ago. First customers."

"Where are they?"

"In the manager's office."

"How many other guards?"

"Three at the vault."

"Do me a favor," Shaye said. "Without attracting any attention, go and see if they're all there."

"Where would they go?"

"Humor me."

The guard, a man in his mid-thirties, said, "Okay, Deputy."

As nonchalantly as he could, the guard walked across the floor. He had to go behind the tellers' cage to check on the vault, which was not visible from this part of the bank. In a few moments he came back, looking worried.

"There's only one man there."

"Okay," Shaye said, "again, without making a ruckus, I want you to get the tellers out from behind their cages and I want all employees and customers against that wall." He pointed to his left. That wall appeared to be the safest place for bystanders to be able to avoid flying lead. "Do it now."

"Yes, sir."

Shaye put his badge back on.

Cotton rushed up the alley, but stopped short at the end of it. He peered around the corner and saw one man standing with five horses. He knew there was no back door to the bank. It had been built that way on purpose. But there were windows. He just couldn't remember where they led.

Cotton didn't think he could take this man quietly.

There was too much space between them. He was going to have to wait for something to happen before he made his move. It was in the hands of Dan Shaye, inside the bank.

Farther down the street, in front of and across from the saloon, men were getting impatient.

"This ain't right," Samms said. "Somethin's wrong."

"I know," Leslie said. "But what?"

"We oughta go to the bank," Samms said. "Maybe we got it wrong."

"I don't know..." Leslie said.

Across the street Thomas and James, secreted in a doorway, were feeling the same way.

"What do we do, Thomas?" James asked. "They're just sittin' there."

"They're not sittin', they're gettin' antsy," Thomas said. "Let's make somethin' happen, James."

"Like what?"

"Let's step out and let them see us."

"Anythin's better than just standin' here."

"Okay, then..."

Shaye didn't know if the vault and the single guard left there were being watched, so he couldn't go back there. Instead, he joined the front guard behind the tellers' positions.

"Now what?" the guard asked.

"Now we wait," Shaye said. "Something's going on, so we'll have to let it play out. Can we see the bank manager's office from here?"

"Yeah," the guard said, pointing. "That doorway over there."

Shaye could see the doorway, but not the whole door. He was about to change position, though, when the door opened and Lou Tanner stuck his head out.

"Get ready," Shaye said. "I think they're coming out. Don't do any shooting unless I do, understand?"

"I understand."

Shaye kept his eyes on the doorway and the first person he saw come through was Belinda Davis.

74

"Roy," Bill Samms said.

"I see 'em," Roy Leslie said.

"Whatta we do?"

"Just move slow, Roy," Leslie said, "slow and easy."

"This is a crap plan."

"Yeah," Leslie said, "I know, but it's the only one we got."

"We shoulda went and grabbed the kid."

"Jeb wouldn't let us do that," Leslie said. "We got to play it as it lays, Bill."

"They're not doin' nothin'," James said.

"Give it a chance," Thomas said. "They'll panic."

"And then what?"

"And then," Thomas said, looking at his brother, "we'll plant 'em."

"Put him down, Vic," Jeb said and suddenly the other guard was on the floor. Delay's knife had fresh blood on it, so he leaned over and wiped it on his own pant leg.

"Okay," Jeb said, "we're goin' out. Belinda, get over here. Tanner, you take the manager."

"Right."

Jeb put his arm around Belinda from behind and said, "Don't worry about nothin'. Just open the door."

There was a man's arm across Belinda's shoulders. As they came out the door, Shaye could see it was Jeb Collier's. Belinda didn't look scared, but she looked puzzled. Then, behind them, came the bank manager, Brown, with Lou Tanner right behind him. Jeb's last move before leaving the office had been to club Alvin Simon into unconsciousness. He'd decided not to waste a bullet.

"You!" Jeb hissed to the lone vault guard. "Drop your gun." Shaye figured Jeb was trying not to be overheard by the front guard.

The guard turned, pointed his gun, but then realized there were two hostages.

"You heard me. Drop it!"

Shaye couldn't see the guard, but heard his rifle hit the floor.

"Now call the other guard," Jeb said, "and then we'll have the tellers start filling bags with money."

Shaye heard a man call out, "Hey, Jack!"

Shaye looked at the guard next to him, who nodded. "Answer him."

"Whataya want, Lew?"

"I—we—need ya back here."

The guard lowered his voice, "What do we do?"

"We'll have to call them out," Shaye said. "If you go back there and they disarm you, we'll be at too much of a disadvantage."

"Jack!" The guard's voice sounded strident.

Shaye drew his gun and called out, "Jeb, can you hear me?"

He was greeted by silence.

* * *

"Shaye?" he called back. "Is that you?"

"It's me," Shaye replied. "It's all over, Jeb. Put your guns down and come on out."

"What do we do?" Lou Tanner hissed.

Jeb waved a hand impatiently. This should have gone smoother. They should have been able to get away before the law and Shaye knew what they were doing. Or maybe he just hadn't planned it as well as he should've. Had he gone soft in prison? If so, he was about to find out if it was fatal.

"We've got hostages, Shaye," Jeb said. "We'll kill them."

"Who are you kidding, Jeb?" Shaye said. "We know Belinda's in on this with you."

"We got the bank manager," Jeb said. "I'll put a bullet in him."

"That won't do you any good," Shaye replied. "You can't get out."

"Oh, we'll get out, all right," Jeb said. "Just stay where you are. You might be right about Belinda, but she's still a woman. I'll put a bullet in her. You wouldn't want that."

"Jeb!" Belinda said, catching her breath. She'd made her decision and thrown in with him. Her plan all along had been to get them all into place—the Shayes, Simon, Jeb—and then make her best play. Finally, the lure of the bank money had overwhelmed her. She'd been willing to leave town with Jeb and the money, leaving Little Matt to either the sheriff and his wife or to the Shayes, whoever wanted him. She just wanted to get out of town with the money. She hadn't expected Jeb to use her, though. She was supposed to be the one using him!

"Shut up," he told her. "Bank Manager, you better get that vault open... now!"

"I—I can't," the man said, "it's on a time-lock."

"Right," Jeb said, "and the lock would be set for the time the bank opens, so you can do business. I ain't stupid, manager. Open it!"

"Get the manager over to the vault, Lou," Delay said.

"Vic?" Shaye called. "You want to die in this bank today? How about you, Tanner?"

"I don't plan on dying, Shaye," Delay said. "I plan on killin' you, though."

"You'll have to, to get out," Shaye said, " 'cause we're not letting you out."

Tanner turned to Jeb.

"We can still go out the window."

"Not without the money," Jeb said.

"Vic?" Tanner asked, looking at his boss. "It's too late, Vic. We gotta get out!"

"We've got the back covered, Jeb," Shaye said. "You can't make it out that way."

"There's only one way out of here, Tanner," Jeb said, ignoring Shaye, "and that's through the front door, with the money." He released Belinda and pushed her into a corner, then pointed his gun at Brown. "Open it... now!"

Jeb looked at Delay.

"You gotta kill him," Jeb whispered to Delay.

"How?"

"Face him," Jeb said. "Man to man."

"He won't agree to that."

"Sure he will," Jeb said, "and while you're doin' that, we'll get as much money from the vault as we can. Once he's dead, we'll be able to get past the rest."

Brown was working on the vault, but he was sweating so much his fingers were slick.

"Talk to him," Jeb said.

Delay nodded, holstering his gun.

"Shaye!"

The guard looked at Shaye, who waved at him to be quiet.

"What is it, Delay?"

"You and me, Shaye," Delay said. "I want out and I'm comin' through you—unless you're scared."

Shaye thought about it. If he could put Delay down, it might make Jeb think differently about the whole thing.

"Who is this guy?" the guard asked. "Can you take him?"

"I guess I'll have to see."

"If you agree," the man said, "he'll step out and I can gun him."

"No," Shaye said, "if I agree, then I'll face him—one on one. If he beats me, you'll be on your own—unless you want to leave now."

The guard considered the offer.

"You'll have to put your gun down," Shaye added. "If I agree, this is not a good situation for you. If you want to leave, I'll understand."

"Is it just you and me?" the guard asked.

"The sheriff is around back," Shaye said, "and there's three more deputies outside."

The guard started to sweat and for a moment Shaye thought he'd take him up on his offer.

"Okay," the man said, "I—I'll stay."

"Good man."

"Shaye! What's your answer?" Delay shouted.

"You step out, Vic," Shaye said. "We'll do it."

Shaye didn't know what he'd do if Delay told him to come back there, instead. If he agreed, there'd be two other guns back there and he couldn't depend on them to play fair. But he figured Jeb would send Delay out, so he could start on the vault.

"Okay," Delay said. "I'm comin' out. I'm gonna take you at your word, Shaye."

"I give you my word."

Shaye holstered his gun, motioned the guard to move out from behind the tellers' cages, and then followed. There was room for all of them back there, but he wanted more.

Then, as an afterthought, Shaye turned to the people against the wall and said, "Everybody out—now!"

They didn't wait to be told twice. The employees and

the only customer ran for the door, shocked into movement despite the fear that had them frozen in place.

Samms and Leslie began to slowly walk up the street in the direction of the bank. Across from them Thomas and James kept pace. All four knew that the minute one of them stepped into the street it would be time for guns.

"What are we doin'?" James asked.

"We'll just follow them," Thomas said. "Just keep up with them and see what they're gonna do."

"What if they try to go into the bank?" James asked.

"That's when we'll stop them."

So they all kept moving—until they were within sight of the bank. Thomas and James could see the bank from their side of the street. Samms and Leslie could not. And the guard on the roof couldn't see the outlaws, just the lawmen, but still had no reason to think anything was amiss.

And then all of them saw people running from the bank.

Shaye heard the shots from outside just as Vic Delay stepped out from the vault area. He was still partially hidden by the tellers' cages.

"Tell the guard to put his rifle down," Delay said.

"Do it," Shaye said.

The guard set his rifle down on a nearby desk.

Delay came out from behind the cages, his gun in his holster.

"Sounds like some excitement outside," he said. "Your sons?"

"Probably taking care of the rest of your gang."

"Or bein' taken care of," Delay said. "Wanna check?"

"I'll check," Shaye said, "after we're done here."

Delay was trying to distract Shaye from the task at hand, gain a little edge.

"Come on, Vic," Shaye said. "You're the one with the big rep as a killer. Let's see if you deserve it."

"I deserve it," Delay said and drew...

Outside, as soon as the people ran into the street, Samms and Leslie reacted by drawing their guns.

"What the hell—" Leslie said.

When they drew their weapons, Thomas and James stepped into the street and produced theirs. They thought the two outlaws were going to shoot at the fleeing people.

"Hold it!" Thomas shouted.

The two men turned to face them and the four guns began to blaze. Having learned a valuable lesson once before, James moved before he fired. He stepped left, dropped to a knee, and fired two shots at Leslie. Both struck home, putting the man on his back in the street. On his back Leslie pulled the trigger of his gun twice, firing harmless into the dirt.

Thomas drew easily, standing fast, and put a bullet in the chest of Bill Samms. The outlaw pulled the trigger of his own gun once, but he was dead before the bullet struck a building across the street.

At the sound of the shots, Jeb Collier turned and shot Lou Tanner in the head. One less person to share with.

"Wha—" Belinda snapped, not believing her eyes.

The bank manager turned from his task of filling a money bag and Jeb shot him as well, grabbing the bag of money.

"Jeb—" Belinda said.

He turned to her and said, "This is for not tellin' me about my boy."

"No!" she screamed. Belinda put her hands up, but they were no match for the two bullets he fired. One went through her palm and into her chest, the other hit her in the abdomen.

Jeb ran for the bank manager's office.

Inside the bank Shaye drew his gun very deliberately. In his haste to beat him to the punch, Vic Delay's first shot went wide. Shaye, slower but more accurate, shot the killer in the chest.

At that moment he heard the shots from the vault area and the girl's scream.

"Come on!" he said to the guard.

Behind the bank Ben Collier heard the shots from inside. He ran to the window and at that moment Riley Cotton stepped into the open with his shotgun.

"Right there!" he said.

Ben turned, saw the sheriff, and went for his gun. Cotton triggered both barrels and Ben was flung away from the window, landing in a bloody mess several feet away. The horses, spooked by the shooting, ran right over the body in their haste to get away.

Jeb Collier entered the bank manager's office carrying one bag of cash in his left hand and his gun in his right. He saw Ben looking in the window, but before he could say a word his brother disappeared in a red mist. Jeb figured his only chance was to get out, so he ran and leaped head first out the window.

Cotton lowered his now-empty shotgun and started walking toward the body, but before he took two steps, a man came flying out the window. He rolled, came up on one knee, and pointed his gun at Cotton, who figured he was dead. In that split second he thought of his wife, then dropped the shotgun and grabbed for his pistol, even though he knew it was too late.

Shaye came through the door in time to see Jeb dive out the window. He ran to it, saw Jeb on one knee pointing his gun, and fired twice. Both bullets struck the bank robber. His blood sprayed the cash bag, which fell to the ground a second before he did. It spilled its contents and Jeb fell onto a blanket of cash.

Shaye stuck his head out the window, looked both ways, and saw Cotton to his right.

"You okay?" he asked.

"Thanks to you. Inside?"

"They're all dead," Shaye said. "You better come in."

Instead of using the window, Cotton went around to the front of the bank, where he ran into Thomas and James.

"Where's Pa?" Thomas asked.

"Inside," Cotton said. "He's fine. You boys?"

"We got the other two," James said.

They all went inside.

"Back here," the guard called.

They entered the vault area and found Shaye standing over Belinda's body.

"What happened?" James asked.

"I guess Jeb wasn't so forgiving, after all," Shaye said. "He was going to use her to rob the bank and then kill her anyway."

"Looks like he didn't want to leave any witnesses," Cotton said, looking at the dead bodies of Tanner and Brown, "and didn't want to share the money."

There were two other bags of cash on the floor near the bank manager, as Jeb had only been able to handle one.

"Speaking of witnesses," Thomas said, "where is the hardware store guy?"

They all went back into the manager's office and found Alvin Simon hiding underneath the manager's desk. He was alive...

Shaye looked down at the coffin that contained the body of Belinda Davis, then across the graveyard at the small group gathered around the bank manager's resting place.

Thomas and James were beside him and across from him was Sheriff Cotton and his wife, Marion holding the child in her arms. They had already decided to adopt the baby and to keep the name Matthew.

When the first shovel of dirt struck the casket, Shaye turned and started walking away. He could still hear his own handful of dirt as it landed on the coffin of his wife—and later Matthew. The pain of their deaths never seemed to go away.

Thomas and James followed, then came the sheriff and his wife.

They walked back to town, where their horses were already saddled. It had been two days since the shooting in the bank. The town was grateful to the sheriff and his deputies for saving the deposit money. Cotton was hailed as a hero who led his men against the bank robbers.

Their horses were waiting in front of the sheriff's office. There they said good-bye to Marion and to Little

Matt. Just the night before, James had asked Shaye, "Do you think she ever really even knew Matthew?"

"It really doesn't matter, James," Shaye replied, "does it?"

Now they turned and each shook hands with the sheriff as Marion returned home with Little Matt.

"I can't tell you how much I appreciate what you all did," the sheriff said. "It's ironic how it was Belinda who brought you here."

"I don't think she really knew what she wanted," Shaye said, "and because of that she brought us all to this place to meet."

"What will you do now?" Cotton asked. "Go back to your ranch and try to make a go of it?"

"Only to sell it," Shaye said, looking at his sons. "We've decided to find someplace that needs a sheriff and a couple of deputies. Wearing a badge gets into your blood."

"Well, I wish you luck, wherever you end up," Cotton said. "If you ever want to come back here, I've got three badges waiting for you."

They all mounted up and looked down at Sheriff Cotton.

"Try to make a lawman out of young Thad," Shaye said. "Tell him we said good-bye."

"I will."

They turned their horses and rode out of Pearl River Junction. There had been no grandson, but since they had decided once again to uphold the law, the entire trip had not been such a waste.